T0243457

Also by Steven Millhauser

DISRUPTIONS

DISRUPTIONS

Stories

Steven Millhauser

Alfred A. Knopf
New York
2023

Some of these stories originally appeared, in slightly different form, in the
following publications: "Late," *Harper's,* Oct. 2015; "Thank You for Your
Patience," *McSweeney's* No. 50, 2017; "Guided Tour," *Tin House* 75, Spring
2018; "A Haunted House Story," *The Sewanee Review,* Fall 2019; "Theater
of Shadows," *Guernica,* Feb. 2020; "The Summer of Ladders," *Zoetrope,*
April 2020; "Green," *A Public Space,* Sept. 2020; "After the Beheading,"
Salmagundi, Oct. 2020; "A Tired Town," *Monkey* (Japan), Oct. 2020; One
Summer Night," *Sewanee Review,* Fall 2020; "A Common Predicament,"
Zoetrope, Jan. 2021; "The Little People," Audible Originals, Jan. 2021;
"The Column Dwellers of Our Town," *En Bloc,* Summer 2021.

Library of Congress Cataloging-in-Publication Data
Names: Millhauser, Steven, author.
Title: Disruptions : stories / Steven Millhauser.
Description: First Edition. | New York : Alfred A. Knopf, 2023.
Identifiers: LCCN 2022024579 (print) |
LCCN 2022024580 (ebook) | ISBN 9780593535417 (hardcover) |
ISBN 9780593468883 (trade paperback) | ISBN 9780593535424 (ebook)
Subjects: LCGFT: Short stories.
Classification: LCC PS3563.I422 D57 2023 (print) |
LCC PS3563.I422 (ebook) | DDC 813/.54—dc23/eng/20220623
LC record available at https://lccn.loc.gov/2022024579
LC ebook record available at https://lccn.loc.gov/2022024580

Jacket illustration by Dylan C. Lathrop.
Courtesy of The Verge and Vox Media, LLC
Jacket design by Janet Hansen

Manufactured in the United States of America
First Edition

To Kate

CONTENTS

V

Kafka in High School, 1959 191

VI

I

ONE SUMMER NIGHT

In the summer of my sixteenth birthday I fell in love with the night. Day after day I waited for the sun to go down. I liked the brilliance and languor of long blue summer afternoons, which reminded me of childhood trips to the beach, but night was my time for visiting Helen. She lived on the other side of town, beyond the high school and the throughway overpass, beyond the park with the gazebo and the picnic tables, in a neighborhood of large houses and towering trees. We had been high-school friends since the start of sophomore year, and one day in spring I asked if it would be all right for me to walk home with her. After that, we were always together. I had never had a girlfriend before, though I did have friends who were girls. The thought that I had a girlfriend at last, a real girlfriend who lived in a real house on a real street, filled me with such exhilaration and deep calm that it was as if everything in my life would be all right from now on. We held hands, though only when we were alone. We kissed. Nothing more. I was patient and grateful, content for things to develop slowly over the course of the next hundred years, though at times a restlessness came over me, a tremor of impatience, as if happiness could never be enough.

The night was ours. I slept far into the morning and worked

six afternoons a week at the town library. Helen was taking a summer course in biology, helping her divorced aunt with one thing and another, and spending time at the beach with friends. Sometimes we saw each other in sunlight, but in the day she seemed a little unreal, like an overexposed photograph. At night we sat in her backyard on reclining lawn chairs and talked with her parents before going for a walk, holding hands as we watched our shadows grow longer and shorter under the streetlamps. Later we sat on the couch in the living room, with space between us, while her mother sat talking to us or washing up in the kitchen or bringing in cookies on a tray and her father read the paper or watched TV with the sound turned low. Sometimes Helen excused herself and led me up to her room. Leaving the door open a crack, she sat on the bed with her back against the headboard and told me about her day. I sat facing her, straddling the desk chair with my arms folded on top of the chairback. When the mood was right, I would make my way over to the bed and sit next to her, leaning in for a kiss, while she listened tensely for the sound of footsteps on the stairs. At eleven her parents went up to get ready for bed, leaving the living room to us. At midnight I rose to take my leave, since Helen had to get up early. I loved walking home from the house of my girlfriend in the radiance of the dark-blue summer night, passing lamplit living rooms glimpsed beneath partially raised blinds, listening to the quiet rush of traffic on the distant throughway.

One night when I arrived at Helen's house, at the end of the red slate walk, her mother answered the brass knocker.

"Come in, Robert, come in. Helen said to tell you she'll be back in ten minutes. That was over an hour ago. Some trouble between her aunt and that daughter of hers." She rolled her eyes and gave a deliberately melodramatic sigh. "Those difficult teen-age years. You probably can't remember how it was back then. But why on earth are you standing there like that? Is this a stickup? Are you carrying a gun? You can take my money, you can take my life, but please, spare my china. Come in, come in. You'll catch your death of cold."

"If you don't mind me waiting, Mrs. Chapman," I said, fol-lowing her through the entry hall into the living room.

"Always the gentleman," Helen's mother said. She was wearing dark-blue jeans with cuffs rolled up to mid-calf and a light-blue blouse with sleeves pushed up to the elbows.

On the oval table in front of the couch stood a half-empty glass of wine and a dark wine bottle. Beside them lay an open book, facedown.

"The suburban housewife," she said, sweeping out an arm, "drinking alone in her Connecticut living room. Can you think of a more perfect cliché?"

She turned to me. "Sit. Sit. Can I get you something? Some wine? A glass of beer? God, you should see your face. Relax, Robert. Relax. Life is too short. Ginger ale? Lemonade? A nice glass of air? Come, take a load off your feet. She said, collapsing onto the couch."

Helen's mother sat down and took a swallow of wine. She patted the couch and settled back.

"Roy's in the city tonight. Some last-minute thing at work. Strange. All winter long I look forward to these summer nights, and once they're here, what happens? They drive me mad. How can anyone sit still on a night like this? So, Robert. Talk to me. Tell me your deepest secrets."

She placed her chin on the back of one hand and blinked at

me in a parody of flirtation. She took another sip of wine and leaned back.

"Well," I said, "I know what you mean. About these nights. They feel peaceful, drowsy. You want to lie down and close your eyes, like a cat. But they don't really leave you alone. They keep pushing at you, like a hand on your back. If you know what I—"

"A hand on your back. Exactly." She looked at me sharply. "There's hope for you yet, sir." She leaned forward and filled her glass. She took another sip and leaned back, closing her eyes. "When I was your age . . ." she said.

She opened her eyes. "Don't you find it stifling in here?" She reached over her shoulder and pushed at her back. "Get a move on, old girl. Times's a-flyin'." She stood up. "Who can stay inside on a night like this? Let's step out back." She looked at me. "Oh, come on. I won't bite you."

I followed her through the kitchen and onto the wide back porch, which led down four wooden steps to the backyard. I had never been there without Helen, and for a moment it seemed a new, undiscovered world: the blue-white splashes of moonlight under the branches of the Norway maple, the long parallel shadows of the rope swing, the three reclining lawn chairs with backs at different angles, the dark coil of hose around the hook at the side of the porch.

Helen's mother walked over to one of the recliners. She stopped and stood with her hands on her hips, looking up at the night sky. "That's better," she said. "That's so much better." She flung herself onto the chair, settled against the backrest, and stretched her legs along the seat. She shut her eyes against the brightness of the moon.

"When I was a little girl," she said, "I would rub lotion all over my face and sit outside on nights like this. If you could get a suntan, why not a moontan? I wanted my face to turn white, like the moon."

She sat up, swung her legs over the side, and paused as if listening. She rose to her feet and looked around. She walked over to the swing, hanging from a high branch of the maple. "Come on. Give a girl a push."

I stood behind her, trying to push only the edges of the wooden swing. "Sorry," I said, as the ball of my thumb pressed against something soft.

"How can I ever forgive you?" she cried, sweeping into the air. I stepped away as she swung higher and higher, leaning far back until she was sideways. She rushed forward with her legs stretched out as if straining to reach the sky. Her auburn hair flew out behind her. Her blouse tightened against her as she swung forward, loosened as she swung back. At the end of a forward swing she suddenly let go. She seemed to hover in the air as the empty seat swung shakily back behind her, then she was landing on the ground with bent knees, falling forward onto her hands. She rolled over onto her back and stared up at the night.

"Look, a star. How does that thing go? 'Star light, star bright. First star I see tonight. I wish I may, I wish I might.'" She sat up and hugged her raised knees. "Flying through the air. I haven't done that for ages."

"You're in a good mood," I said. "A night mood."

"A moon mood."

She stood up and wiped her hands on her hips. With three fingers she thrust a loose edge of blouse into her jeans. She glanced over her shoulder and slapped at her behind. She pointed to the grass where she had landed.

"Beat that!" she said. "Go on! Dare ya!"

I threw myself onto the swing and pushed off. She stood behind me, pushing against my hips. "Higher!" she said. "Don't hold back! Higher!" After a while she came around to the front of the swing and stood facing me. Back and forth I swung, from shade to moonlight, higher and higher, and all at once I let go. I imagined myself moving steadily through the air, sailing over the hedge, traveling through yard after yard, lingering between heaven and earth, but already my feet were striking the ground, I was falling forward onto my palms, rolling onto my back. I looked up. Helen's mother was standing near my face, her hands on her hips. She rose high over me, her eyes shining. I felt that if I didn't turn my eyes away, they would be burned by her brightness.

She bent over me and helped me to my feet.

"Only a few bones broken," I said. "Nothing serious. You won, by the way."

"We both won. Let's rest. No, not there. There."

She pointed to the porch. I liked the idea of sitting on the porch, which was much longer than the one at the back of my house and, like all porches, gave you the sense of sitting indoors and outdoors at the same time. But Helen's mother was walking away from the door, toward one end of the porch. The pockets of her jeans moved a little from side to side as she walked. A small ladder stood leaning up against the edge of the porch roof.

"This way, ladies and gentlemen," she said, stepping over to the ladder and sweeping out her hand. "Ta-da!" She began to climb. At the top she stepped onto the slightly sloping roof and began moving forward on all fours. She sat down, hugging her raised knees.

I climbed up after her and sat down a few feet away, raising my knees and leaning back on my elbows.

"This sure as hell beats the living room," she said. "I ought to move the furniture up here."

"I'll carry it up," I said. "Just tell me where to put things."

"Careful what you promise."

I looked around. "It's perfect up here. It reminds me of a flying carpet. Without the flying."

She lay back and stretched her arms above her head. "My mother used to say, 'A living room is for living.' All I ever wanted to do was get out of the living room."

"I liked our living room. The one in the first house. The fireplace. The old phonograph. The mahogany bookcase against the stairs."

"I said to my dolls: 'That one's called the kitchen. That one's called the den. And this one over here, with the couch? That's called the dying room.'"

I laughed. "Here's something I just remembered. Our house had a garage with a chicken coop at the back. A chicken coop! Who had a chicken coop? It was empty, but there it was. I used to climb onto the roof of the coop and sit there, just like this, looking down at the backyard."

"My father once took me up to the top of the roof. I was five, six. He pointed down. 'Don't ever be afraid,' he said. 'Be smart, but never afraid.' By twelve I was sneaking onto the roof alone. I wasn't afraid of anything. He would've killed me." She sat up. "All this chitter-chatter about roofs. It's making me want to go higher." She stood and turned to face the house. "Blame the night, not me." Her head was a few inches below the second-floor windowsills.

"I'll need a hand," she said. "Two hands, actually. Did you remember to bring both hands with you?" She positioned herself directly beneath a window.

"I brought three, just to be on the safe side."

Placing one palm on my shoulder, she stepped nimbly onto my interlocked fingers and grasped the windowsill. As I raised my palms, she pulled herself up, pushed open the window, and began climbing inside. For a few moments she lay flat across the sill, wriggling and kicking, before she disappeared into the room. Seconds later she looked out at me.

"Come on. I'll help pull you up. What's a cracked rib or two?"

I gave a small jump that allowed me to rest my forearms on the sill. Pushing with my shoes against the shingles, I squirmed my way awkwardly up as Helen's mother gripped an upper arm and pulled.

"Up you go," she said. "Easy does it. Steady, now."

Flat on my stomach in the window, I wriggled my way through, scraping my ribs and hips. I seized the edge of a table and managed to plant my feet on the floor.

The dark room was striped with moonlight. I was facing the end of a bed, with its headboard against the far wall. The table on my right held a box of tissues.

Helen's mother, standing before me, slapped her hands together.

"Well done!" she said. "Mission accomplished. Welcome to the guest room."

She stepped past me to the window and leaned forward with her palms on the sill. She took a deep breath.

"Mmm, smell that air. Heavy with honeysuckle. You could almost walk on it. Anything's possible, on a night like this."

She pushed herself up. "The door to the attic is down the hall. Thataway. The attic gets us up to the roof." She turned and seemed to hesitate. "Let's sit for a second." She took a few steps over to the bed and sat down, leaning back on her elbows.

"Come," she said. "Take a load off." She patted the bed beside her. In the moon-striped dark, she crossed her legs and began swinging her calf back and forth.

Slowly I stepped over to the bed. It struck me that I didn't know Helen's mother's first name. How was that possible?

I sat down at the edge of the bed, a few feet from the swinging leg. Was it Mary? Marian? Through the window I could see the leaves and branches of the Norway maple and bits of brilliant dark-blue sky.

"You need to relax," she said. "Remember. This is the only night that ever was."

We sat without speaking, listening to the sounds of the night: a passing car, a shut window, the distant cry of a cat.

I felt a stirring on the bed. She seemed to be bending toward me. Something pressed against the side of my mouth. My body stiffened.

She leaned back on her elbows. Her blouse was pushed back against her, as if she were swinging on the swing.

"In case you're wondering," she said, "this isn't something I do."

I sat motionless. I could feel a trembling in my body, as if I'd been running for a long time.

"Such a good boy! Honorable. An example to us all."

She stood up without looking at me. She clapped her hands

together. "So! Time for the living room. I believe that's the proper destination."

She walked over to the closed door. As she began to open it, she suddenly held up her other hand. "Shhh. Hold on." She listened. "Helen's back. What could be more perfect? You go down. Go. I said: Go. I'll be down later."

I hurried down the stairs as Helen stepped from the front hall into the living room. What had just happened? "I'm so sorry," she said, turning up both palms. "It was hard to get away. Were you waiting long? Where's my mom?"

"Upstairs," I said, pulling her in for a hug. She was wearing loose jeans with the cuffs turned up once and a white shirt folded back at the wrists.

"I'm glad you waited," she said. She fanned her face with a hand. "It's muggy out there. You know what I could use? Some ice cream. Come on."

In the kitchen we sat at the Formica table, eating scoops of butter pecan and chocolate and pistachio. I ate quickly, anxiously, hungrily.

"Time to relax on the ol' couch," Helen said, laughing and pushing away her bowl.

I tried to imagine sitting next to Helen on the soft, familiar couch. "It's stuffy in there," I said. "Can we go out back? Just for a little while."

"Really? Okay. If that's what you want."

Outside, I looked around at the yard, as if trying to figure out where I was, and headed over to the swing. I leaped on and began to pump my way up toward the level of the porch roof. The air felt thicker, heavier, as if I were pushing my way through a net.

The window above the porch was dark. I wondered whether Helen's mother was still there, leaning back on her elbows. Swinging high, I let go of the ropes and hurled myself forward.

I landed in a crouch, rolled over, and lay on my back with my arms stretched out to the side. I stared up at the night sky. It glowed as if lit from within. Helen came running toward me.

"Are you all right? Is anything—"

"I'm fine, fine," I said, sitting up quickly and thrusting myself to my feet. "Come on. Your turn."

"I don't really—"

"I'll push."

I stood behind her, pushing against her lower back.

"Easy," Helen said. "Not so hard." As she swung, she sat almost upright.

"Lean back," I said. "Stretch out your legs. More. Let me know when you're ready to jump."

After a few more swings, she dragged her feet across the grass and came to a stop.

"That's it for me. You're in a funny mood. Let's get out of this heat."

In the living room she turned on a window fan and threw herself down on the couch. She leaned her head back and closed her eyes. "That's more like it," she said. As I sat down next to her, I could feel the couch pulling me in. She reached over and we held hands. Through the parted curtains of the two windows across from me I could see light from a streetlamp shining on the side-yard hedge.

"You seem quiet," she said. "Is everything all right?"

"It's fine. Fine. A little tired, is all."

"Me too."

After a while she said, "Let me go up and check on Mom. She must've heard me coming in. Be right back."

I listened to Helen's footsteps as they climbed the carpeted stairs and moved along the hall. I imagined her mother sitting on the bed, leaning back on her elbows. How could I not know her name? I stood and began walking up and down the living room, back and forth, pausing to glance out of windows. The room seemed smaller than before, as if the four walls were moving closer. Hadn't I once read a story in which someone was crushed to death in a room like that? The fan made a clicking sound, like an insect trapped between windowpanes. I needed to breathe fresh air. I imagined the pillows of the couch pressing against my mouth as I struggled to draw a breath.

I found myself at the front door. Opening it, I stepped out into the night. I could feel a tightness flowing out of me. I'd planned to stand there for a minute or two before going back inside, but when I turned to face the half-open door it seemed to loom over me with its arms crossed.

I pushed the door shut quietly and began walking fast along the slate path, forcing myself not to run. Tomorrow I would explain to Helen that I'd been very tired. I would apologize for my rude departure. She would forgive me. We would sit on the couch and hold hands. The thought of sitting on the yellow-brown couch filled me with restlessness. At the end of the path I glanced back at the house before turning onto a sidewalk of branch-shadows and patches of light from the streetlamps. What had happened in that house? Had I really climbed onto the porch roof with Helen's mother, whose name I still didn't know? Had we really crawled into that room? Did she lean toward me and press her mouth against the side of my mouth? I had sat stiffly there. Earlier I'd swung through the air and let go. Now I was walking along a dark sidewalk. What had she called it? "The only night that ever was." What was I doing down here on the sidewalk, on the only night that ever was?

I stopped, looked up. I seized the branch of a great dark tree and pulled myself up along the trunk. I was a squirrel. I was a cat. Up on my branch I looked around and began to climb higher. Higher. At last I leaned back and stared through the upper leaves at the night sky. I could feel the summer night streaming through me. "Moon mood," she called it. Was the night my wine? She had leaned back on the bed, swinging her leg. The bed was swinging, the room was swinging. She had looked over at me, leaned toward me. At that moment, the room had changed. Everything had changed. I could feel it in me, like the night. I would never go back. I would go back tomorrow. She would be there, in the house. Would she ever look at me again? Up in my tree, high above the world, I wondered what was happening to me. I closed my eyes to keep out the night. She was leaning back on her elbows, swinging her leg. I felt a quiver pass through me, and throwing back my head and looking up into the dark-blue sky, I watched the summer night burst into blue fire.

AFTER THE BEHEADING

After the beheading, which took place at 11:14 a.m. on Saturday, June 1, in the middle of the town green, some of us remained seated in our folding chairs, trying to understand what we had just witnessed, others came forward to look more closely at the guillotine, mounted on its platform splattered with blood, still others headed home to their families or set out on solitary walks or gathered at the Black Cat Tavern to talk or forget. Parents who had left their children at home tried to imagine what they might say about the morning's event, while those who had made the decision to bring their children with them wondered whether they'd done the right thing. Whatever our response to the public execution, which for many months had been the subject of heated debate, we all recognized that a turn had taken place in our town, one that we did not yet fully grasp.

The idea had evolved gradually and gathered momentum over the past year and a half. A wave of break-ins and robberies, unusual in our quiet town, had made many of us feel unsafe in our tree-lined neighborhoods, and at every town meeting there was talk of strengthening our police presence, increasing the severity of punishment, enforcing the law more rigorously. The turning point had come a few months later, when Dennis

Caldwell, thirty-six years old, who lived in a modest neighborhood out by the new mall, quarreled one night with his live-in girlfriend, whom he proceeded to hit in the face with both fists, rape, burn with cigarettes, and beat to death with a hammer. The jury, after a brief deliberation, found the defendant guilty, the judge imposed the death penalty, and within days a movement had arisen to make the death of Dennis Caldwell serve as a warning to our town that such acts would not be tolerated. The idea of a public execution was one among many, but it began to attract serious attention as petitioners went door-to-door soliciting signatures. At a crowded town meeting, the final vote was 39 percent in favor, 37 percent opposed, and 24 percent abstaining. In the weeks that followed, we debated the merits and shortcomings of death by hanging, death by lethal injection, death by electrocution, and death by firing squad, before settling on the guillotine for a number of reasons, chief among them its dramatic swiftness and its power to leave a lasting impression. Members of our town board, acting with uncharacteristic decisiveness, gained permission from the governor and appointed a Special Projects Commission to oversee all arrangements.

The work of constructing a guillotine was awarded to a local carpentry firm, Stanford & Sons, noted for innovative designs in porch swings, octagonal gazebos, and backyard arbors with built-in benches and planters. The finished structure, with its fourteen-foot posts, its diagonal blade bolted into a steel weight, and its latched opening for the neck, was transported by truck to the edge of the town green, carried by eight workers across the grass, and set on top of a raised wooden platform with steps going up in front and back. Our green is bordered by a row of sycamores on Beach Street and is overlooked on one side by our town hall, which dates from the seventeenth century, and on another by our Historical Society, originally an eighteenth-century inn. For this occasion, rows of folding chairs were set up to face the front and sides of the guillotine, so that the audience could see the victim's head clearly, but by dawn of execution day it was evident that the gathering crowd had exceeded all expectations. Additional folding chairs were brought over from the basement of the nearby Presbyterian church and hastily set up in rows that covered the entire green, so that many who attended were forced to sit behind the guillotine and could not directly witness the severing of the head. Some sat on the tops of cars in the two parking lots that bordered the green, some brought towels and blankets and tried to find empty spaces on the grass, others watched through binoculars from the porches of houses across the street. It was a sunny June morning, the kind of day when many of us drove past this very green on our way to the beach a half mile down the road, and in the air you could feel a mood not only of tense anticipation but of festivity, as if we had come out to celebrate the splendor of the blue spring day.

Shortly before eleven o'clock, three police cars and an ambulance drove into the town-hall parking lot. From one of the cars emerged two officers and Dennis Caldwell, wearing an orange prison jumpsuit, his hands cuffed behind his back and his ankles shackled. He was led across the lawn to the back steps of the platform, where he was handed over to two assistants who guided him up the steps to the rear of the guillotine. The condemned man's face, which was difficult to see from my seat near the edge of the green, held no expression, or perhaps what it held was a stern refusal of expression. His eyes looked straight ahead. We watched as he was strapped facedown onto a tilted board that was lowered toward the opening. A third assistant unlatched the top of the opening, set the condemned man's neck in place, and closed the top. The executioner, wearing black pants and a long-sleeved black shirt, stood at the side of one post and silently raised his right hand to a lever. The blade dropped swiftly between the grooves of the posts, blood flew up, the head dropped into the basket with a sound everyone could hear, it was all over quickly. Two men covered the basket and carried it across the green to the ambulance. Two other men placed the headless body in a coffinlike box and carried it to the ambulance, which drove away.

I was one of those who sat without moving, trying to take in the meaning of what I had just seen, trying, already, to recall exactly what had happened from the moment the blade struck the neck, while all around me people were standing up, gathering their things, pushing past knees. Had his eyes remained open the whole time? I had faithfully attended all the town meetings, I had argued forcefully against the idea of a public execution, and at the last moment I had voted yes. After a while I stood up and walked over to the platform. Town employees in dark-green uniforms were scrubbing away stains of blood and spraying the sides of the platform with hoses. A revulsion came over me, or maybe it was less a revulsion than simply a desire to get away from it all, to breathe fresh air, though in fact I was breathing fresh air on the town green under a blue sky on a warm morning in June. Two acquaintances invited me to join them for lunch in town, but I was in no mood for company. I set off alone.

My walk took me along Beach Street to neighborhoods near the shore, where boys were playing basketball on the driveways of two-car garages as sprinklers sprayed arcs of water on green lawns. When I grew tired in the heat, I returned to my car and drove to the other side of town, where my house stands on a street of older houses and shady sidewalks. Since the death of my wife I have lived alone, and though I spend much of my free time with friends I was glad to be by myself on this afternoon, to sit without talking in the shade of my porch and to lean back with half-closed eyes, like someone who has been lifting heavy loads for many hours and is entitled to a long rest. I had seen the blade fall, I had watched it slice through the neck, but everything had happened so quickly that I found it difficult to recall things with any precision. Was it possible that for an instant I had shut my eyes? I remembered the head falling into the basket with a small, decisive thump, but my seat was so far from the guillotine that I'd had only a distant sense of the condemned man's face. What stayed with me was something else. When Dennis Caldwell's neck was fixed in the opening, one of the assistants on the platform took hold of Caldwell's hair, evidently in order to steady the head in preparation for the descent of the blade. The assistant had put on a full-length rubber apron to protect his clothes from the burst of blood, and as the blade plunged toward the neck he drew back his own head and bent it to one side, as if to get out of the way of death.

In the middle of the night I woke and remembered the expression on Dennis Caldwell's face. He lay strapped to the board with his neck in the opening and stared out at the crowd. I saw a look of ferocious judgment in his eyes. Even as I reminded myself that I could not possibly have seen the features of Dennis Caldwell's face from where I sat, that I could see his brown hair falling over his forehead but not the shape or color of his eyes, I saw them now, as the blade dropped like the slash of a sword in an old movie that I had watched as a child.

On that first day I obeyed my sharp need to be alone, to hear
no talk, to stay away from my phone and laptop and TV, but by
Sunday morning I was seized by the desire to hear what people
were saying. The phone kept ringing, text messages kept popping
up, friends needed to talk, my brother-in-law's family wanted to
know every detail. What was it like? How did it feel to watch
something like that? The town was alive with voices. Despite
announcements forbidding the use of cameras, many in the audience had used concealed smartphones to capture bits and pieces
of the execution and posted them online. Most were blurred or
shaky images of people's heads and shoulders, with a glimpse of
the top of the guillotine high above, but one six-second sequence
posted on YouTube had already been viewed eighty thousand
times. It showed the blade, at a distance, clearly plunging down,
but just as it was about to strike the neck, someone blocked the
view, so that you saw the blade vanish behind a blurry shoulder,
followed by a moment when something that might have been
dust or pollen or spots of blood appeared in the air. Along with
images of this kind, vigorous opinions poured forth freely. Many
in our town deplored the beheading as a sickening return to the
barbaric past, while others praised it as a long-overdue response
to the loss of respect for law. On the local radio, a mother with
a shaky voice said that her daughter was now afraid to pass the
town green on her way to the beach. An air-conditioner repair-
man said that people got what they deserved, a realtor expressed
the fear that property values would fall, and a member of the
town planning commission said that the execution was the greatest thing the town had accomplished in his thirty-four years of
service. Local news reported that protesters had been gathering
at the green since Saturday afternoon, carrying signs with mes-

sages like "Day of Shame" and "Execution Is Murder." Several protesters had clashed with police and had been removed from the scene.

I suppose it was inevitable that rumors about the event should begin to circulate. At the office the next morning, where I work as an accounts manager for an insurance firm, I was startled by the wide discrepancy in eyewitness reports. One of my colleagues claimed that he'd seen the eyes blink twice, after the head had been severed but before it had dropped into the basket. Another said that she'd heard the sound of a word emerging from the severed head, a word that sounded like "crime" or "climb." Someone started to explain to us that the brain remains alive for a short time after the head leaves the body, someone else declared that the brain dies but the facial muscles continue to twitch. There was disagreement about how much blood had been spilled, about the look on Dennis Caldwell's face as the blade began to fall, as the blade struck, as his head separated from his body. I tried to hold on to what I'd seen, I clung to any detail I was able to remember, but already I felt things shifting, growing uncertain, like a landscape dissolving into dusk.

I made a point of avoiding the town green that day, but dissatisfaction with my evasiveness and a kind of fury of curiosity drew me back the next afternoon. Had there really been a public beheading in our peaceful town? The green had changed. It was now blocked off by yellow-and-black tape attached to steel stanchions. Uniformed police stood guard all around, and on the sidewalk of Beach Street and in the parking lots of the town hall and the Historical Society, angry protesters shouted and pumped their arms. In the middle of the green, the guillotine stood high on its platform, its diagonal blade gleaming in the sun. Two birds sat on the top crossbar and suddenly flew away. A groundskeeper seated in a riding mower rode slowly across the grass, throwing up sprays of green. Across the street, a group of counterprotesters stood holding signs with messages like "Death for Death" and "No Mercy for Murderers." Cars passed slowly, heading out to the beach.

A few nights later a troubling incident took place on the green. Shortly after three in the morning, the guillotine burst into flames. The fire department, located a few blocks away, extinguished the flames within minutes, no damage was done apart from minor charring of the platform and one post, the two teenage boys responsible for the act were quickly apprehended, but the attack made its impression and for a while strengthened the hand of the pro-guillotine faction, who argued in favor of broadening the death penalty to include crimes against property. Others insisted that the guillotine had itself been responsible for the incident by the sheer fact of its blood-soaked existence, which was nothing less than a continuous incitement to violence. The result of it all was a stricter patrolling of the green and an increased presence of night guards.

Toward the end of the first week, a story began to circulate that left many of us uneasy. Mary Lou Wharton was the eleven-year-old daughter of Charles and Helene Wharton, who lived in an old neighborhood within walking distance of the green. The Whartons had attended the beheading but had chosen to leave their daughter at home. Shaken by what they'd witnessed, they returned to their house before noon and were surprised not to find Mary Lou waiting on the front porch or playing in the yard or reading in her room. Only after a thorough search did they discover her in the basement playroom, sitting quietly on the couch. Before her on the rug stood the oval table around which, at the age of six, she had liked to arrange her dolls before serving them imaginary tea and cake. Six of the old dolls were seated neatly on six small chairs around the table. All the dolls were without heads. Some held an arm raised, others rested a hand on the edge of a teacup. Each head sat beside a teaspoon. On the end table beside the couch lay a kitchen knife.

The story of Mary Lou Wharton, passed on by a gossiping friend, spread quickly and led to new clashes of opinion. If even one of our daughters could behave in this way, who knew what emotional damage had been inflicted on the children of our town? The beheading had already caused many of us restless nights, but angry voices now urged us to take charge of our lives by voting to make public executions illegal and by removing and destroying the monstrous guillotine, visible reminder of our disastrous mistake. Defenders argued that Mary Lou Wharton's parents were entirely to blame for their ill-considered decision to spare their daughter instead of taking her to the green. Left to her own devices, she had fallen prey to an imagination that would have been strengthened and disciplined by the experience of the event itself. Others, while acknowledging the unfortunate nature of May Lou Wharton's behavior, begged to point out that the vicious and drawn-out assaults committed by Dennis Caldwell were in no way similar to the merciful swiftness of his own punishment, and they urged that the guillotine be proudly preserved as a symbol of justice.

Although the protests at the green continued, a tapering off was noticeable as June advanced toward summer. A faithful dozen or so, standing about with signs, lingered outside the barrier tape at the edges of the green, mostly ignored by people strolling past on their way to the beach, glancing up for a moment at the guillotine, nodding to a groundskeeper or to one of the few remaining policemen. Now and then a young mother or father would point at the guillotine and say something to an upward-gazing child. Cardinals and sparrows sat in the overhanging branches. A smell of summer was in the air.

It was toward the end of June, not long after high-school graduation, that we heard reports of a Guillotine Party, held one evening in the backyard of Ray Anderson, a popular senior who was captain of the swim team. Apparently he and a few friends had managed to cobble together a crude guillotine, composed of two upright posts fastened to the sides of a wooden crate and connected at the top by a board. On the crate stood an old tire, through which the victim's head had to pass. A bucket of water was secured by straps to the top of the upper board. When the victim, who had lost a contest of some kind, was tied up and placed facedown on the platform, so that head and neck emerged from the tire, the executioner pulled a rope. The high board tipped forward, water from the bucket poured down onto the victim's head, cheers and whistles erupted. The game was harmless enough, a way to pass time with friends in a backyard on a summer evening, but I wasn't the only one disturbed by this travesty of our public execution, for not only did the game tame down the fierce act of beheading, infecting it with an air of playfulness and mockery, but even as it did so you could sense, beneath the shouts and the lighthearted laughter, the memory of a bloody blade drifting through the darkening air with its scent of hedge blossoms and cut grass.

Influenced perhaps by their older brothers and sisters, younger children were beginning to behave in odd ways. One afternoon a mother bearing a tray of cookies and lemonade entered the room of her eight-year-old son, only to discover that he and his friends had painted bright red circles of lipstick around their necks and were staggering around in the throes of pretended death. One boy with a splash of red on the back of his neck lay facedown on the bed with his head hanging over the side and his arms dangling. In another part of town, a babysitter, checking up on the children, found the five-year-old girl trapped in a window with her neck held down by the bottom pane, while her brother stood next to her wearing a black mask. It was about this time that Angelina's, the toy shop on Main Street, began selling little guillotines in two sizes, the six-inch and the twelve-inch, supplied with safe plastic blades and gel-necked victim figurines. Sometimes I had the sense that the guillotine on the green was multiplying itself in grotesque forms, in order to demonstrate its power.

And yet, for all that, as the hot days of summer settled in, it was clear to most of us that the sway of the guillotine was gradually diminishing. Yes, there were incidents here and there—a red swastika painted one night on the front of a guillotine post and removed by a groundskeeper the next morning, a headless cat nailed to the trunk of a tree beside its severed head—but on the whole, we could feel our world returning to its familiar ways. We went to work, strolled in town, spread out our towels on the beach, mowed our lawns, argued about the proposed meters for Main Street parking. A guillotine stood in the middle of our green, but it had grown less visible, obscured by familiarity. It was like the front of the town library, with windows topped by elegant designs of brick and stone that most of us could not visualize with any precision. The day itself, though hardly forgotten, seemed to have taken place long ago, like a childhood visit to a museum.

We were shaken out of our apathy by an incident that erupted one day in late July. Richard Penniman, a semiretired handyman who had worked in many of our homes, was rushed to the hospital in critical condition. A neighbor had discovered him in his backyard at dawn. The story, which emerged gradually, was this. For two months Richard Penniman had spent long hours in his basement workshop, constructing a guillotine. Penniman's skill as a craftsman was well-known to us—he had once built a dollhouse village for a neighbor's daughter, including a gas station, a grocery store, an elementary school, and three streets of houses—and the construction of a secret guillotine would have seemed less ominous in retrospect if his intention had simply been to display it as an object worthy of our admiration. Whether he had planned from the outset to demonstrate its perfection is unknown. As always, he traveled in his pickup to lumberyards and hardware stores in nearby towns, choosing material carefully. At least part of what compelled him, in my view, was the desire to build a guillotine superior in every way to the one on the town green. Only afterward did a neighbor realize that the shrill whining sound emerging from Penniman's workshop at night must have been the sharpening of the steel blade. Late one night, Richard Penniman carried up the separate parts—the polished posts with their grooves, the latched opening that allowed the head to pass through, the diagonal blade, the supporting base, the basket lined with oilcloth—and laid them out on his back lawn, which was enclosed by a high wooden fence. In the darkness before dawn he began assembling his masterpiece. It rose sixteen feet into the air. In the predawn light, Penniman stepped onto the base, lay down on his stomach, and opened the top half of the neck hole. He inserted his head over the bottom half-circle and closed the top over the back of his neck. A lever near his right hand enabled him to release the blade into the grooves of the posts.

The operation proved flawless except for one thing: the blade, dropping swiftly and smoothly between the posts, failed to cut all the way through the neck. Cries of pain alerted the same neighbor who had heard sounds from the workshop at night and who now rushed outside and made his way through Penniman's front yard into the back. There he found Richard Penniman's body thrashing on the platform and the blade sunk into his bloody neck. At the hospital Penniman remained in intensive care for two weeks before beginning his imperfect recovery. But what haunted us was the vision of the guillotine at dawn, maiming but not killing its victim.

Even activists most violently opposed to the presence of a guillotine in our town had never imagined its failure. It was the successful beheading itself that was the focus of moral revulsion. The wounded neck, the thrashing body, the face twisted in anguish, seemed far more sinister than the cleanly beheaded body of Dennis Caldwell, as if the guillotine had at last revealed itself to be an instrument of torture, or a creature from outer space whose mission it was to mangle earthlings. Crowds of protesters gathered again at the town green, chanting and raising their fists. Parents took away toy guillotines and threw them in the trash.

Despite the revival of outrage and dismay, most of us continued to go about our usual business. Gradually the new protesters drifted back to their customary lives, leaving only a handful of stubborn loyalists, who stood for an hour or two talking quietly among themselves in the warm shade and opening backpacks to remove bottles of water that glistened in the sun. A few sat on the curb, with their signs against their knees, and looked at passersby or glanced at their watches. The possibility of new occasions for protest hung in the air, but we understood that we were in the last weeks of summer and had only a short time in which to savor the lazy peaceful days of backyard barbecues and trips to the beach before being swept up into the rhythms of autumn. A passion for the everyday came over us, as if we'd been confined to bed for months with a debilitating illness and were eager at last to get up and greet the new morning.

This embrace of the normal was itself cause for concern, since at its heart lay an acceptance of the guillotine as part of ordinary life. The post office, the library, the high school, the beach club, the guillotine, the bank, the movie theater, the Historical Society, the Presbyterian church, the new stop sign out by the hardware store—it was the town we all knew, the town most of us had grown up in, with its familiar monuments, its careful preservation of the past, its openness to reasonable change. A guillotine on the town green was beginning to seem no more remarkable than the new crosswalk between Vincenzo's Drugstore and the Downtown Diner or the new post-office branch out by the renovated junior high. What really occupied our attention wasn't the blade and the bloody neck but the new parking meters installed on two downtown blocks and the road-repair project that closed off half a dozen streets and produced traffic jams causing ten-minute delays.

On the last day of August, the annual end-of-season craft fair opened at six a.m. on the town green. The barrier tapes had been removed, and booths appeared all across the lawn. Soon families were strolling from booth to booth, examining wine bottles decorated with yarn and seashells, oil paintings of local scenes, handmade coasters shaped like apples and pears. The three protesters laid their signs against the trunks of sycamores and entered the green, stopping at tables, chatting with friends. The guillotine was surrounded by an orange mesh fence and watched over by a single guard in a dark-blue uniform, who sat on the steps of the platform and answered questions put to him by adults and children about how guillotines work. High above, the diagonal blade hung in the morning sun. A woman pushing a stroller bent over and adjusted her daughter's baseball hat.

Scarcely had the fair ended when the town became caught up in Labor Day get-togethers and preparations for the new school year. One afternoon toward the middle of September, when the air was still warm but the first leaves were beginning to turn, I parked near the library and took a walk up Beach Street, as I liked to do at this time of year. I passed the Presbyterian church with its well-kept lawn, strolled past the Historical Society, and came to the town green, which remained free of yellow-and-black tape. I paused on the sidewalk to look across the green at the guillotine. It was cordoned off on all sides by a single rope, attached to black corner posts. A woman in jeans was standing outside the rope, gesturing at the guillotine as she spoke to a man with a jacket slung over his shoulder. Piles of tarpaulin lay on the platform, perhaps in preparation for repairs or bad weather. An aluminum ladder leaned against one of the posts. I looked up at the top of the guillotine, where a bright red water bottle sat on the crossbar.

I continued on my walk, past the town hall at the other end of the green, past the Revolutionary War graveyard, past the cluster of historic mansions and the newer blocks of ranch houses and split-levels down by the beach. I walked through the open gate and up the short path that led to the top of the sand, which stretched away in both directions and sloped down to the water.

A few people in bathing suits sat on towels in the mid-September sun, though the lifeguard stands were empty at this time of year. At the water's edge, low waves breaking, I tried to make sense of it all. We had executed a man in public. We had spilled his blood. Was our town safer than before? I had argued against public execution and voted for it in the end, for reasons I could no longer remember clearly. I tried to recall our green without the guillotine, but the memory was penetrated by a sense of distortion, as if I were deliberately rearranging the actual world in order to escape into a dream of innocence. I had seen a bloody head fall into a basket. I had watched men in dark-green uniforms cleaning up the blood. Had we prevented future Dennis Caldwells from committing torture and murder? Had we harmed our children? Would the guillotine be used again? Or was it destined to become a well-preserved artifact visited by sixth-grade classes, like the pillory in the basement of the Historical Society? All I knew was that we were a peaceful town, with a guillotine on the green.

After a while I turned back along the sand and walked down Beach Street toward my car. As I passed the green, I glanced over at the guillotine. A squirrel sat on one corner of the platform, scampered in the direction of another corner, and abruptly stopped. Two boys on skateboards came clattering up behind me and swept out of my way. I had two more hours of work to do before picking up a few shirts from the cleaners and meeting a friend in town for dinner. A slight pressure in my sinuses made me wonder whether I had time to stop off at CVS and pick up a packet of decongestant tablets. I watched the skateboards rush into the distance and continued on my way.

GUIDED TOUR

Fifteen, sixteen, one more and we're good to go. There: seventeen. All present and accounted for. You, sir. In back. May I ask you to step forward a little? We don't want to lose anyone. So. We're now ready to begin the walking portion of our tour. For those of you who may have concerns, I can assure you that it won't be strenuous. It's no more than two miles to our final destination, with plenty of stops along the way. The bus will remain here, outside the wall, to await your return. At that time all cell phones and smartphones will be handed back to you at the guardhouse. The driver is authorized to leave the vehicle but will of course lock both doors securely. I need to remind you that AuthentiTour is not responsible for any personal items that may remain on board.

Before we begin, please take a moment to observe the *Stadtmauer*, or town wall. It completely surrounds the town, which stands near the river that flows past on one side. Medieval rivers are good for trade but dangerous as routes of invasion. Our wall is nine meters high, or twenty-nine-and-a-half feet, with twenty-two observation towers, each manned by a small garrison. As you know, AuthentiTour prides itself on providing its customers with an authentic experience of historical events. That is why we've bypassed the sprawling contemporary town that clings to the same name but has expanded far beyond the original walls and is built up on both sides of the river. It bears little resemblance to the thirteenth-century world we're about to enter. Our researchers and architects, using all available evidence, have spared no effort in reconstructing the town as it was in June of the year 1284, when the stranger first appeared.

Please follow me through this *Tor*, or gate. Note the high, curved arch, typical of the period. There are four gates in the wall, all kept open during the day to allow townsfolk to pass out into the surrounding fields and farms. Take a look at the thick doors as you pass. At sunset they're swung shut and barred to protect the town against unknown visitors or armed invaders.

Please observe the guard, who in those days would have stopped us and demanded to know the purpose of our visit. He'd then have inspected our belongings and collected a toll. No, we're fine. You can enter. Just follow me.

Here we are, at the beginning of the high street. Let's stop for a moment and take it all in. Note the many horses, the carts full of goods, the merchants in their fur-lined cloaks. Look at the tanners and weavers in their shops, the stable boys, the dogs, the chickens, the geese. Chicken feathers everywhere. This street won't be paved for another century. Over there, that sign hanging over the doorway—do you see the mortar and pestle? That's the apothecary shop. I'm sure you've noted the piles of filth, typical of this period. Don't be alarmed. The masses of animal and human excrement, the rotting vegetables, the fish entrails, all are hand-painted plastic models made from vinyl chloride by our highly skilled replica artists. Concealed odor machines produce a mild approximation of the original smells, which in their full force would cause attacks of nausea and vomiting in most of you.

Please stay close behind and follow me to the church square, directly ahead. Note the narrow side lanes, the wooden houses crowded together on both sides. See how the second stories jut out beyond the first, almost meeting in the middle of the lanes. Over that way, just before we reach the church, you'll see another gate in the wall, with a view of the river. That's where the rats were drowned.

Here is the church square, where we'll pause for a few moments. All here? Fifteen. Sixteen. Seventeen. Good. Apart from the fortified wall and a few houses owned by the wealthier merchants, the church is the only structure built of stone. It's the tallest building, as you can see, though much lower and narrower than it's destined to become in the next couple of centuries. At present, in the year 1284, the church is undergoing a slow transformation from Romanesque basilica to Gothic cathedral. But we're not here because of the church. We're here because of the children. For it is here, on that fateful June morning, that the stranger appeared for the second time, no longer in the many-colored costume of his first visit, but in the dress of a hunter, dark green, with a brilliant red hat. He is angry. He raises his wooden flute.

Remember. Three days earlier, the stranger led the rats and mice through the streets of the town and down to the riverside gate. He passed through the gate to the bank of the river. There, still playing his flute, he walked slowly into the water up to his waist. I like to think of him that way, standing in the river on a sunny day in June, playing his wooden flute. You all know what happened. The rats and mice plunged after him and drowned. But when the piper went back through the gate to collect his reward, the leaders of the town laughed at him and refused to keep their promise.

Now he has returned in anger. He raises his flute and begins to play. I ask you to imagine that music. Is it the same music that enticed the rats and mice to follow him through the gate into the river? It can't have been the same. It can't have been, because not a single child followed him the first time. It must have been a music for them alone, for the children of Hamelin, a piercing, seductive music, a music that passes through the skin and makes your blood restless, a summons, a promise, a call, an enchantment. Imagine the children. Imagine them. They are the children of cobblers, weavers, tanners. They are the children of butchers and bakers, of blacksmiths and coppersmiths, of tavern keepers, of silk merchants. They are in the shops and stables, they are in the narrow lanes, they are in the upper rooms of the merchant houses being read to by governesses. They hear a sound they have never heard before. They stop. They lift their heads. They listen. What is that sound? It is the sound buried in the depths of rainbows. It is the sound of setting suns, of the shadows of birds in flight. It is the sound of blue skies on long summer afternoons. It is the sound rising from beneath the sun shining on the river, the sound coming from the bowels of stones. They must follow that music.

They hurry into the street. They gather around him, the stranger in the red hat. His right elbow is raised. His fingers are fluttering over his wooden flute. He begins to walk. The children follow. We're told that one hundred and thirty children came forth that day.

Where are the parents? The parents are watching. They're watching from doorways, they're watching from the shops and market stalls, but they cannot move. The music that has the power to stir the children has closed around the parents like twists of rope. They can do nothing as the children follow the stranger along the high street toward the gate that leads to the forest.

Can you hear that music? Can you feel it? It is the sound of the other side of sunlight.

We'll now proceed along the high street and out through that gate, which you see straight ahead. Observe the narrow lanes on both sides, the shop signs hanging from poles, the second stories built out over the sunless streets. Please stay close behind me.

Let's pause here, outside the gate. You'll notice that the ground near the wall has been cleared all around, for purposes of defense. Over there is the river. No enemy can approach the wall unseen.

In a moment we'll be making our way across the clearing and over to that meadow. We're fortunate to have such lovely weather for our walk, don't you think? It may be that some of you find the sunshine a bit strong out here, so I'm pleased to see so many hats. That straw hat, ma'am, with the wide brim—a very good choice for our excursion. Please take a moment to make any adjustments to your clothing that you care to make. If any of you are carrying sun block, you may want to apply it now. But let me assure you. Our path lies directly through the meadow and over to that forest, which you can see from here. It isn't far. Take a moment to look at the river, winding away in the sunlight, and beyond the river the rolling countryside. Over there, the farms and orchards, the vegetable gardens. This is the kind of day that makes you happy to be alive. Please follow me.

Our stretch of meadow may have been a goat pasture at one time. It leads down to the river on this side. We're almost there.

Here we are, like the children of that far-off summer, at the edge of the forest. Let's stop for a moment and look back at the town. You can see the wall, the towers, the top of the arched gate. And over everything, the steeple of the church. The world the children have left is not far behind. It's right there, on the other side of the meadow. It's the familiar world, the safe world—a world closed off from everything beyond. The children are glad to leave that shut-in place and glad to return to it. Try to put yourselves in their place. You are the children of Hamelin. Before you lies the forest. Behind you, the meadow and the gate. Many of you have come to the forest with your mothers or older sisters to search for mushrooms, to pick berries, to gather kindling. But you are never allowed to walk unattended among the high trees. You've also heard the stories. The stories come from the mouths of nursemaids and servants, from the throats of blue-eyed grandmothers sitting at your bedside as you fall asleep. The stories are about creatures of the forest. Elves with crooked noses who lie in wait for you with their sacks. Witches who will entice you into their cottages and snatch you up and eat you. But you aren't thinking of the dark forest now. You're thinking of the pleasant shade at the edge of the trees. You're following the stranger with the flute, you're following the music that is like soft fingers against your faces, music that whispers: "Come with me, oh come with me." You don't hesitate to follow the stranger into the trees.

Please stay close behind me. The forest path will soon disappear. Many of these trees are hundreds of years old. Observe those oaks, so high that you can barely see the tops. Over there, a thicket of firs. Spruce, beech—have you ever seen trunks so thick? The forest has its dark places, but sunlight still strikes the upper branches and falls in bright patches down here with us among the ferns and the dead brown leaves.

Let's stop here, in this clearing. Four, five . . . nine, ten . . . and seventeen. Excellent. We're almost there. If any of you are tired, please feel free to rest on one of these enormous roots. Nature's chairs, I call them.

I ask you again to imagine the children. You are following the stranger, whose music draws you forward. The farthest thing from your minds is that he might wish you any harm. But even as you follow, you're aware that you can no longer see the town, when you turn your heads for a moment to look back. Turn your heads. Look back. What do you see? Nothing but mossy trunks, thick branches, a chaos of leaves. You are deep in the forest, a world you know and do not know. It's possible that, in the midst of your enchantment, a ripple of uncertainty passes through you, a touch of fear. But almost at once you fall under the spell of the music, which beckons you to an adventure you cannot refuse.

And what of the piper? Think about him. He is not angry at you, the children. His rage is directed elsewhere. The adults have wronged him and he will never forgive them. But as he leads you away from the familiar world, through the woods, how can he not be aware of his terrible power over you? How can he not rejoice in that power, as he pulls you forward by the force of his breath alone? How can he not feel, in the depths of his being, a certain contempt for you, his victims, as you follow him all too meekly to an unhappy end?

Please follow me. We'll soon be arriving at our destination.

Up ahead there. See? The trees are thinning out.

And here we are, at the foot of the mountain. A high hill, really, or call it a low mountain, rising up before us and covered with trees. Near the top you can see down into the town: the church, the street where we walked a short time ago, the steep roofs of the houses. Do I see a hand? Sir? My apologies. I didn't mean to cause you any anxiety. We're not going to climb the mountain.

Look straight ahead. There where the land begins to slope upward. Do you see where I'm pointing? That cluster of high bushes. If you look carefully, you can make out an opening. That is the entrance to the cave. Follow me.

We'll stop here for a moment, before the cave mouth. Please be patient while I count you one more time. We certainly don't want to lose anyone! Fourteen, fifteen. Sixteen. Seventeen. Very good. In just a moment I'll be leading you into the cave. Keep in mind that it's very dark inside. You'll be safe with me, but please: stay close.

What do we know about the children's entrance into the mountain? We know that the mountain opened at the playing of the flute. But how it opened is far from clear. Did the mountainside rip apart with a loud cracking of stone? Did trees shake and fall? Or was there, as some say, a great door in the mountain, which gradually swung open? We simply don't know. We also don't know about the music. Did the stranger play a new melody on his wooden pipe, addressed to the mountain alone? Was it a darker melody, an inhuman melody, drawn from all that lies hidden in the world? And let's not forget the children. What were they thinking, the children of Hamelin, as they watched the hillside open to receive them? Was there the thrill of a new adventure about to begin? Or was there a moment of doubt, as they stared into the darkness? We know only that the mountain opened and the children followed the stranger in.

Please follow me. This way. We have room for two abreast. Right through here. Careful. Watch your step. The light from outside will guide you in.

Are we all safely inside? Sixteen. Seventeen. You can still see a bit of light from the opening. It doesn't reach far. Please come forward a little more. Slowly. Slowly. That's right. Easy does it. Take your time. Good. Let's stop here, at the threshold of darkness.

Have any of you been in a mountain cave before? They vary widely. Some are immense as dreams. Others take the form of smaller chambers, with passageways leading to open spaces that contain stalactites, stagnant pools, even waterfalls. But the secret places of mountains always have one thing in common: once you make your way inside, past the dim light of the entrance, you can see nothing at all.

Think of the children. They have come into the mountain, behind the stranger with his magic pipe. They will follow him anywhere, even here, but as the music draws them forward they are aware that they've come to a place of utter darkness. This is no longer the shady forest, lit by bars of sunlight that lean through the high branches like ladders of brightness. This is a darkness deeper than the darkness of starless nights. This is a darkness darker than dark. It is a darkness so dark that it has a heaviness they can feel. It presses against them. Can you feel it pressing against you? It is the darkness on the other side of everything that is known.

The stranger is no longer visible. He is still playing his flute. Slowly, like a sun slipping behind a hill, the entrance closes. The children are half aware of the closing of the mountain, but they're still under the spell of the music. They can no longer see one another's faces. They have stopped moving. There is nothing left in the world but that music.

And now something happens. It is something more extraordinary than the closing of the mountain. It is something that has never once entered the minds of the children, as they followed the piper through the forest and into the darkness of the cave, for their minds have been possessed by an unworldly music. But now it happens, as it was destined to happen from the beginning: the music stops. The stranger has lowered his pipe. His work is done.

Imagine that moment. The children have come into the mountain. The music that filled them with longing has suddenly stopped. They are not frightened, not yet, but they are unsure. The silence is like a sound they have never heard before. They listen to that sound, that silence, and do not know what it is. All around them is darkness. They are beginning to understand, but they do not yet understand. They do not yet understand that the stranger has deceived them, that they will never return to the world of sunlight.

Ladies and gentlemen, I thank you for your patience. We're almost done. I ask only that you remain where you are for a moment while I slip outside.

Can you hear me? That is the sound of the inner partition sliding down. It's the last sound you will hear from the outside world. And that? That is the sound of the outer partition sliding down. It is a sound you cannot hear. The partitions are made of oak from the forest and are one meter thick. They can never be moved.

Although you can no longer hear me, I'm still speaking to you. These words are part of your tour. I am addressing you through the doors of the hill. In a few moments I'll make my way back through the forest and into town. The bus driver and I have a long way to go.

No one knows what became of the children. We know only that they were never seen again. We can imagine the first cries, the shouts, the desperate search for a way out. Did they beat their hands against the walls of the cave? Did they stumble and fall? Did they sit down and weep bitter tears? We have no way of knowing. But you will soon know. You will know what no one knows. You will know what no one can bear to know. We here at AuthentiTour don't pretend to have all the answers. We promise only to provide you with an authentic experience of events that took place long ago. These events have come down to us in the form of tales or legends, of stories to be told to children safe in their beds. But beware of stories. Stories have teeth that can sink into your flesh. If you try to tear yourself away, blood will spill. Think of the children of Hamelin. Think of them. They are alive in the dark, like you. They have been betrayed by a stranger, like you. They cannot see their own hands. They cannot see the ground. A terrible knowledge is growing in them.

Our tour is done. Thank you for choosing AuthentiTour. It has been my pleasure to serve as your guide.

LATE

Because Valeria is always late, because I'd like to have dinner with her at seven, and because, if I ask her to meet me at the restaurant at seven, I might not have dinner until eight, I ask Valeria to meet me at the restaurant at six. This plan, I tell myself, is a bold and ingenious way of defeating lateness. Even if Valeria arrives forty-five minutes late, for our six o'clock dinner, she will, without knowing it, be fifteen minutes early, for our seven o'clock dinner. I'll then feel grateful to her, for being fifteen minutes early, instead of impatient with her, for being forty-five minutes late, and the evening, rather than beginning with unconvincing excuses on her part and suppressed irritation on mine, will be perfect from the start. I enter the restaurant at ten minutes to six. This is not because it's important for me to be early, but because it's important for me not to be late. I'm soon seated at a table for two, where I take sips from a glass of water brought to me by a friendly waiter, to whom I've explained that I am meeting someone at six. From my table I can see the glass entrance door, through which three customers are entering, and part of a second room, where the tables are full and where I can see, on the far wall, part of a big-screen TV, on which a blond anchorwoman is moving her mouth silently above a news crawl. As six o'clock draws near, customers continue to enter, including one unaccompanied woman, who looks in my direction. She is not Valeria. I study my glass of water. I glance up, from time to time, at the opening or closing door, and down, now and then, at my watch. At six o'clock I deliberately look over at my waiter, who is standing at another table and writing on his pad, before I turn my attention to the door. No one is entering. By 6:10 I feel a first faint stirring of impatience. I remind myself that Valeria is only ten minutes late, that traffic is always unpredictable, that it's often difficult to find a parking space near the restaurant, that the parking garage is always full at this hour, that, although Valeria is ten minutes late, it feels like twenty minutes because I arrived ten minutes early, a fact that should not, in all fairness, be blamed on Valeria, and that, apart from such considerations, if she'd arrived at 6:10 she would have been a mere ten minutes late, for our six o'clock dinner, but an immense fifty minutes early, for our seven o'clock dinner, in which case my plan would have been a disastrous failure, since it would now be necessary to have dinner almost an hour earlier than I'd like to do. It is, therefore, I say to myself, pleasing to me that she hasn't yet arrived, and I should be grateful to her for not disappointing me by an unexpectedly early appearance. At 6:15 I order a cup of coffee and apologize to the waiter. He holds up the palm of one hand and closes his eyes for a few moments in a sign of understanding, sympathy, and amicable patience. In the second room, the blond anchorwoman has become a dark-haired anchorman with thick eyebrows. By 6:30 I can no longer repress an irritable restlessness. Valeria is now half an hour late, although she is also half an hour early, and despite the fact that I'm dutifully working my way through a second cup of coffee, which I do not want, in order to legitimize my occupation of the table, I feel that I'm taking unfair advantage of the restaurant's hospitality, especially since three couples are looking around and checking the time as they wait behind the blue velvet rope for a table to be free. At 6:35 the door swings open and Valeria enters. She is, I quickly see, not Valeria. She resembles Valeria, though only a little. She is so different from Valeria that I can't understand how I could possibly have mistaken her for Valeria. I remind myself that if Valeria were to step through the door at this very moment, she'd be only thirty-five minutes late, which, for her, is practically on time, while simultaneously, so far as my dinner plans are concerned, she'd be an astonishing twenty-five minutes early. Even if she were forty minutes late, I say to myself, for our six o'clock dinner, she'd still be twenty minutes early, for our seven o'clock dinner, and with this thought in mind I make every effort to assure myself that all is well, despite my awareness that she has made me wait thirty-five minutes at a table for two on a busy night in a crowded restaurant. By 6:45 I've become so impatient that I begin to entertain thoughts of leaving. What is the point, I ask myself, of sitting alone in a frantic restaurant, glancing now at my watch and now at the door, while waiters are striding briskly back and forth, and customers behind the blue velvet rope are flinging looks in my direction, as I wait for Valeria, who was supposed to meet me at six, who is already forty-five minutes late, and who, in only fifteen minutes, will be late by an entire hour? I remind myself that to leave now would be to defeat the deeper purpose of the evening, which is to meet Valeria, not at six, but at seven, so that, if she arrives in fifteen minutes, she will actually be on time. If I look at things calmly, without giving way to an understandable but unhelpful resentment, I can see that my plan is succeeding brilliantly. Then again, I can't help thinking, if Valeria is already forty-five minutes late, for our six o'clock dinner, though fifteen minutes early, for our seven o'clock dinner, there's no reason to think that she won't be as late for dinner at seven as she already is for dinner at six, in which case it's entirely pointless to continue sitting here like an idiot, wasting my precious time and taking up valuable space on a busy night in a crowded restaurant, though it's important to remember, I say to myself, that even if she turns out to be forty-five minutes late, for dinner at seven, she'll be no later for dinner at seven than she already is for dinner at six, and since I've now waited forty-five minutes, for the six o'clock dinner I did not want, I can easily wait forty-five minutes, for the seven o'clock dinner I've been eagerly looking forward to. The best thing to do, under the circumstances, is call the waiter over and order a glass of white wine. As he returns with the wine, I keep my eye steadily on the door. It strikes me as astonishing that I've somehow failed to bring a newspaper with me, or a good book, so that I might occupy the time that I knew was bound to pass before her late arrival, because the one thing you can count on, when it comes to Valeria, is that she's always late, although a book or newspaper, it now occurs to me, might have the disadvantage of concealing the visible impatience that serves as a continual, quiet apology to the staff, the manager, and the waiting customers. At 6:50 I glance up at the door. The door is quiet. No one is standing on the other side, raising a hand to grip the vertical brushed-steel bar that runs the length of the glass and serves as a handle. At 6:55 I begin to feel, beneath the tight surface of my fierce-willed calm, a ripple or flutter, as when, in the fourth grade, I rode for the first time on the roller coaster and felt it climbing higher and higher before the unthinkable plunge. Below me, I could see my parents growing smaller and smaller as they stood with their heads tipped back, looking up at me, and I could also see, far down, the top of the merry-go-round. As the hour approaches, I refuse to turn my attention to the door of the restaurant but stare tensely at my watch. At exactly seven I raise my eyes, as if to catch Valeria in the act of entering. Valeria is not entering. Of course Valeria isn't entering. Why would she be entering? My feelings are far from simple. I'm upset, even angry, that Valeria is one hour late for dinner, while at the same time I feel entirely justified in having asked her to meet me at six, since, had I asked her to meet me at seven, it would now be eight and my hunger would be unbearable. Immediately I remind myself that, though she is one hour late for dinner at six, she is not yet late for dinner at seven, so that my impatience, however reasonable, is uncalled for. Shouldn't I be pleased, even joyful, that everything is taking place as I foresaw? At 7:10 a new impatience stirs in me. Now Valeria is not only late, by one hour and ten minutes, for our six o'clock dinner, she is also late, by ten minutes, for our seven o'clock dinner. Ten minutes late, of course, is laughably early, for a woman like Valeria, but I am growing hungry and can't forget that I asked her to meet me, not at seven, but at six. At 7:20 I order, reluctantly, a third cup of coffee. At 7:30 a new thought arises: is it possible that something has happened to Valeria? After all, though she's only thirty minutes late, for our seven o'clock dinner, she's now ninety minutes late, for our six o'clock dinner, and, even for Valeria, an hour and a half is a lateness that has to be taken seriously. Maybe, at this very moment, she is standing helplessly at the side of the road, beside a flat tire, her emergency lights blinking, her cell phone uncharged. Maybe she's been in an accident and remains unconscious in the car, slumped forward with her face pressed against the steering wheel, the horn blasting steadily into the night. As I sit here, feeling ignored and mistreated, she might, for all I know, be lying in an ambulance that is speeding through red lights, stop signs, and crosswalks on its way to the emergency room, while an anxious medic stands over her, watching a screen. The possibilities, which alarm me, also annoy me, since they undermine the exasperation that I feel is justified by her extreme lateness, unless of course something has really happened to Valeria, in which case my exasperation is not only irrelevant but offensive. I know I should call her, right now, this very second, but as I reach for my cell phone I understand that I can't bear the thought of listening to Valeria make excuses, once again, for being late. I decide that I'll wait until exactly 7:45, at which time I will either call Valeria or get up and leave. But as the hands of my watch approach the final minute, I become aware of a change in the restaurant. No customers stand behind the blue velvet rope, several tables are empty, and the waiters, who moments ago were rushing about, are now moving quietly, as if they have all the time in the world. If I remain at my table, I am no longer interfering with business, as I was at 6:30, when I began to feel that I was taking unfair advantage of the restaurant's hospitality, and it might even be argued, I say to myself, that I am helping business, in a small way, by showing passersby, who glance in the window, that the restaurant is doing a lively business, even at this hour. Although Valeria is now nearly one hour and forty-five minutes late, for the six o'clock dinner I did not want, she is not yet forty-five minutes late, for the seven o'clock dinner I've been counting on, and I am certainly used to waiting forty-five minutes for Valeria to arrive at whatever place I have arranged to meet her. At eight o'clock she is two hours late, for our six o'clock dinner, and one hour late, for our seven o'clock dinner. I remind myself that I expected her to be one hour late, for our six o'clock dinner, so that if she is now one hour late, for our seven o'clock dinner, it's only to be expected. The one course of action open to me is to call the waiter over and order a second glass of wine. At 8:30 I ask myself, for the first time, whether Valeria might have mistaken the day, even though she never mistakes the day, or whether I'm the one who has mistaken the day, even though I never mistake the day. At nine o'clock the thought crosses my mind that Valeria is not coming to dinner. This thought, which disturbs me, is quickly followed by a second thought: that her arrival is not, considered objectively, out of the question, or even unlikely, since she is always late, though not this late. In that case, I say to myself, I wonder whether it would be better for me to order a fourth cup of coffee, which will keep me up all night, or a third glass of wine, which will make me drowsy. I decide to order a fourth cup of coffee, come what may. At ten o'clock Valeria is four hours late, for our six o'clock dinner, and three hours late, for our seven o'clock dinner. Now there are only a few couples seated at the tables, speaking quietly, and one man with neatly combed gray hair, who sits alone, reading a newspaper and nursing a beer. A waiter leans against a counter and stares out the window at people walking by. There are cars parked on both sides of the street, with spaces here and there, and, if I lean forward, I can make out part of my own car, parked on the other side of the street, a block away. In the other room, the television screen shows a center fielder moving gracefully to his left under a high fly ball. At 10:15 I order a fifth cup of coffee, which I have no intention of drinking. By now I feel certain that Valeria is not coming to dinner, though it remains true that I can't claim to know, with the degree of assurance that would put my mind at ease, that she absolutely won't be coming to dinner, even at this late hour. At the same time I've grown so hungry that my stomach has begun to hurt. Although it's impossible for me to order dinner, since I am waiting to have dinner with Valeria, it's also impossible for me to go without dinner, since I can feel myself growing dizzy from hunger while sitting at a table in a restaurant, like a man dying of thirst at the edge of a stream. I can, true enough, no longer imagine eating a full meal, because of the pain in my stomach, and so, when I call the waiter over, I order only a bowl of onion soup and a small salad. When I've finished my meal, which I think of as a pre-dinner, or a second lunch, I continue to sit at the table, glancing out at the street and occasionally at the door. At eleven o'clock only I and the man with neatly combed gray hair remain in the restaurant. Outside, two teenagers walk by, holding hands. At 11:45 the man with gray hair folds his newspaper in half, stands up, pushes his chair in, and, without looking at me, walks toward the door. As he passes the counter where the cash register sits, he reaches into a small bowl and removes a mint. At 11:50 an elderly waiter, whom I haven't seen before, tells me, in a melancholy voice, that the restaurant will be closing at midnight. I glance at the door, where Valeria is not entering, look down at my watch, which has shifted, very slightly, from the center of my wrist, and ask him to bring me the check. The check arrives promptly, in a green leather booklet resting on a small black tray. I pay cash, leaving a large tip, and then, after a pause, a larger tip. At one minute before midnight I walk out of the restaurant and head for my car. From the driver's seat I can see the plateglass window of the restaurant, the red neon sign, and the entrance door. It's only a little past midnight, and it isn't beyond the realm of the possible, I say to myself, that Valeria, who is always late, might finally arrive. Since I've already waited five hours, for our seven o'clock dinner, and six hours, for our six o'clock dinner, a burden of waiting that, as I'm fully aware, deserves to be called unreasonable, it is, I assure myself, no more unreasonable, logically speaking, to wait still longer. At one in the morning I take note of a temporal symmetry: I have now waited seven hours, for our six o'clock dinner, and six hours, for our seven o'clock dinner. At two in the morning I'm still in my car, watching the dark restaurant, which turned off its lights long ago, except for a small, luminous sign, ice blue, in one corner. At 3:30 in the morning I feel myself growing sleepy, despite the four-and-a-half cups of coffee that ought to be agitating me into alertness. I remind myself that, if I yield to my desire to fall asleep, I will never know whether Valeria has come to dinner. Two hours from now, dawn will break. When the restaurant opens, at seven in the morning, I can leave my car, walk across the street, and order a delicious breakfast of blueberry pancakes with crisp strips of bacon on top, over which I'll pour, from a small jar with a retractable metal spout, maple syrup the color of amber. The waitress will smile at me as she bends forward to refill my cup of coffee. The breakfast will, in a sense, be my dinner of the night before, and after breakfast I can stop waiting for Valeria to arrive yesterday and begin waiting for her to arrive today. After all, I say to myself, no matter how late Valeria is, for our six o'clock dinner, she will always be one hour earlier, for our seven o'clock dinner, so that, whenever she arrives, she'll be earlier than she would have been, on some other occasion. It is, in any case, far better to wait for Valeria, who is always late, than to have no one to wait for, at any hour, and with this thought in mind I lean my head back against the car seat, glance down at my watch, and turn my face toward the dark restaurant, which will soon be ready to begin a new day.

II

THE LITTLE PEOPLE

Who They Are

They are citizens of our town, who own property, pay taxes, and vote. They dress like us. They speak like us. They eat like us. They are two inches tall. They educate their children in their own schools, which by all available criteria are superior to ours. They have jobs like ours: doctors, teachers, computer programmers, bricklayers. They do not own or operate cars, preferring to walk or ride bicycles. They are wary of us, though friendships sometimes happen. Their voices are difficult for us to hear. In their presence we feel immense, ugly, loud, coarse, and menacing.

Where They Live

They live on a two-acre lot in the northwest section of our town, not far from the old mall. Last year they purchased an additional half acre, adjacent to one side of the lot and now in the final stages of preparation for housing development and the construction of a major shopping center. A few still live in undeveloped parts of town, like the woods behind the reservoir or the banks of West Creek, but life in such places is difficult, impermanent, and dangerous. Sometimes a family is invited into one of our homes for dinner and conversation, and may even spend the night before returning to their own community.

Their Community

Because our laws do not require residents to indicate religious belief, political affiliation, or height in inches, we would have no way of knowing their population were it not for their street addresses, all of which indicate residence within the two-acre lot. The latest census lists their number as 2,157, out of a total population of 32,476. In addition, a small and unknown number, probably between two hundred and three hundred, live in less civilized circumstances, without addresses, in other parts of town. The known citizens produce children at the same rate we do, with the difference that their children do not move out of the community, so that their population is increasing more rapidly than ours. On their two-acre lot, commonly known as Greenhaven, we can see a busy downtown avenue filled with shops and restaurants, with narrower streets leading to residential areas. In the northeast corner are smaller houses and rental apartments occupied by sanitation workers, firefighters, hospital employees, and street-repair personnel. The buildings of Greenhaven include two elementary schools, a middle school, and a high school, as well as a microchip plant, a waste-management plant, a four-year college with MA programs in business and engineering, a hospital and clinical research center, a library, two banks, a mall, and a new research facility notable for innovations in nanotechnology. Greenhaven is in many respects self-sufficient, though the larger town supplies its water and electric power by means of miniaturized pipes and wires designed by Greenhaven engineers.

The Enclosure

In response to the dangers presented by squirrels, chipmunks, skunks, and occasional rabbits, by birds that can swoop down at any moment, by unleashed dogs and outdoor cats, and by our own mischievous children, the inhabitants of Greenhaven agreed forty years ago to work with us in erecting a brick wall four feet high, pierced by four entrance gates and topped by a row of cast-iron spear-point finials. At each of the four corners rises a watchtower. The enclosure is equipped with an electronically operated retractable plexiglass roof, which can rise to cover the entire community for protection against violent downpours and heavy snowstorms. Teams of workers regularly scale the wall in order to clear the slanted glass panels of bird and squirrel droppings, stray twigs and leaves, and accumulations of snow. Many residents of Greenhaven object to the wall, which emphasizes their apartness. They call for a return to an earlier time, when inhabitants battled the weather bravely and guards armed with entrapment wire and tranquilizer guns surrounded and killed any animal that entered the grounds.

Our Town

Our town is for the most part white and middle-class, with a small percentage of African Americans and Asian Americans who work primarily in the legal and medical professions or run their own businesses. We are fiscally conservative but socially liberal and pride ourselves on welcoming to our community anyone who wishes to come here and can afford to stay. Although most of our places of worship are Protestant churches of the Congregational, Methodist, Presbyterian, and Episcopalian persuasions, we are also home to Congregation B'nai Israel and Temple Beth El, which serve our small but growing number of Reform and Orthodox Jews. At a recent town hall meeting, approval was granted for the construction of a mosque across from the Senior Center. Incidents of racial and religious bias, though rare, do occur and are taken very seriously by political parties of the left and right. But however much we make it our business to be fair to all people and to fight prejudice of every variety, we continually come up against the problem of the Little People. Here it is less a matter of being fair or unfair than of overcoming a sense that they are radically other. When they come into our homes, our chairs and tables rise over them like hills. When we walk over to Greenhaven, our shadows darken whole neighborhoods.

Employment

Although we never enter Greenhaven—quite apart from the existence of the wall, we would fear crushing people with our enormous feet, damaging homes and gardens, smashing street signs and lawn furniture, causing unspeakable destruction—members of their community often come to us. Many are skilled at tasks for which we eagerly employ them. Expert plumbers can enter the clogged pipes beneath our sinks and clear away obstacles more swiftly and thoroughly than our plumbers are able to do, with their crude plungers and clumsy snakes. Highly trained mechanics enter our vast refrigerators, stoves, and washing machines to remove dirt and grime, touch up scratched surfaces, and perform thorough inspections. Greenhaven women, in search of secondary incomes, advertise online an array of housecleaning skills, such as removing undetected particles of dust on mantelpieces, candlesticks, door handles, vases, and the tops of baseboards, or polishing hard-to-see places on countertops or chair legs. To watch a group of three housecleaners with their hair up in buns and their white aprons tied behind their backs as they push their meticulously crafted dust mops across tabletops or bend over with cloths the size of flies' wings to remove dots of dust between the fringes of a throw rug is a pleasure and a revelation. Teams of window washers with ladders as tall as drinking straws and an ingenious system of ropes and pulleys are able to remove every visible and invisible smudge or spot from our suddenly gleaming windows. Meticulous gardeners disappear into the depths of our bushes and cut away dead leaves and rotten twigs before climbing down to chop lumps of soil into sand-fine particles. Our children's birthdays are made memorable by intricate designs on the icing of pastries the size of bottlecaps and by ribbons on birthday presents tied by a team of ribbon masters to form lions, dragons, and rearing horses. The expert help provided by workers from Greenhaven is far more satisfactory than that provided by our own community, and we are continually discovering new tasks that demand their dedication and skill, such as cleaning the insides of our downspouts, removing lint from our laundered clothing, polishing our eyeglass lenses, and searching our cellars and attics for ants and mouse droppings.

Other Encounters

In addition to enlisting their help in a host of tasks, we regularly welcome the inhabitants of Greenhaven as equals on social occasions. We invite them to attend our places of worship, our town meetings, and our civic events, which include concerts in the park, parades on Main Street, charity fundraisers, and visits to historic houses; often special conveniences are provided, in order to make them feel comfortable and protect them from the many dangers of our world. One minister has paid for the construction of a miniature set of pews that he has placed on the bench of a front-row pew and that can be reached by a banistered stairway leading from floor to seat. Many of our clothing stores have set aside areas where specially manufactured shirts, blouses, dresses, suit jackets, jeans, and chinos are displayed on little shelves or hung from quarter-inch wooden hangers. Supermarkets, computer stores, restaurants, and furniture stores now offer arrangements of their own. Indeed, the manufacture of small objects suitable for the inhabitants of Greenhaven is a fast-growing industry in our town, where a new company called Design Innovations has led to more than two hundred jobs for members of both communities. In addition, our Department of Public Works has supplied many of our streets with carefully marked lanes for the bicycles of visitors from Greenhaven. One of the delights of a summer day in our town is strolling along a tree-shaded sidewalk while, just below the curb, a row of little bicycles moves along. Once, walking with my young daughter, I saw a disturbing sight. From the other side of the street a squirrel rushed toward six bicycles. The squirrel seemed to grow larger and larger; his head rose over the cyclists like the face of a monster in a bad movie.

My daughter screamed and clung to my arm. Suddenly the squirrel lay twitching on its side with its front legs bound together as the six cyclists continued on their way. It all took place so swiftly that I remember only the glittering lines of thread or wire twisted around the squirrel's legs.

Friendships

Mingling with members of the Greenhaven community often leads to more intimate occasions. Some of us, perhaps through a closeness formed with a houseworker or through repeated public events like Sunday sermons or town hall meetings, will invite a family to our homes for dinner. The initial awkwardness of such occasions is usually not difficult to overcome, especially if we have ordered a set of appropriately sized chairs, tables, dishes, and utensils, which can be arranged on our dining-room tables. The voices of our guests are so low that we are forced to bend forward with our monstrous heads and vast fleshy ears, but we are able to follow the conversation after some effort and are careful to speak in lowered voices. Our guests are invariably lively, intelligent, humorous, and well informed about all things pertaining to our town. Sometimes these visits develop into lasting friendships and a sense of deep loyalty. Quite apart from everything else, we admire the sheer physical beauty of the Little People, the elegance of their eyes and mouths, the delicacy of their fingers, the silken perfection of their skin. We want them to be happy. We want them to love us. We want them to forgive us.

Names

Their names are like ours, with two exceptions. In the matter of surnames, theirs take only the form of the patronymic: Johnson, Robertson, Carlson, Edwards, Williams, Richardson, Peterson. The reign of the patronym suggests an early tribal culture, long before the present era. In the matter of first names, theirs are the same as ours—Mary, Brian, Karen, Steven—except in the case of working-class males, whose names sometimes refer to the type of work done by the father or grandfather: Brick Edwards, Stone Jameson, Shingle Johnson. These work-related first names have attracted interest in our community and are sometimes given to our newborn sons.

The Story of Catherine White and Shingle Johnson

Catherine White was a forty-two-year-old widow who lived alone in one of our better residential neighborhoods. Her husband, Edward White, an investment banker, had died in a car accident two years earlier, leaving her a secure monthly income and a diversified portfolio of stocks and bonds. After a period of mourning, Catherine resumed her active social life and spent her spare time refurbishing the house. Among the help she hired was Shingle Johnson, an expert woodworker from Greenhaven who had been named for his father, a skilled carpenter. He was employed by Catherine to remove scratches on mahogany table legs, repair the patterned wooden strips between the glass panes in the dining-room hutch, and replace the plain wooden knobs on the drawers of her bureau with a series of handmade knobs carved with intricate scenes showing village dances, bathers in lakes, and riverside cafés. Catherine White was so taken by the work of Shingle Johnson that she kept finding more for him to do. She paid him to repair her childhood collection of wooden animals from Germany and to build a complete set of doll furniture for her niece's ninth birthday. She asked him to create three teakwood chests that rose to the height of his shoulders and were useful for storing paper clips, postage stamps, and duplicate keys. Shingle Johnson began spending so much time at Catherine White's house that now and then she would invite him to stay overnight in order to spare him the effort of returning to Greenhaven, where he lived with his aunt and uncle while expanding his business and saving up for a down payment on a home of his own. On such nights he slept between two folded handkerchiefs on the seat of the leather chair in her late husband's study. It was about this time that people began noticing a change in Catherine White. She had always been an attractive woman who dressed well. She now began dressing more daringly, though with impeccable taste, in skirts and silk blouses that emphasized her fine figure. She seemed more youthful; her skin was said to glow; she gave off an intensity and excitement that no one could miss, though at the same time she would often fall into states of abstraction in which she would stare out of windows or sit silently among friends. Exactly when she became aware that she was in love with Shingle Johnson is not clear. As we now know from her diary, she was struck one day by the sheer grace and beauty of Shingle Johnson as he stood in a shaft of sunlight at the base of an end table. But all of us are struck by the grace and beauty of the Little People. Catherine White, seated on the Oriental rug beside Shingle Johnson as she gave instructions about repairing the front feet of the clawfoot couch, or bending toward him as he knelt on a coaster on the lamp table examining a scratch on a cherrywood bowl, was startled by the perfection of his eyebrows, the bones of his cheek, his elegant wrists, his barely visible fingernails. One day, when he asked whether he could step onto her hand in order to be lifted from the base of the fireplace to the top of the upholstered armchair, so that he could set up his ladder and reach the bottom strip of an oak-framed painting, she nearly fainted as she felt the pressure of his feet against the skin of her hand. She could not bear to be away from him for a single moment, while at the same time she felt so gross and fleshy in his presence, despite her slenderness, that she wanted to rush out of the house and never return. She ate less and less; she weakened; she took to bed. One morning, waking after a night of restless half-sleep, she saw him standing beside her on the bedspread, looking at her with concern. Unable to stop herself, she blurted out her love for him, heard her words with horror, burst into apology, and covered her face with her hands. He told her that he had been in love with her from the moment he saw her bend her head to inhale the odor of a chrysanthemum in the vase on the sideboard. Tears streamed along Catherine White's cheeks. He began sharing her bed; each morning she would wake up and find him lying beside her on her pillow. She loved him in a way that pierced her to the center of her being, but her feelings for him were not only spiritual. He liked to climb naked onto one or the other of her breasts as she lay naked on her back; once on top, he would seat himself on the areola and embrace the nipple with his legs. Holding the sides of the nipple with the palms of both hands, he would rub his face back and forth across the sides and top, rousing her to shuddering paroxysms that she had never dreamed possible. We know less about how he satisfied his own strong desire. From hints in the diary, it appears that he liked to lie on her stomach and make love to her navel, but sometimes he preferred a more daring method: he would kneel naked on her lower lip as she lay back in bed with parted lips, and from there he would lean forward against her upper lip with both arms spread in order to steady himself as he thrust against the tip of her tongue. Their love was joyful but not without difficulty. She required continual reassurance that her towering face, her nostrils the size of caverns, her massive fingers thicker than his thighs, the bloody gashes in her slimy eye-whites, did not fill him with disgust and revulsion, while he, a lean and powerful two-inch man, was troubled by his sense of smallness and weakness. They loved doing things together: reading side by side, speaking about their childhoods, taking rides in her car to have a picnic lunch on the bank of West Creek, discussing home improvements, and solving crossword puzzles (he with the aid of a demagnifying glass that reduced the words and squares to readable size). She loved looking at his face, with its tanned and glowing skin, its strong, delicate cheekbones that looked as if they had been carved by a master, and its teeth so small that she could distinguish them only when she bent close; he loved lying on his back in the palm of her hand with his hands clasped behind his head. One day she drove home from a garden store with a potted chrysanthemum and found Shingle Johnson lying on the bottom step of the porch with his legs shattered and blood pouring from his chest and neck. In terror she called an ambulance and accompanied him to the east gate of Greenhaven, where a team of medics placed him on a wheeled bed and rolled him swiftly to the hospital. A stray cat had snatched him up as he was strolling in the yard and had dropped him onto the porch step. Shingle Johnson survived, but both legs had to be amputated and an artificial lung implanted. He did not leave Greenhaven again. Catherine White never forgave herself for leaving him alone that day. She vowed to take care of him for the rest of her life, but his aunt and uncle blamed her for the accident and stopped all communication between them. Catherine White dressed in black for twelve months, during which she scarcely left the house. When she came out of mourning, her face had changed, as if she had aged ten years. She dressed carelessly, in loose-fitting smocks or baggy jeans, saw few people, and died six months later. Rumors of suicide made the rounds, but we knew she had died of grief. A long obituary in the local paper spoke of her years as an elementary-school teacher, her marriage to Edward Pearsall White, and her many contributions to local charities.

History

The two-acre lot later known as Greenhaven was turned over to the Little People some seventy-five years ago by a philanthropic businessman who owned a few hundred acres in different parts of town. He paid for the vacant lot to be cleared—trees cut down and stumps uprooted, boulders removed, an old rusted shopping cart hauled away—before the parcel of land was divided into small units by its new owners. The progression of the two-acre lot from a stony field to a village of primitive farmers to a fully modern community over the course of seventy-five years is one of the remarkable developments in the history of our town. The property was officially named Greenhaven at a town hall meeting in the year of the American bicentennial. Today the inhabitants are in certain respects more advanced than we are, especially in the fields of microelectronics and software design. Not long after the clearing of the land, the settlers erected a large stone wall, two inches high, around the entire lot, but the wall proved ineffective against animal invasion. Squirrels in particular had always been a menace, though a specially trained force of guardians quickly became expert at trapping and killing them in a ditch skirting the inner wall. The controversial four-foot brick enclosure was in part a response to the attack of a neighbor's cat, who smashed several houses and mauled dozens of inhabitants before the guards secured it with ropes and put it to death. The earlier history of the inhabitants of Greenhaven is less well documented. They appear to have lived in temporary communities all over our town, in woods, vacant lots, and even in backyards; evidence suggests they were present at the time of the Revolutionary War and of our town's origin as a farming village in 1696. One respected Greenhaven historian traces the presence of his people back several centuries before that, to a time when the land was inhabited by roaming tribes of Native Americans, and still earlier, to a world of forests and streams inhabited by deer and wolves. There is every reason to believe that the ancestors of the people of Greenhaven were here long before our earliest settlers and that our forebears drove them from their land.

Money

Their money is identical to ours in all respects except one: it is so minuscule that we can barely see it. A Greenhaven quarter is only a little larger than a grain of sand. For this reason our banks and businesses own Converters, machines that accept Greenhaven money and convert it to the size we are accustomed to, as well as Enhancers, machines that magnify Greenhaven credit cards and debit cards so that we can read them. The machines are also programmed to work in the opposite direction, thereby enabling us to purchase goods sold by Greenhaven merchants in our stores. Online transactions between both communities have become more and more common. Those of us who employ Greenhaven workers pay them by notifying the Greenhaven Accounts Department of any of our banks, which in turn transfer the sum to the main bank in Greenhaven. Before this arrangement, we were required to drive to a bank and convert our bills and coins to miniature dimensions, storing the barely visible money in envelopes the size of postage stamps, in order to have a supply of wages on hand. The recent connection between our banking systems, supported by both communities, is a development that many of us see as an encouraging sign of increased interdependence.

Plants and Animals

For most of their history, the Little People have lived among soaring blades of grass, wild berries bigger than their heads, leaves the size of porch roofs, and trees so vast that small hollows were sufficient for sheltering many families. Precisely when the smaller strains of plant life were developed is a matter of debate among Greenhaven historians, but most agree that it began soon after the two-acre lot was turned over to its inhabitants and became their place of settlement. Within a generation, the new grass, the new dandelions, and the new violets had begun to appear. By the time the four-foot wall was erected, more than two dozen varieties of plants and flowers were growing in the yards of Greenhaven, along with three varieties of maple tree, eight to fourteen inches in height, and two of spruce. Greenhaven researchers work tirelessly to cultivate miniature strains of all flora that grow in our town, as well as new cross-strains unknown in our community. The fate of Greenhaven fauna is less clear. At present, genetic scientists have failed to produce a single successful animal, though recent laboratory experiments have led to predictions of a Greenhaven German shepherd within the next five years. Greenhaven is still not safe from our enormous insects, in particular our mosquitoes, ants, spiders, and flies, which are trapped and killed swiftly, or from our dangerous birds, which are caught in nets, taken outside the gates, and released. At town hall meetings, frequent debates about how to control the flights of our birds have led to no useful answers.

Outsiders

Very little is known about the two hundred to three hundred inhabitants who live outside the walls of Greenhaven. They appear to be descendants of roaming tribes that chose not to settle on the two-acre lot when it was turned over to their community seventy-five years ago. Now and then a rebellious Greenhaven adolescent, male or female, will escape from life behind the wall and join the outsiders, who fend for themselves and live off the land, though more often than not the experiment does not outlast a year. More rarely, a youthful outsider will ask to be admitted to the enclave of Greenhaven, with or without parental consent. The usual fate of such youngsters is to be adopted by a volunteer family and enrolled in a special school program, with varying degrees of success. Dr. Henry Josephson, a leading Greenhaven neuroscientist, is the most remarkable example of radical transformation. Sometimes at dusk, when we glance out at our darkening backyards, we are aware of a slight movement in the grass, which might be a chipmunk or a sparrow or, as we secretly desire, a group of outsiders, passing through.

Greenhaven Homes

Although it is impossible for us to enter their homes, whose chimneys rise to the height of our knees, we are familiar with their rooms and furnishings through photographs taken by Greenhaven residents and sent to our computers and mobile devices. We observe the kitchen cabinets, the dining-room tables, the wickerwork patio chairs, the flat-screen TVs, the shower stalls with sliding glass doors, the double beds with quilts and headboards, and understand that they live just as we do. But gradually we become aware of small differences, especially if we zoom in on the images. Then we notice details that were invisible before: the carved arabesques on window muntins, the painted rural scenes on the edges of bookshelves, the circus animals carved in cameo along the tops of baseboards in dens and playrooms. As we continue to enlarge, we discover new details within the details, such as wooden eighth notes carved along the sides of the vertical grooves of a piano leg, with an occasional mischievous face peeking out from behind a note. Many of us adopt in our own homes the hidden designs we discover in theirs, hiring experts from Greenhaven to bring about the desired effect. We admire the perfection of complex small objects like laptops or televisions that can rest on the tips of our fingers, but what fascinates us is the sense of an invisible world perpetually on the verge of becoming visible.

Eric Lindblom and Mary Robertson

Mary Robertson of Greenhaven was hired by Denise Lindblom to microdust the grooves, runners, and lion-head finials of two antique mahogany rocking chairs inherited from her late mother. Denise was so pleased with the work that she asked Mary to come twice a week for a number of cleaning tasks, especially that of dusting the tops of the more than three thousand books that sat in a dozen bookcases throughout the house. Denise Lindblom worked as a reference librarian in our town library. She was married to Mark Lindblom, a high-school English teacher, who was fond of saying that he and his wife lived in a world of books. They had one child, a son named Eric, a high-school sophomore fifteen years old: a shy, lanky, somewhat dreamy young man who had a few friends in the neighborhood and a few at school but who would just as soon sit alone in his room with a book in his lap as go outside and shoot hoops or hang out in town. He sometimes talked to girls but that was all, and he had never gone on a date. He was usually home when Mary Robertson was in the house, kneeling on the tops of books with her mop and dust rags or climbing the shelves of bookcases by means of a rope ladder with hooks on top. He enjoyed watching her work. They exchanged a few words, and he discovered that he could speak easily to her. He admired the perfect cuffs of her rolled-up jeans and the supple movements of her reaching and bending form. He began looking forward to her arrival. She was twenty-one years old, a graduate of Greenhaven College who was working part-time while training to be a research assistant at TomorrowCorp, a new company specializing in the reorganization of existing spaces, in particular the development of aerial bicycle paths. As she spoke in her lively, playful, barely audible voice, Eric felt in his body a vast stillness. One afternoon he saw her resting on a bookshelf. She was leaning back against the spine of a book, swinging her calves slowly back and forth, and the sight of her there on the shelf, with her head tipped back, her brown-black hair falling across one shoulder, and her eyes half closed, filled him with a kind of desperate happiness. He dreamed about her night after night; one night she looked at him sadly, turned into a butterfly, and flew away. He found himself wanting to stroke her hair with the tip of his finger, and the thought of it filled him with a shame so unforgiving that he bit down hard on his fingertip, bringing tears to his eyes. One day, as he adjusted a book for her on a shelf where she was working, something brushed lightly against the side of his hand. He understood that it was her hair, or a piece of her blouse; he felt light-headed and had to brace himself to keep from falling. The daily sight of her anklebones above her white sneakers troubled him as if he had caught glimpses of a forbidden part of her anatomy. In the long days of her absence he fell into states of dullness and apathy so extreme that the act of suicide seemed to him a form of exertion beyond his capacity. These states alternated with sudden eruptions of restlessness that raged in him like attacks of madness. In her presence he felt that he was hovering oppressively close, like a bear bending over a goldfish in a bowl, or remaining at a discourteous distance, huddled in a corner like a homeless man in a bus station, while she, nearly invisible on a distant shelf, seemed no more than an optical disturbance caused by a flicker of light and shade. One day, as she was preparing to leave, he heard something that sounded like "sssooo" in the air of the room. He realized in a rush of panic that he had said aloud the words "I miss you." She turned to him with a look he could not see clearly and said something that sounded like breath blowing on a candle. On her next visit he stayed in his room, sprawled on his bed reading one page of a book over and over again without knowing whether the dinner conversation at an English country house was witty and cheerful or sinister and tense. He sensed Mary Robertson in his room and felt her climb up the side of his bed by gripping the spread. Once on top of the bed, she began walking forward beside his leg, grasped his shirt next to his belt, and climbed up onto his stomach. There she took several steps forward and sat down facing him, with her legs drawn up under her. She was wearing a white blouse with black buttons and a knee-length pleated skirt. She looked at him kindly. She said that he was a friend, a dear friend, that she loved him as a friend, but only as a friend, and feared that her friendship might have been mistaken for something else. As she spoke, the sound of her voice soothed him, while the actual words she was uttering seemed to contain something dangerous that he would have to return to at a later time and examine with extreme care. He was a lovely boy, she said, who would delight many women, and she would always think of him fondly. But she was a Greenhaven girl, and there could be no crossing over. She hoped she had not encouraged in him a sense that more than friendship was possible. When she was done speaking, she remained sitting with lowered eyes. After a while she stood up, walked forward across his chest, laid the palm of one hand for a moment on his chin, and quickly descended to the bed. She climbed down the side and left the room. She never returned to the house. Mrs. Lindblom complained that the girl had given abrupt notice for so-called "family" reasons and asked her son if he had been aware of anything unusual in her behavior. Eric refused to leave his bed for five days; his mother leaned over him tenderly, feeling his forehead with her palm. He said to himself, over and over again: "I'll kill myself tonight." The words helped him get through the next difficult months.

Difficulties

The inhabitants of Greenhaven provoke in us feelings of admiration and envy: we are moved by the perfection of their bodies, the smoothness of their skin, the elegance of their movements. Such feelings often lead to self-loathing, since even the smallest and thinnest of us, in comparison, rise to dizzying heights, move cumbrously, and carry masses of jiggling flesh. Some of us attempt to combat self-loathing by reminding ourselves that the perfection of the Greenhavenites is an inevitable distortion caused by our coarseness of perception, and that among themselves they are surely aware of rough or pimpled skin, hairy nostrils, and unclean teeth. But self-loathing can quickly turn into resentment. What right do these people have to make us dissatisfied with ourselves, in ways for which we are in no way responsible? Wouldn't we be better off if they simply disappeared? We could squash any one of them with a single blow of the fist. The violence of the thought fills us with anxiety and remorse, and we reproach ourselves for emotions we judge to be savage, vicious, and cruel. These emotions, of course, are precisely what one might expect of enormous creatures who stride violently through the world, crushing insects and blades of grass beneath their feet, slaughtering trees, ripping up the ground, grunting with pleasure. Is it a wonder that we want to be someone else?

The New Shortness

Although many of our teenage boys still long to be tall, a new appreciation of shortness has begun to spread. Shortness, it is felt, is less wasteful of space, more efficient in design. Shortness puts you closer to the earth, where real things happen, while tallness carries you off into the clouds. Above all, shortness decreases your distance from the Little People. Our high school now has a Shortness Club, open to male students five feet two and under. It is considered so great an honor to be a member of the Shortness Club that students are often caught cheating as they stand to be measured; many train themselves to walk and stand upright with deeply bent knees, in order to remain below the dreaded cutoff mark. One troubled boy, a proud member of the club in his freshman year, grew two inches over the summer and was ejected from the club at the beginning of his sophomore year. That afternoon he went home and began cutting off his feet with a hacksaw before his mother found him and called an ambulance. Another boy, confined to a wheelchair, argued that in the name of fairness his height should be measured from a sitting position. Short girls, who are planning to form a club of their own, are treated by taller girls with new respect. New kinds of attractiveness are becoming fashionable: barely developed breasts draw admiring attention; small penises are the envy of locker rooms; little thumbs, small eyes, and narrow shoulders are noted with approval.

Giants

In an effort to experience what they must feel in our presence, we sometimes attempt to imagine smallness. If I am six feet tall, I rise to a height thirty-six times greater than the height of a resident of Greenhaven. A comparable giant, for us, would attain a height of 216 feet. I imagine standing at the foot of such a giant and looking up at a knee that is higher than the crossbars at the top of a telephone pole. My chin reaches partway up the side of a towering shoe. The stench of leather and excrement is so powerful that I can barely breathe. Suddenly the foot rises into the air like a house in a tornado. I want to rush for cover but there is nowhere to go. The foot crashes down like a couch falling from an apartment window. Shudders twist along my legs and up into my chest. From high in the clouds, something massive is coming toward me. Just as it is about to crush me to death, it stops above my head. Long slabs of cracked red meat begin to separate. A row of yellowish white tombstones appears. Between them sit stinking chunks of cheese. The smell of rot and filth thickens the air. Above the teeth I see an ugly wet red quivering mass. A roar fills my ears with pain as a hot wind burns my face. He has said hello. My face is wet with fear.

Deeper Changes

The current fashion for shortness may be a superficial sign, but other shifts suggest more lasting effects. Because of the barely audible voices of the Little People and the virtual silence with which they move about, a new quietness has begun to appear among us. Bursts of loud laughter are frowned upon. Conversations are conducted in low voices. Music no longer blares from open windows. Lawn mowers, hedge trimmers, vacuum cleaners, and snow blowers now come with mufflers. The increased quietness permits us to hear new sounds in our neighborhoods, like the quiver of a grasshopper leg rubbing against a forewing or the sound of a falling maple leaf as it lands on the floor of a porch. More important is the new visual alertness. We pay attention, as never before, to small details of our world, such as the stitches in a window curtain, the shape of a blade of grass, the shadow cast by a hair lying across a cheek. Sometimes we have the sensation that the world has become sharper and more detailed. It's as if we had been walking in the rain and now the sun has come out. The world bursts out around us. We are born anew. We see.

Thomas Gebhardt and Janet Peterson

At the age of thirty, Thomas Gebhardt began searching for a wife. His life was secure—he had already risen to the position of director of software development at New Directions Software—and he was tired of starting things with woman after woman only to break it off a few months later with the familiar sensation of diminishing excitement. At the advice of a friend and against his own nature, he signed up with Do It or Rue It, a new online dating service known for absolute privacy and a 97 percent rate of success. He was quickly drawn to Janet Peterson, a twenty-eight-year-old website designer with a degree in computer science and a lively online personality. Her one oddity was her refusal to submit a photograph before meeting in person; she would explain when they met. Gebhardt's instinct warned him to put an end to it now. He was a good-looking man who had always dated good-looking women, and Janet Peterson's refusal to reveal herself in a photograph was not a promising sign. But he was already so attracted by her words that he decided to cancel an evening with friends in order to risk a single dinner with a woman who might turn out to be missing an eye or an ear. At the restaurant he was conducted to a corner table in an alcove, where he came to an abrupt halt. At one end of the tabletop stood a miniature table and chair, and in the chair sat Janet Peterson. Thomas hesitated. He glanced about, looked at his watch, started to leave, and sat down. As Janet Peterson began to speak, he moved closer and bent toward her. She explained, without apology, that she had arranged her little deception because she wanted a chance to present her case. After the first few emails, she had felt the flow between them. She had dated many men from Greenhaven, always with the result that within two weeks she had lost interest. She was ready for something new. She had read dozens of online profiles before she found his. She felt they had known each other for their entire lives. Yes, of course, there was the question of size, but she preferred to think of it as an accident, whereas the essential things were what mattered. He was welcome to leave now. Thomas, listening carefully, was struck by her intelligence, her animation, her confidence, and her delicate, fierce beauty, which seized him like two hands gripping his arms. He felt an odd desire to lift her in the cup of his hand and cover her with kisses; a sudden sense of his freakishly large mouth filled him with confusion. After this meeting, Thomas and Janet began seeing each other every evening. He was hopelessly in love; life without her was no longer conceivable. She was thoughtful and earnest and tender and funny and strong. She was unafraid of his massiveness and proud of her own size. In her presence he felt something that at first he failed to recognize, until gradually he understood what it must be: joy. He proposed marriage two months after their first dinner. She accepted by climbing onto his shoulder and touching his lip with a hand. They were married by a judge in the town hall, in a quiet ceremony attended by his best friend and her best friend. She moved into his house on a leafy street lined by sycamores and arranged for the transportation of her clothes and possessions from Greenhaven. Thomas immediately set to work clearing out the upstairs guest room and transforming it into a vast workspace for his wife. He hired a skilled carpenter to build into the base of one wall a row of spacious six-inch closets with sliding doors. He hired an electrician to rewire the electrical system for her use. Another carpenter, who for years had produced objects for sale in Greenhaven, was put to work constructing miniature bookshelves, file cabinets, and a computer desk under the supervision of Janet Peterson-Gebhardt. The room was so large that she oversaw the building of a three-sided inner wall with its own ceiling; in the outer space she supervised the construction of a gymnasium and a private bathroom with shower. At night she slept beside him in his bed, on her own small pillow that touched the edge of his. Well before marriage they had discussed frankly the question of sex. At first they had agreed to do without it for the sake of deeper and more important feelings, but they soon found themselves moving from cautious experiment to bold strategy. Thomas would lie naked on his back while Janet crawled among ropy growths to sit at the base of his stiffening penis, which she embraced with her legs and arms. As it hardened and expanded, she would rub her breasts against it and sometimes ascend along its swaying length, in a way that made him erupt in so powerful an orgasm that she would often be flung into the air and land laughing on the bed. This method of lovemaking frequently resulted in her own explosive orgasms. At other times she would climb onto the top curve of his ear and straddle it while sliding back and forth and flinging back her head. Thomas could not bear to fall asleep until his beloved wife was sleeping peacefully beside him. In the morning they shared breakfast—she at her own table and chair on top of the breakfast table, a daily reminder of their first date—and then went to work, he at New Directions Software at one end of town and she in her upstairs workspace. A motorized platform attached to the stairpost and the banister permitted her to travel up and down the staircase with ease. In the evenings they liked to entertain. At first there was some resistance in the neighborhood to the strangeness of the marriage, but Thomas made it very clear that if you did not accept his wife you were not only banished from his list of acquaintances but were likely to face a lawsuit on the grounds of prejudice, harassment, or discrimination. Greenhaven guests were provided with tables and chairs on top of the dining-room table, to which they ascended by means of motorized platforms attached to the table legs. Six months after their marriage, the Gebhardts consulted with doctors from both communities and arrived at the decision to have a child. The research laboratory of Greenhaven Hospital had recently developed a method of drastically reducing the size of sperm donated by our hospital, without any lessening of reproductive power; an early experiment in artificial insemination had proved successful, though the child was stillborn. A year later, Janet gave birth to a healthy son, William. Ten months later, Jane was born. Both children, now six and five, are of Greenhaven size and attend school in Greenhaven, though most of their time is spent in the large house in town. Often we see Thomas lying on his back with outstretched arms in the backyard while Will and Janey, not yet one inch tall, run up and down the length of his body, laughing wildly. Despite some early uncertainty, the neighborhood has come to adore this family, the only one of its kind in our entire town. Whether it is a sign of things to come, no one can say. What we know is that they are happy, happy. At a recent weekend barbecue, after Will and Janey were put to bed, Thomas rose in the summer night, raised his glass, and said that he had been a dead man until he met his wife. At those words Janet leaped onto his belt, nimbly climbed his shirt, and pulled herself onto his shoulder. Standing with her fists on both hips, she looked down at the guests, burst into a smile, flung back her head, and let out a laugh of joy, sheer joy, into the dark-blue glow of the summer night.

Resistance

Although members of both communities support the breaking down of barriers, there are those in both groups who feel that things have already gone too far. It is one thing, they say, to mingle socially and vote together at town meetings; it is quite another to indulge in twisted sexual practices or live together in a mockery of marriage. Discrepancy in size should never lead to unfair treatment, but the discrepancy is real and can only be heightened by attempts to pretend it doesn't exist. They point out that inhabitants of Greenhaven are always at great risk when entering our homes and yards, with our monstrous children, our cats and dogs the size of buffalos, our sneezes like windstorms, our deadly air-sprays, and our habit of suddenly dropping murderous objects: coins the size of manhole covers, ice cubes like concrete blocks, spilled peanuts the size of baseballs. At the same time, members of our community go about in continual fear of crushing one of them to death with a careless footstep or knocking one of them down with a sudden movement of the arm or hand. Far more hurtful and destructive is the emotional turmoil stirred up in both communities by excessive proximity, since inhabitants small and large become acutely aware of their size and are made to feel awkward, inadequate, and ashamed. People who present such arguments find themselves in the curious position of asserting that attempts to bring the communities closer together do nothing but strengthen their sense of apartness; only strict rules of separation can bring an end to the feeling of separation.

165 Charles Street

A recent development has generated a great deal of discussion in both communities. In a heated bidding war set up by an agent at Franklin Realty, a group of Greenhaven businessmen outbid all rivals for the property at 165 Charles Street, in the heart of one of our most desirable residential neighborhoods. Despite a lawsuit filed against the selling agent by a group of concerned citizens, the sale was perfectly legal. The new owners intend to rent the seven-room neocolonial to an as yet undisclosed number of Greenhaven residents, a plan that may run into obstacles stemming from occupancy regulations. Even if the house is rented or sold to a single Greenhaven family, the neighborhood will be radically affected. Our children and pets will have to be closely supervised, since parents and pet owners are legally responsible for any harm inflicted on Greenhaven citizens. Whether the new residents will work at home or ride their bicycles each day to Greenhaven remains unclear. The deeper reason for purchasing the property also remains unclear. Do the owners wish to be able to extend social invitations to residents of our community, in a way not possible in their little homes behind the wall? Perhaps, as some have speculated, the experiment will fail and the owners will end up living in Greenhaven and renting to us. Even in the event of such an outcome, the symbolic significance of Greenhaven ownership will be impossible to ignore.

Think Big

One troubling response to the increasing presence of the Little People among us is the Think Big movement, started by a bartender who lost his license because of his refusal to serve any person who, in his words, was shorter than a glass of beer. Members of Think Big are known to use disparaging expressions when referring to the inhabitants of Greenhaven: the Itsy-Bits, the Weensies, the Mighty Mites, the Pixels. They are aggressive proponents of big bodies, big houses, big public buildings, and big ideas, all of which, in their view, are threatened by the cult of smallness. One member recently decided to challenge our town's building code by adding two stories to his Victorian home, located one block from Charles Street; partway through the construction he was ordered to return the house to its original size. In response he hired a contractor to design and build an immense wrap-around porch, which spread over his entire front and side lawns and proudly displayed a row of Corinthian columns two stories high. A group of tall men in their early twenties, wearing Think Big muscle shirts, left a popular bar one night, linked arms, and walked side by side across the entire street and both sidewalks, knocking down anyone who stood in their way. On another night, the police were called to a house in the neighborhood of Thomas and Janet Gebhardt, where a Greenhaven woman was discovered in the rain gutter, crying for help and weeping hysterically. She told the police that a man in a Think Big hoodie had snatched her up as she was taking a stroll just outside of Greenhaven and had driven her to a house where a ladder stood against one wall; after climbing the ladder but before placing her in the gutter, he had held her upside down and looked at her underpants. In an interview with the local paper, the founder of Think Big said that he did not condone such behavior but went on to insist that the movement was a necessary response to attempts to belittle true human beings, who walk with their heads high in the air.

Think Again

In the wake of the Think Big movement, our community has seen the rise of several pro-Greenhaven groups, among them Think Again, whose members challenge every statement of Think Big and retain a team of high-level lawyers to investigate any assertion deemed to be libelous or defamatory. One argument of Think Again is directed against the notion that inhabitants of Greenhaven live in a small world. They point out that the height and proportions of a Greenhaven house bear the same relation to the size of the house dwellers as our houses bear to us. Not only that, but Greenhaven Hospital, though it reaches no higher than our knees, is far larger, in proportion, than our Walter J. Nash Memorial Hospital. It is also true, they argue, that the continual exposure of Greenhavenites to our massive objects and mountainous houses has begun to influence their own architecture, as seen in the recently opened Greenhaven Hilton, which has three more floors than our highest hotel. Another line of argument insists that it is by no means true that our own community values only largeness, as may be seen by our devotion to semiconductors, our interest in genetic engineering, and our dedication to research in fields such as microsurgery, bacteriology, and neuroimaging.

A New World

The signs of unrest are everywhere, but of one thing we can be certain: the Little People are here to stay. Their presence among us seems to grow by the day, though it may simply be that our awareness has become more acute. They do not come to us bearing unfamiliar religions, exotic styles of dress, or unusual forms of behavior; they are like us in every way, except one. It is this difference that creates unease and fascination in equal measure. If, by some miracle of science, they could suddenly grow to our size, we would experience a terrible sense of loss, though exactly what would be lost is difficult to say. Are we drawn to them precisely because they are not us? Sometimes we suspect that they are happier than we are, though this may only be because we cannot always see the expressions on their faces. At other times we fear that our presence fills them with unhappiness. What do we know about them, really? We know only that they are here. In quiet moments—say, when we find ourselves turning over a burger in a backyard barbecue, or standing on a ladder clearing leaves from the rain gutter—a fantasy comes: we are as little as they are. We live with them in their houses, which are spread all over our town. We play baseball in their park. We swim in their pools. We lean back in their lawn chairs in their green backyards. We are happy. The sky is blue. Then a doubt comes over us. What does it mean that we wish to disappear into their world? Does it mean that our own world is no longer enough? Do they have the answer to a question we don't even know we have? At once we resolve to welcome them even more eagerly into our lives, to greet them with open arms, at the same time reminding ourselves to open our arms very slowly and carefully, for fear of shattering their bones as we knock them across the room with our forearms bigger than porch posts and our knuckles like knee-high boulders.

THEATER OF SHADOWS

How delightful, the Theater of Shadows!—and yet, in the end, how serious and unforgiving. Even today, after so much has changed, I find it difficult to account for the turn in our lives, brought about by so innocent a pastime. Was it really so innocent? We embraced it for the sake of our children, we hurled ourselves willingly into the Theater of Shadows, but in that embrace, wasn't there something for us as well? Shouldn't we have warned ourselves to move more slowly? To yield, if we had to, less completely? Even then we must have sensed the uneasy nature of shadows—those creatures born of the sun, but rebelling against the light.

When I look back to that first performance, I'm astonished to recall a time before it all began. I was young, I was ambitious, my wife hummed as she slipped into her bathing suit. Our children laughed in the sun. We welcomed things, we and our friends, we seized whatever life had to offer, while at the same time we never felt the need to step outside certain unspoken bounds that struck us as natural and healthy. We knew a little about the Theater of Shadows, the way you do when you're reading the morning paper while glancing at your watch. It had finished a run in New York and was making a three-day visit to our town. The one-man show, operated by someone from Romania or Hungary, was said to be ideal for the whole family. The performance was to take place in the old Arts Building, used at that time by the local film society, by visiting lecturers, by actors reading plays at two podiums—by anyone who cared to rent space before an audience.

When we arrived, the stage was hidden behind its sagging dark-blue curtain. Most of the seats were taken. We smiled, we waved to friends, we settled the kids. Everyone continued to whisper as the lights grew dim.

The curtain rose crookedly. On the half-dark stage stood what appeared to be a small theater, about the height of my shoulders, with a black curtain of its own, closed above a narrow proscenium. Slowly the black curtain halves began to part, revealing a whitish rectangle that might have been paper. It was painted with a black scene showing a tree and a wall.

Now the theater lights went out completely. In the dark you couldn't hear a sound. From the depths of the small theater came a sudden glow that threw the screen into brilliant whiteness. A moment later two ink-black figures appeared, facing each other beneath the tree. The sharply outlined figures moved toward each other, moved away, while their arms and legs lifted and lowered, their heads leaned forward and tipped back. Could we make out the pale shadows of strings? From behind, a voice spoke a few words for each shadow in turn. Somewhere a tinkling music played. It was a drama of hopeless love, of repeated misunderstandings, with a comic beating or two, but the power of it all lay less in the story than in the sheer fact of the dark silhouettes moving in light, hidden and visible at the same time. The piece lasted eleven minutes. The whiteness of the screen faded away, and as we sat in darkness before the theater lights came on, we were aware of a hush that revealed not confusion or uncertainty but a kind of reverence, before we burst into fervent applause.

Again the theater lights went out, and again a shadow piece began, this time with a painted scene that showed a black house with two black steps. I remember nothing of the play except a moment when a silhouette leaped from the roof onto the back of a goat. Again the hush, followed by grateful applause. Four pieces were performed that evening, and when the final lights came on we rose from our seats and clapped with high-raised hands, we shouted our approval, we called for the hidden puppet worker to come out and take his bow.

Slowly the black curtains closed over the white screen. We heard a noise as of shaken paper. When the curtains parted, the screen was no longer there. In the empty rectangle appeared the head of a man with dark eyes, thin black hair combed to one side, and a drooping black mustache. High above, our dark-blue curtain came creaking down.

Did we sense that something had shifted in our lives? I suspect we simply opened ourselves to an enchantment we felt no need to understand. The next two evenings, people stood in line for three hours. Children were allowed to sit in the aisles. When the Theater of Shadows left to continue its run in the suburbs, our town board met. The rest is well known: the negotiations, the startling offer, the establishment of permanent residence, the building of a new theater.

Fads come and go. The Theater of Shadows stayed. One reason for its extraordinary success was the energy of the Shadow Master, as he came to be called, for he never performed the same piece twice. Night after night we witnessed new ingenuities of presentation. The figures, said to be of leather or wood, had always presented themselves in clear outline, illuminated from behind and thrown up against the translucent white screen, but one night a second pair of shadow figures appeared, slightly blurred, behind the foreground silhouettes. We speculated that the second set of figures was being worked by a hidden assistant, at a distance behind the first set. The blurred look gave to the scene a new appearance of depth. Other innovations, which we found more difficult to explain, included shadowy spirits who appeared in the whiteness above the black figures, sometimes emerging from their heads or bodies. There were also effects of a kind that might be called realistic: the crumbling of a shadow tower, the eruption of a volcano, the explosion of a mysterious box, whose separate parts could be seen rising into the air and slowly falling.

Such inventions drew us repeatedly to the Theater of Shadows, as if we couldn't bear to miss a thing. They also began to draw people from nearby towns, who had heard stories of our theater and were eager to see for themselves. Not the least wonder of the Theater of Shadows was its success purely as a business venture. Especially in the summer, when our town has always attracted visitors to its upscale restaurants and wine bars, its spacious parks, its venues for visiting musicians and troupes of actors, the Theater of Shadows was forced to turn away long lines of people who had waited for hours and who were willing to pay outrageous prices for tickets hawked by young boys striding up and down the sidewalk, passing out circulars announcing the summer program.

But ingenuity and professional skill go only so far in explaining the dominance of the Theater of Shadows at that time.

Beneath or beyond the performances lay the fascination of the shadow world itself, with its hiddenness, its refusal of color, its indifference to familiar effects of visual precision and detail. We who loved the brilliance of summer light, of sun burning on beach sand, we who loved to photograph our wives and children, to marvel at the beauty of faces, of tendrils of hair falling along a cheek—did we ever stop to wonder what it was that compelled us toward the shadow world, which stood apart from the realm of sunlight while offering ungraspable seductions of its own?

I don't mean that we withdrew at first from our usual pastimes. The Theater of Shadows was simply another pleasure, among many. And so we mowed our lawns, trimmed our bushes, organized birthday parties and trips to the beach, coached our baseball teams, went ice-skating in winter, and every night took our families to the Theater of Shadows, where we fell under a spell we never thought to question.

I suppose it was inevitable for a rival theater to appear. Demand for the Theater of Shadows far exceeded its capacity; people grew tired of learning that a performance had been sold out weeks in advance. The Rainbow Theater opened to a full house and offered a striking innovation: its shadows contained vivid details in red and blue and green. Sometimes an entire shadow was itself a single brilliant color. Most of us attended a performance or two out of curiosity but soon found ourselves back at the Theater of Shadows. The Rainbow Theater, we felt, was amateurish in its art of manipulating figures and embarrassing in its reliance on stories that strove solely for exaggerated effects. But what truly spelled the end of the Rainbow Theater was the fact of color itself. After the shock, not without its pleasures, of red or green or blue glowing against the white, the presence of color seemed only an intrusion of the sunlit world, and we found ourselves longing for the deeper, quieter, more dangerous attractions of pure shadow.

The rival theater held on for a couple of months before vanishing forever. Its significance lay less in its memorable failure than in its very existence: it was our first revelation that we wanted more of what we already had. For didn't we carry the Theater of Shadows home with us night after night, didn't we dream of shadow people and shadow countrysides, didn't we yearn for more, always more, as if, in some way, the familiar world were no longer enough?

A few weeks after the closing of the Rainbow Theater, an event in a different part of town drew our attention. In an abandoned church that had been purchased and improved by a group of civic-minded businessmen who rented space for cultural activities, actors from the area regularly auditioned to put on two or three plays a year. One night the director announced to the half-empty rows of seats that an experiment was about to take place. The curtain parted to reveal a second curtain, plain white, stretched tight across the entire stage. As the theater lights went out, a brightness appeared behind the white curtain. The actors performed the play in silhouette, with no other changes. The event was attacked, praised, mocked, cheered; in the next two weeks the house was packed. Such was the beginning of the Company of Shadows. If in one sense it was an adult rival of the Theater of Shadows, in another it simply went its own way, since its actors weren't jointed puppets operated by a hidden master but real people performing familiar full-length plays. It's also true that the Company of Shadows quickly grew impatient with traditional forms and began producing shadow dramas of its own, with long stretches of silence and with scenes shaped to the demands of silhouette.

If the failed Rainbow Theater and the successful Company of Shadows were public signs of the widening influence of the Theater of Shadows, there were private indications as well. In basement playrooms, in garages and attics, in backyards at night, white sheets and translucent white screens had begun to appear, behind which teenagers would experiment with shadow-performances presented to friends and family seated on couches, rugs, or folding chairs. High-school seniors with training in theater were especially devoted to these events, often adding musical embellishments by friends who played drums or guitar. Soon children at birthday parties or in their rooms at night began throwing themselves into spirited imitations. We watched as Ping-Pong tables standing in cellars and garages were folded up and left to lean against walls, as badminton nets stretching across lawns were wrapped around their poles and put safely away. Such variations in the history of family games are difficult to trace and shouldn't be overstated. We still played backyard baseball, watched TV, leaned over board games and card games at the cleared-off kitchen table. But most of us who lived through those times remember a sense of difference, as of some change in the weather.

The shadow parties sprang directly from these amateur performances. College students, bored after a day at the beach, appear to have started the trend. In a basement playroom at night, a sheet or translucent screen was hung, behind which shone a bright lamp. A few couples danced on the illuminated side of the screen. On the dark side, partygoers seated on pillows watched the silhouettes, some sharp and some blurred, while talking among themselves and waiting their turn. The dancers, aware of being watched, and equally aware of being hidden, liked to imagine their silhouettes moving voluptuously against the whiteness. Sometimes, aroused by the music, by punch spiked with gin, above all by the sense of acting a part, the dancers would slowly begin to remove their shirts and blouses, at last flinging them into the air to wild applause. Girls thrust out their breasts and buttocks, boys gyrated their hips. In the dark, friends watched the shadows of friends act out secret desires. It was at the shadow parties that the eroticism of shadows first became evident, though exactly what was so alluring about those shapes, exactly what drew the attention of couples in the dark, who were touching each other's bodies with hands and mouths but kept pulling away to watch the shadowy presences moving against the whiteness, no one could say.

At about this time we first began to hear talk of shadow practices in the bedrooms of our town. Here and there a married couple, perhaps feeling a slight loss of excitement, perhaps aroused in some fashion by the dark figures in the Company of Shadows, would set up in the bedroom a translucent screen of linen or oiled paper, behind which husband or wife would slowly undress. The disrobing partner, who was silhouetted against the whiteness, moved with unnatural deliberation, sometimes pausing to pose against the screen, and was said to cause in the watching spouse such deep surges of desire that the lovemaking which followed was like nothing that had happened before. In one variation, a light was placed on each side of the screen, so that one partner's shadow undressing could be succeeded by the other's, the first now seated in darkness as the second performed behind the white divider.

Sometimes, moved by irresistible longing, a watcher would approach the screen and start to touch the shadow, an act invariably accompanied by disillusionment and a kind of despair. For some, this was the first experience of what came to be called the cruelty of shadows. In a much-talked-about play, *The Cruelty of Shadows*, the Company portrayed its own version of the remoteness of shadow: as actors performed behind the tight-stretched white curtain, a male actor concealed in the audience began to stare with terrible yearning at one of the shadow actresses, with her waves of hair and her long, flowing arms. At the height of the performance, the man rushed up onto the proscenium and hurled himself against the white curtain, which came down with loud ripping sounds, exposing to the audience a view of actors staring open-mouthed in alarm, a harshly bright light, and a cellist seated on a stool, gripping the neck of her cello as she held the bow motionless in mid-stroke.

The migration of shadows to the bedrooms of our town was only one manifestation of their increasing presence among us. Stimulated by the Theater of Shadows, people had begun looking at their familiar surroundings in a new way. Some took to painting their houses deep shades of black, set off by white shutters and white chimneys. Beds of black calla lilies, black roses, and black orchids appeared. In green backyards, you could see the shiny black swing sets, the black Wiffle ball bats, the sandboxes filled with black sand. One maple-lined street became famous among us when every one of its houses was painted black, with neat white trim. Black flagstone paths led up to white-and-black porches.

It was during this move toward decorative darkness that a local business known as Crown Glass, which supplied us with panes for our windows and glass panels for our doors, began to advertise a product called Shadow Glass. This smoky glass was said not simply to darken the brightness of objects but to drain color from them as well. Here and there, in the houses of our town, a darker window would appear in a row of windows overlooking the front lawn. These early shadow panes were widely criticized for not performing as advertised—colors grew dim but failed to disappear. In response, Crown Glass produced a new, improved version of Shadow Glass, which did in fact remove every trace of color and permitted the viewer to see nothing but black objects standing or moving in grayish light. The result was a distant and not very convincing variation of the Theater of Shadows, but our interest was awakened, and now kitchens, bedrooms, playrooms, and porches began replacing traditional glass with darkened panes. Soon downtown storefronts began to experiment with Shadow Glass, led by Keene's Drugstore and quickly followed by restaurants, clothing shops, and business offices. The new glass worked in both directions: people passing a house or coffee shop fitted with Shadow Glass saw dark figures moving within.

As improved Shadow Glass began to spread among the windows of our town, we became aware of another product sold in the hardware store out by the strip mall. Packaged in individual rolls like aluminum foil, Shadow Wrap was a dark, translucent plastic sheeting that prevented colors from showing through. It was intended for vases, scenic lampshades, framed paintings, and other indoor objects, as well as for outer parts of the house like porch posts and chimneys, though some people tried wrapping it around tree trunks, telephone poles, and corner mailboxes, where it worked for a while before coming undone and giving things a wrinkled look.

Shadow Wrap was finally an unsatisfactory product, which remained all too visible and was significant only as a clumsy expression of our desire. A far more successful item was Shadow Shellac, a colorless liquid that could be brushed directly onto any surface and immediately turned the color to shadow. Houses and garages coated with Shadow Shellac soon lined many streets of our town, which even in bright sunshine took on the look of a grainy movie filmed in black-and-white. The new substance worked also on leaves, bark, and grass. For a while it became fashionable for high-school football players to paint Shadow Shellac onto their bare biceps and forearms; cheerleaders darkened their cheeks and throats. One day a tall, thin senior, who spoke very little and always kept to himself, came to school with his face and hands and clothes coated entirely with Shadow Shellac, so that he resembled a phantom. Shouts and applause erupted in the corridors, before he was sent home with a note.

This brief vogue for shadowing the body was only another sign of our growing impatience with the old look. First in high school and then in lower grades, students had begun dressing in shades of black: black blouses, black skirts, black button-downs, black cords, black shoes. Blond-haired girls, once highly popular but now embarrassed by their look, sought out powerful jet-black dyes, often adding a stylish streak of white. One morning a well-liked basketball player came to school on black metal crutches, his foot raised in a black cast. Friends signed their names in white ink.

The fashion for darkness spread quickly, in all directions—to young couples starting out, to patients in our elder-care facility, to waitresses, bank tellers, and highway-maintenance crews. Babies wore soft black diapers. People blew their noses into black tissues. On summer afternoons, in our lively downtown, you would see crowds in black straw hats and black polo shirts and long black dresses moving past store windows darkened by Shadow Glass, while in the outdoor cafés, at ebony tables, under black awnings that cast a deep shade, customers sipped dark drinks in smoky glasses.

Meanwhile, at the beach, girls in Shadow Sunglasses strolled along the water's edge, displaying the latest in nylon Shadow Wear, which covered their bodies in glistening black from neck to toe.

And yet this gradual draining of color from our town, exhilarating though it may have been, was accompanied always by a sense of dissatisfaction. Despite our clever inventions, we knew that our dimming streets and darkening bodies remained dense and substantial, without the impalpable mystery of shadow. Sometimes it seemed to us that what we wanted wasn't so much the absence of color as the blurring of hardness and definition. The sunlit world oppressed us with its sharp lines and edges, its brilliant details, which seemed to us nothing but knife blades piercing our skin. It was as if what we longed for was release from the fierce precision of things.

Driven by such moods, we sought out forms of weather we had usually complained about, in the days before the Theater of Shadows. We became celebrants of fog, especially the dense, billowy fog that came rolling in from the Sound, causing cars to pull over and streetlights to tremble like dim candle flames. We walked in our fog with outspread arms, watching our fingers fade into ripples. One evening the Company of Shadows surprised us with a fog machine. It produced new undulations behind the white curtain and slowly spread a vapory grayness into the audience itself, so that you could no longer make out your neighbor. But such impressions could take us only so far, and we soon found ourselves searching for less obvious effects. Drizzles under dark-gray skies offered their own quiet attractions, though some preferred the drama of sudden thunderstorms, with rain slashing against windows as shadowy trees bent low in high winds. In white blizzards, when snow came blowing and swirling down, we liked to see shadow people making their way along sidewalks, like background figures in the Theater of Shadows.

If we found much to admire in these natural performances, we also knew that they couldn't satisfy us for long. We who were devotees of the Theater of Shadows, we who had been present from the beginning, craved nothing less than an uninterrupted world of shadow, as if the truth of things lay only there. In our beds at night, we lay awake dreaming of dim streets barely visible in the dark light of streetlamps coated with Shadow Shellac. We imagined ghostly citizens moving through a world of blacks and grays, shadows sliding into shadows. A few enthusiasts, in the extremity of their longing, sought to transform themselves into shadow beings by extravagant methods that were bound to fail. Some replaced the inner walls of their houses with silk hangings that encouraged the sensation of passing through solid walls. Others numbed their fingertips with the new Shadow Spray in order to deaden the sense of touch and create an illusion of immateriality. Such actions, most of us believed, represented a serious misunderstanding, for they undermined the feeling of distance that was an essential feature of the Theater of Shadows.

In our impatience with the old way of seeing, we became alert to inner shiftings. An inclination toward daydreaming had grown noticeable among us. Hardheaded businessmen who prided themselves on habits of discipline would look up from their work and gaze for a long time at a mark on the wall that resembled a branch or a river. One afternoon a workman repairing a slate roof fell and broke his leg; in the hospital he reported that he had been "thinking of other things." The owner of a downtown hat shop wandered out the back door and across town into a park, where she sat down in the shade of a tree while customers kept pressing a silver bell on the counter.

Such alterations in our way of looking at the world began creeping into our public institutions. College graduates hired by the local paper to report on mundane incidents, like traffic accidents and minor arrests, were urged to suppress the merely factual and develop the personal and impressionistic. The Senior Center offered a popular art class in the construction of deliberately incomplete work: fragments of ceramic figurines, half-finished drawings of faces, stories that broke off in the middle of a scene. In high-school English classes, teachers encouraged students to avoid the tedious method of careful analysis in favor of a looser, more intuitive engagement. Some teachers attacked the old rules of grammar as forms of constriction, intended to conceal the free-flowing nature of language. Others questioned language itself, which was said to be nothing but a noisy invasion of the country of silence.

Broader intellectual disciplines, such as history and religion, were also succumbing to the new spirit of shadow. The director of the Historical Society gave a well-attended lecture in which he described the town's past as a time of few lights and deeper darkness, when many shadows inhabited the house. The growth of vivid modern lighting, he said, had destroyed our intimacy with shadows and damaged our ability to comprehend the past. Meanwhile the minister of a new church that met in the basement of a retired policeman preached to his congregation about the New Heaven and the New Hell. The New Heaven was a realm of whiteness inhabited by shadowy spirits. The New Hell was a world that resembled a sunny afternoon in an American town, with its sharp outlines and vivid colors, its relentless pressure of hard-edged detail.

Today, as advances in technology permit images of the outer world to rush in on us at every moment, groups of concerned citizens have searched for ways to protect our town against a return to the past, with its surfeit of sunlight, its assault of color. One group has developed a Shadow App, which turns all images on mobile devices into silhouettes against a white background.

We watch them, the new children. They seem quieter, more contemplative, than we remember ours to have been. They rarely attend performances of the Theater of Shadows, preferring to spend six or seven hours a day absorbed in the new shadow games, which they follow on their laptops and smartphones. The new children live indoors. In day-long dusk, behind windows of Shadow Glass, they play alone. The new games have complex rules and can last for months at a time. The new children are pale. They are growing dim. We see their faces flickering in screen light.

Some say that our passion for shadows has gone too far. They point to our darkened streets, the rows of houses and trees that are barely visible, our sidewalks vanishing into blackness. Whole neighborhoods, they warn, are slowly disappearing. They propose shutting down the Theater of Shadows and transforming the building into a fitness center. They urge us to replace our windows with the old glass and let the sun back in. Our town, they say, is in danger of fading away.

Those of us who defend the art of shadow believe that a new town is emerging, that the visible world is itself a form of deception.

Let others decide such questions. We know only that we no longer see the world in the old way. I'm not now speaking of our Shadow Glass, our streets artificially darkened by Shadow Shellac, our tastes in weather and entertainment. Such things never last. No, I'm speaking of a street untouched by our arrangements. The house fronts brilliant in sunlight, the sharp blades of light-green and dark-green grass, the edges of maple leaves precise against the blue sky—we acknowledge them, we know they invite our full attention. But what draws us is the half of the rose petal closed in shadow, the blurred grass dissolving in the shade of a garage, the dark figure seated on a porch behind the blazing white posts. We who have been marked by the Theater of Shadows search only for things that are scarcely there. Is it possible that our bright town is only the shadow of a town we have never seen? What stirs us is the hint, the suggestion. We are connoisseurs of intimation, sensualists of the half-seen. Sometimes we long for that other world, for your world, when sunlight on a beach in summer was enough. For then our eyes were unopened, but now we see. We may remember it, the old way, but we're no longer what we were. Look! The lights are growing dim, the black curtains have begun to part. The time for talking is over. Let the new world begin.

THE FIGHT

The fight between Frank DeCiccio and Johnny Carwin took place on the sidewalk, at the school bus stop a block from my house. It was 1956. We were nearing the end of eighth grade. A group of us quickly formed a half circle around Frank DeCiccio and Johnny Carwin, closing them off but not crowding them. They stood trapped between us and the low pricker hedge that grew along the edge of the sidewalk. Someone shouted, "Hit him!" I'd seen plenty of playground fights in elementary school and a few recent ones in junior high, but never outside of school bounds. I watched in fierce silence, feeling my blood beating in my neck.

Frank DeCiccio had been in my class the last two years of elementary school, fifth grade and sixth, a dark unsmiling boy who said nothing. He had one friend. You'd see the two of them walking silently together on the playground or standing under the maple tree next to the chain-link fence that looked down on the candy store. We all knew that Frank DeCiccio's older brother had been arrested for robbing a candy store. He'd pulled out a gun. It gained his younger brother a certain respect. You didn't want to mess with Frank DeCiccio, though he wasn't the type who went looking for trouble. His dark eyes kept to themselves.

He had a thin hard face, with skin that looked as if it had been pulled tight over the bones. His close-cut black hair seemed to grip his head. Under each sideburn you could see a pressure of bone.

Once, in fifth grade, he had taken part in a playground ritual organized by two older boys who were later suspended. You were invited to step up to the brick wall of the school building, hit it with your fist, and display your bleeding knuckles. If your hand was unharmed, one of the leaders would spit on your shoe. The art was to draw blood without breaking your hand. Frank DeCiccio walked up to the wall and stood looking at it while a crowd of us watched. He stayed like that for what seemed a long time. No part of him moved. All at once he smashed his fist against the bricks. Turning around, he allowed his hand to be examined by the two older boys, one of whom held it up in triumph so that we could see the streaks of blood. Frank DeCiccio pulled his arm away and walked unsmiling back into the crowd.

What struck me about Frank DeCiccio, what made him interesting to me, was his thinness. He was a skinny boy, like me, but with a difference. In eighth grade he wore tight white T-shirts with the sleeves rolled up over his shoulders, and on each of his narrow brown arms you could see a raised vein, running along his thin tight biceps and down along the forearm. My own arms were thin without signs of strength, not good for much except practicing the piano, playing Ping-Pong in the basement, or slapping a badminton birdie over the net in the backyard. They hung from my shoulders a little uncertainly, not really sure what they were doing there. Frank DeCiccio's arms knew exactly what they were doing there. I was a head taller than Frank DeCiccio, but my height served only to make me feel more visible than I wanted to be. In the dangerous world of junior high I walked the halls warily, careful to avoid eyes that lay in wait to challenge you. Frank DeCiccio walked at his own pace, alone. He stared straight ahead, looking at nothing.

Johnny Carwin was the new boy on the block. I'd taken an instant dislike to him. He was tall, as tall as I was, a good five ten, with dark blond hair that he combed up in a wave. Yellow-brown strands of it were always falling onto his forehead, and he kept sweeping them back with an easy motion of his hand. He was broad-shouldered but soft: his shoulders were round and soft, his upper arms were large and soft, his cheeks were soft, his stomach, without being heavy, had a softness you could see. He wore short-sleeved button-down shirts with the sleeves turned up once, and cuffed chinos with big-buckled belts. What bothered me about Johnny Carwin wasn't his softness or his clothes, but his smile. It was a good smile, with well-shaped white teeth, a smile that welcomed you in. But he kept showing it, eager to make you like him, eager to let you know that it would be worth your while to have him as a friend. I understood how hard it must be to move to a new town with a school full of strangers, especially in the middle of the eighth grade. I understood. But that smile of his, the too-easy laughter, his way of putting himself forward, of inviting attention to himself, it all scraped against my nerves. Life was more difficult than that. We spoke easily enough at the bus stop each morning, but after school he went around with others in the neighborhood.

On the afternoon of the fight, a warm day in spring, the usual crowd of us got off at my stop and began forming groups before heading home. Johnny Carwin was laughing as he stepped off the bus with Tom Saksa, a friend of mine since second grade, though grown distant since the start of junior high. Frank DeCiccio had started down the sidewalk alone, as he always did. Against one hip he held a three-ring notebook with unraveling threads and a single schoolbook with a brown paper cover. Carwin, walking between Tom Saksa and Billy Stoccatore, suddenly shouted something at Frank DeCiccio's back. A silence came over us.

DeCiccio kept walking. He wore cheap black pants without cuffs, the familiar white T-shirt with the sleeves rolled up over his shoulders, and dusty black shoes with worn-down heels. Johnny Carwin looked at Billy Stoccatore and gave a thoughtful frown. He said, in a loud voice intended for everyone: "He must not've heard me." He took a few steps forward and came up directly behind Frank DeCiccio. Reaching out a hand, he pushed three fingers against DeCiccio's back. Johnny Carwin was a head taller than Frank DeCiccio, and his soft upper arms were as broad as DeCiccio's neck. Tom Saksa and Billy Stoccatore stood watching, waiting. We were all waiting.

When Frank DeCiccio felt the fingers against his back, he took one more step forward and stopped. Turning to one side, without looking to see who had pushed him, he bent over and placed his notebook and book on the curbside grass. This was the sign for us to begin forming our half circle. Suddenly DeCiccio spun around. He stood crouched in a fighter's stance, hands raised in front of his body, palms open. He swung his left palm hard against Johnny Carwin's left cheek. We could all hear the loudness of the smack. Carwin jerked his head away and raised an arm to protect his face. DeCiccio hit him in the side with his open right hand. He began moving quickly forward and back, side to side, striking out with first one hand and then the other, filling the air with sharp slaps. Carwin raised his arms to his face, lowered them to his stomach, raised them to his face. "Hit him!" someone shouted. "Hit him back! Hit him!" I had the feeling that if Johnny Carwin just let himself fall forward, he could crush Frank DeCiccio to death. But he kept backing away. Red splotches, darkening, showed on both sides of his face. The smack of skin against face flesh sounded like firecrackers.

With a suddenness that startled me, Frank DeCiccio stopped. He brought his arms down to his sides and stood motionless. He was staring directly at Johnny Carwin's face. Carwin glanced at the half circle of watchers, looked back at Frank DeCiccio, and lowered his eyes. One of his turned-up sleeves had unrolled and he began fixing it. DeCiccio continued to stand there, unmoving, his long hands hanging tensely at a slight distance from his hips. The palms looked ready to spring back to life at any second.

Our crowd was starting to break up. Frank DeCiccio stood looking at Johnny Carwin. Johnny Carwin stood fiddling with his shirt. All at once DeCiccio turned to one side, bent over, and picked up his books from the grass. He rose, looking at no one. He turned his back to Johnny Carwin and walked slowly away.

"He took me by surprise!" Johnny Carwin was saying, as he walked in the other direction with Tom Saksa, Billy Stoccatore, Lou Salerno, and Richie Vance. He raised one forearm in front of his face, lowered it to his stomach, raised it to his face. "Like that! Took me by surprise!" Lou Salerno, shaking his head, struck a stick against the side of a telephone pole.

I walked to my house and let myself in with my key. My mother taught first grade and would be home in an hour, my father taught at the university and would be home for dinner. In the empty house I climbed the carpeted stairs, looking down over the banister at the three bookcases in the living room, the books on the end table by the couch, the piano with its dark-gleaming bench, its metronome sitting on a pile of music books, its Mozart sonatas open on the rack. No one in the neighborhood had a living room like that. My childhood friends accepted me, but they knew I came from a strange world. How deep in me flowed those peaceful winter evenings when I sat in front of the fireplace lining up my British and American soldiers on the warm, flickering bricks, while my father sat in a corner of the couch grading his papers and my mother sat reading in lamplight, looking up now and then to watch over me, before it was time for both of them to read me to sleep. Was I still that little boy?

Upstairs in my room I tossed my books and notebook onto my bed and lay down. The bed sat under two windows with half-open venetian blinds. Stripes of sunlight fell across my arms and stretched along the floor. My body felt like a clenched fist. What if Johnny Carwin had pushed his fingers against my back? I loved my neighborhood, but things had begun to change in sixth grade. A toughness had sprung up. Arm muscles, thrust-out chests, a new swagger. My old friends and I still spoke, but the intimacy, the playfulness, of childhood was gone. In the long halls of junior high, or on the tarred playground where we stood around after lunch, I was aware of trouble waiting to erupt. I'd seen it happen. "You want something?" Shoulders shoved against a wall, books fallen to the ground. The fights out back near the athletic field, hands open in obedience to some unwritten rule. Cheeks flaming, blood bursting from a lip. The threat of fists, of smashed faces. What if I'd felt Johnny Carwin's fingers pushing against my back? I saw myself stopping, turning around, pointing at my chest. Me? The raised eyebrows, the look of innocent surprise. Who, me?

I sat up and swung my legs over the side of the bed. My room steadied me. The two bookcases with their crowd of books, standing in tight rows or lying sideways in uneven piles. A heap of old board games on a bottom shelf, next to a shoebox full of baseball cards in neat piles bound by rubber bands. The wobbly folding table behind the chest of drawers. Long summer afternoons playing Monopoly with Tom Saksa and Billy Stoccatore, my mother with the tray of chocolate chip cookies and three tall glasses of milk. My friends all liked my mother, who had been kind to them in school. "Eat up, boys! There's plenty more where that came from." Now Billy Stoccatore wore his hair slicked back on both sides, collar up, sideburns moving down his cheeks. Tom Saksa's high-combed hair, his black leather jacket, dark-blue dungarees with the cuffs rolled up above the tops of his shoes. A silver comb sticking up out of his right back pocket. Childhood friend Jimmy Marcangelo looking away as he walked past the vacant lot with his arm around the neck of Joanna Bassick, fingers dangling at her breast. No one bothered me, I was safe enough in the streets of the old neighborhood, but it was no longer the old neighborhood. My hair was wrong. My walk was wrong. My face was wrong. On the floor at the foot of my bed, a barbell with screwed-in weights sat next to an upside-down slipper. The tips of fingers pressing against my back.

I pushed my hands down hard on the edge of the bed and thrust myself up. I stepped to the middle of the room and stopped, stood motionless. I could feel a ripple in my legs and arms, like something waiting to be released. Through a partly open window I could hear Mrs. Mancini calling for her daughter: "Mary Jane! Mary Jane!" Smell of lawnmower gasoline, hedge flowers, cut grass. "Mary Jane!" I felt my shoulders leaning forward. My knees began to bend. Head up, hands raised. Keep moving. I slapped at the air with my open left hand. I danced away, slapped at the air with my right. Bobbing and weaving, I slapped hard and drew back, slapped harder and drew back. I took a swing at Johnny Carwin's face. The sharp smack tingled across my palm. I danced away, stepped forward, hit him again. Johnny Carwin was holding up both forearms, trying to protect his eyes and mouth. I swung at his soft stomach. Hit him! My hands closed into fists. I drew my left hand back and swung again at his face. My fist hit him in the mouth. With my right fist I smashed him in the cheek. I could feel the bone through his soft flesh. Johnny Carwin began backing away. I kept swinging. Near one of the bookcases I hit him so hard that he dropped to one knee. Looking down at him kneeling there, no mercy in my heart, I punched him in the side of the head. I slugged his bent neck. As he began to fall sideways, I pulled back my arm and aimed my fist at the side of his face.

I was startled to feel my knuckles scraping against a row of books, knocking a few back against the rear of the bookcase. On the shelf I saw my seventh-grade yearbook photo. It sat looking at me from its black wooden frame. The new sport jacket, too large in the shoulders, the weak little ingratiating smile. Fury flamed in me. I snatched up the frame and hit the picture in the face with my fist. The frame came apart in one corner, fell with its glass and photo to the floor. Something rolled away. I grabbed the broken-framed photo, tossed it up in front of me, and punched it as hard as I could. It struck the floor with a crackle of glass. I stomped on it with my right heel, driving the glass into his face. I kicked at the twisted frame and sent it scudding across the room, where it struck the bottom of the chest of drawers and lay still.

I sat down on the bed and rolled onto my back. Lines of sunlight striped my stomach. It was over. I could feel the tension flowing out of me like breath. Soon I would hear the sound of my mother's key in the front door. I would explain to her that I had knocked over the picture by accident, and she would tell me not to worry. All would be well. Something had happened in my room, something I needed to think about. I would think about it later. Tired now, I pulled a pillow under my neck and began to read calmly in the warm light of my room.

A HAUNTED HOUSE STORY

I

One morning when I was eight years old I climbed the carpeted stairs that led from the living room to the second floor, walked along the sunny hall past my room, my parents' room, and the guest room, all with doors half-open, and stopped at the shut door of my father's study. As I raised my hand, I saw the shadow of my arm on the wood. To knock was a punishable act. It was forbidden to disturb my father when he was at work in the morning, except for two reasons: an emergency, which I understood, or an urgent problem, which I did not. I had recently asked my father what an urgent problem was, and he said that it meant a serious matter that didn't require a doctor or a policeman. He paused thoughtfully. "Or the Lone Ranger." I had been thinking hard about "urgent" and "problem" and had decided that the two together stretched wide enough to justify my knock. I was willing to be punished, so long as I could ask my question. I looked away from the shadow of my arm and knocked twice.

"Come in," my father said, and I opened the door.

He was sitting with his back to me at his large desk, bent forward and writing. I knew that he always wrote first in a notebook, with a yellow No. 2 pencil, before turning to his typewriter. The pencil had to have six sides. The blinds were closed, though it was a sunny morning. At the edges of the thin curtains I could see that the two windows were partway open. To his right stood the big black typewriter, which with its rapid clack and banging bell reminded me of the trains at the railroad station in Bridgeport, where we went to pick up the grandmothers. A sweet smell of pipe tobacco mingled with a faint scent of cut grass.

My father looked over his shoulder. "What's up, Ben?" He pushed back in his chair and stood up to stretch his back. My father was a large man, with big hands and glinty eyeglasses. His head was higher than the wood at the top of the windows. He looked at me hard: not with anger but with alertness. He gestured to the deep armchair at the side of the desk, where he always sat when he graded papers and smoked his pipe. The stem and bowl of his pipe curved like the clef signs on my mother's piano music.

I sat down in the saggy chair with my back to a wall of books. I was facing another wall of books, where black-and-white photographs of my mother and me, in dark frames, stood here and there at the front of the shelves. My father liked to develop his own negatives, which sometimes hung in strips in front of the kitchen window. He turned his desk chair sideways to face me. On one bookshelf a pipe rack held four old pipes, their ash-blackened bowls leaning in different directions. My father sat down. He crossed his legs and placed a finger against his cheek.

"Are ghosts real?" I said. I spoke without hesitation. It was the only way.

I saw the look of attention in my father's face, sharp as a touch.

"Let me ask you something," he said. My father settled lower into his chair and began to arrange himself for a talk. He raised his left leg so that the ankle lay across his right knee, grasped the ankle with his right hand, and placed his other elbow on the armrest. As he spoke, he moved his free hand in the air, fluttering his fingers. "Are people real?"

I thought about it. "Yes."

"Very good. And how do you know they're real?"

I thought again. "I know they're real because I can see them."

"Excellent. Anything else?"

"I can touch them."

"You can touch them. Very interesting. People are real because you can see them and you can touch them. Now answer me this. Have you ever seen a ghost?"

"No."

"Have you ever touched a ghost?"

"No."

"Then you already know the answer to your question. Was there anything else you'd like to talk about?"

"No." I started to get up, but he held out a hand, with the palm facing me.

"Are your friends talking about the Harrington house again?"

"Yes. Charley says there's a ghost." I thought about what Charley had said. "He says it's the ghost of the dead woman."

My father moved a forefinger slowly along his chin, a gesture I liked to imitate.

"If Charley said there was a dragon in his basement, would you believe him?"

"No."

"Why not?"

I thought about a dragon, breathing fire in Charley's basement. "Because dragons don't exist."

"Exactly. Because dragons don't exist." He stood up. "Spend your time thinking about people, Ben. People exist. Even if they don't always know it."

I could see my father's attention leaving his face; he was returning to his work. I crushed down my desire to ask him what he'd meant by "even if they don't always know it," thanked him for answering my question, and left the room. With relief, with exhilaration, I hurried along the hall, rushed down the steps, and ran out into the yard, where I welcomed the summer day and looked up at the wide-open sky, as blue and bright as the oceans on the map of the world that hung in my room, and I did not think about ghosts again for the next nine years.

II

In the summer after high school, the four of us—Charley, Tom, Lindberg, and I—spent all our spare time together. We'd been friends since grade school, and we knew in our bones that this summer was different from the others. It was the last of the old summers. It was the last summer of all, since instead of passing on to the next grade in the same town we were headed off to new lives: three of us to colleges in different states, Lindberg on a cross-country journey to discover, as he put it, what it was all about, though the "it" was never clear. Charley and Tom had part-time summer jobs, Lindberg worked at his father's hardware store and had a part-time girlfriend, and I, aside from mowing the lawn every couple of weeks and slapping a little paint on the shingles of the garage, did nothing but loaf and read and dream the time away and practice my backhand serve on the Ping-Pong table in the basement. I told myself that I was preparing my mind for college, but what I was really doing was savoring the last summer of my life. I was also, I suppose, warding off the future, clinging to the very end of childhood, even though I was seventeen and eager to embrace the new life that awaited me in the world outside my Connecticut town.

The four of us did what we'd always done in summer: leaned back on our elbows on towels at the beach as low waves broke against the shore, went bowling at the alley out by the shopping center, banged ketchup from bottles onto plates of fries at Betty's Diner, where we were sometimes joined by girls we knew from school, strolled in town like lords of the universe while wondering how to pass the time, threw ourselves into day-long games of Monopoly and Risk on sunny back porches while mothers in shorts served us lemonade and batches of homemade cookies, took drives on the throughway in the direction of New York or New Haven and swung off at lesser-known exits, which took us into half-familiar towns that felt as if we'd grown up in them but had somehow forgotten the layout of the streets. We liked riding around at night. Sometimes we stayed up till dawn.

It was during this lazy and restless summer that we paid a visit to the old Harrington house, one evening when the sky had faded from blue to grayish blue, and the streetlights had come on. People still called it "the haunted house," though even Charley, now six foot two and skilled in calculus and drawing with charcoal, rarely gave it a thought. The house was the last one on a dead-end street lined with sycamores and old elms. Shady two-story houses were set back from the road. These were the comfortable homes of solid middle-class families, not the mansions of the fancy lawyers and corporate big shots who lived up on Ludberry

Hill or the smaller houses of carpenters and machinists out by the car dealerships. Dr. Harrington, a cardiologist, had moved to town at about the same time as my parents. His wife had died suddenly. Some said she hanged herself; there was talk of murder. Harrington was never charged, though people gossiped. He moved out of state but for some reason refused to sell the house; he rented it, but the couple had scarcely moved in when one of them had a terrible accident of some kind. The next client backed out at the last moment. The agent herself was said to be reluctant to visit the property.

Rumor had it that the house was haunted by the ghost of Mrs. Harrington, a beautiful woman with long blond hair. It was said you could hear sounds at night. Though the house stood empty, Harrington, who had money, held on to it. The town required him to keep the lawns mowed and the porches repaired; once every two months a cleaning crew entered and left. No one had lived in the house for thirty years. It sat away from the road, at the top of a slightly sloping lawn where tall oaks bordered a red slate walk. The nearest house was separated from it by a broad yard with a high wooden fence, over which rose thick spruces.

We parked at the end of the road, where a small woods began, and sat looking at the house. "I used to dream about this place," Charley said.

Someone said, "Do they know what really happened to her?"

Someone else said, "She hanged herself."

"Do they know where?"

"The neck."

"Very funny."

We began talking about ghosts, but Tom grew impatient. "Let it alone. What are we, five?"

"You and Ben," Charley said. "Always so rational."

"You make rational sound like a disease," Tom said.

Charley said, "So you wouldn't mind spending a night there alone?"

That was how it happened: a lazy summer evening, streetlights brightening under a darkening sky, an idle challenge swiftly accepted. The plan was for Tom to enter the house at dusk the next day and stay until dawn. We would park Lindberg's old Chevy at the dirt lot on the other side of the woods and watch from the trees to make sure Tom remained all night.

"You don't have to do this," I told him when we were alone. "Charley's just being Charley. What if somebody sees you? What if they call the cops? What if—"

"No one will see me," Tom said sharply, sweeping at the air like someone batting away an insect.

The next evening we parked at the dirt lot and crept through the trees. Charley, Lindberg, and I took up positions and watched Tom walk up the darkening lawn to the side of the house. He tried one of the windows that faced the woods, but nothing happened. When he pushed at the second window, we saw it begin to rise. Moments later he thrust himself onto the sill and slithered inside. We watched the window slowly go down.

All of us had agreed that light of any kind might attract attention. Tom was to spend the night in the house, in any room, asleep or awake, and to report to us at the first glimmer of dawn. Charley pointed out that the risk was the same for all of us. If anyone saw us lurking in the woods, we could be hauled off by the police. We cared and didn't care; this was the best thing we'd done all summer. Charley had brought a sleeping bag. We agreed to take turns watching.

By three in the morning a terrible boredom had set in. Charley was half-asleep in his bag, like a boy on a camping trip. Lindberg sat back against a tree with his head tipped to the side, one leg stretched out and one leg bent up. As for me, I was tired of watching a dark house that sat there doing nothing. I was also restless and uneasy. It was as if I were pacing up and down, up and down, in a cramped room with no windows, instead of sitting motionless on pine needles and crackly leaves in a stretch of woods at the end of a dead-end road in the middle of a summer night. I tried to imagine Tom in that house, where a beautiful woman had once hanged herself. In the night before the morning when I'd knocked on the door of my father's study, I had lain awake thinking of her ghost drifting through the Harrington house with streaming hair. On her neck was a red mark from the rope. She went from room to room, looking for something, searching for a way out. On the dark ceiling of my room I had watched a rectangle of light from a passing car move slowly along. I heard a sigh and felt something brush my cheek.

Charley woke me. "He's coming out," he whispered. Through the leaves I could see pale spaces of sky. Tom slipped from the sill to the ground, pulled down the window, and walked over to us in the first light of dawn, like someone out for a stroll. We'd all agreed not to utter a word until we were safely in the car. I could see there was something wrong about his face.

"I don't want to talk about it," he said in the car. He didn't look at us. The plan had been to have breakfast at Betty's Diner and get home before our parents were up, but Tom wanted no part of it. I sat next to him in the back and tried to catch his eye, but he looked down at his hand, spread out on his leg.

"Come on, Tom," Lindberg said. "Tell us something."

"Leave him alone," Charley said.

At his house Tom got out of the car and made his way slowly along the front walk, as if he were studying patterns in the concrete.

Charley said, "I knew it."

"What did you know?" Lindberg said.

Charley slammed the heel of his hand against the steering wheel. "The place is haunted."

"You're kidding, right?" Lindberg said.

"Ghosts don't exist," I said; it sounded like a shout. I could smell the tobacco in my father's study.

For the next two days Tom stayed shut up in his room and refused to come out. His mother, standing guard at the front door, said he wasn't feeling well. She looked at us with murderous eyes. "Where were you," she said, glaring at each of us in turn, "that night you never came home?" On the third day Tom agreed to leave his room and go for a short ride. As he came toward us down the front walk, we saw his mother watching from behind a pulled-back curtain.

In the car he said nothing except "Uh-huh" and "Don't want to talk about it." "You can't just not talk about it," Lindberg said. Charley said, "Stop hounding him." Tom sat in the back with me. He looked out the window, stared at his knees, stroked his thigh with a thumb. Ten minutes later he asked to go home.

The next day his mother told us over the phone that she and Tom would be spending the rest of the summer with her sister in Augusta, Maine. She felt it would be a good change for him, under the circumstances. We understood there were no longer four of us. I told Charley and Lindberg that I was going to stay overnight in the Harrington house if it killed me.

III

Under the fading sky of a hot summer evening, I broke into the Harrington house. I did it with such swiftness and ease that I imagined myself bursting into a laugh, as I stood boldly there, on the forbidden side of the window, while Charley and Lindberg watched safely from the woods, but I was in no mood for laughter. Besides, boldness had nothing to do with it. What drove me was some fury of desire that I did not try to understand. In the darkish dusk I could see polished brown cupboards and a teapot on a counter. Along the top of the cupboards ran a narrow decorative band that showed alternating silhouettes of a girl skipping rope and a boy flying a kite. The word "pantry" sprang to mind, though I had never seen a pantry and wasn't sure I knew what one was. I was tense and anxious, fiercely alert to the slightest creak or rustle, as if at any moment something might loom before me or brush up against me from behind. A woman had hanged herself in this house.

Slowly I made my way from the cupboard room to the next room: more rows of cabinets, a wooden table with four cushioned chairs. On the table sat a shadowy sugar bowl. As I stood for a moment, looking warily around, something began to stir in me. It was a feeling I couldn't account for, here in the kitchen's deepening dusk. I had the sensation that I was being welcomed in some way—felt, almost, a kind of pleasure. The mood confused me, even irritated me, since I hadn't come here for pleasure. Who knew what I'd come for? On top of the refrigerator an owl-shaped cookie jar seemed to be watching over things. An oven mitt hanging on the side of the stove looked as if it wanted to shake hands. With surprise and a prickle of delight I saw, suspended from the swing-out wall lamp, a jointed puppet with bent elbows and one raised knee. Even the row of pots hanging from hooks had a somehow festive air, as if they were about to swing into a dance.

As I entered the darker living room, where partly drawn curtains nearly reached the floor, I made out a curved-arm rocker and a puffy armchair, turned toward each other. They seemed to be telling me to come on in and make myself at home. In one corner of the couch sat a big bear wearing a baseball cap. On the mantel over the fireplace I saw what looked like a large box. Stepping closer, I discovered that it was a toy theater with curtains and a stage. A little man in coattails stood before a table. When I bent forward, I saw that he was pulling a rabbit out of a hat.

In the darkening air I passed into the next room, which appeared to be the dining room. On one wall I could make out the portrait of a bearded grandfather in an oval frame. He was staring solemnly across the table at the opposite wall, where a dim circus poster showed a young woman in a top hat and tutu standing on one leg on the back of an elephant.

As I made my way deeper into the house, past windows that admitted shimmers of blue-black sky, I could still see the curves and lines of things, but as the details faded I had the always sharpening sense of an arrangement or atmosphere in which the formal was balanced by the playful, in which ceremony rang with laughter. This was a world set apart from the world. It was a world that released me from myself, invited me to overcome whatever it was I was.

One downstairs room appeared to be a study lined with bookshelves, but in one corner I was able to make out a dressmaker's dummy wearing a tilted fedora on top of its neck.

Upstairs, in a room where the bed had a curved headboard

and footboard, I saw a stuffed monkey hanging by one hand from a curtain rod. When I opened a nearby door, I saw the dim shelves of a linen closet. On top of a pile of folded sheets, two Japanese dolls in kimonos sat upright on their knees, their bodies facing each other and their heads turned in my direction. One doll held up a fan that partly concealed her face, while the other extended an arm toward me, as if in invitation.

Behind another door I discovered a flight of dark stairs going up. As I climbed the steps I used a tiny penlight that I'd brought along, shading it with a cupped hand so that no one outside could see. In the attic I moved past piles of old trunks, on top of which lay straw hats emerging from darkness, ice skates, a ballet slipper, a music box, and I came to a dollhouse higher than my knees. Bending over, I pointed my light through a window.

A man and a woman were sitting at a little table. With one extended arm the man was supporting a violin against his shoulder. With his other hand he gripped the bow. The woman sat with her two forearms raised and her hands holding a flute to her lips. The man was sitting erect and looking straight at the woman. She sat with her head bent slightly forward, her eyes raised to his. A cat with an arched back and shining green eyes rubbed against her leg.

I heard a soft creak in the nearby dark. A second creak came closer. I caught myself thinking that these were sounds that should make my arms stiffen, my head turn in terror. Instead, they were the sounds an old attic had every right to make, in a house I had already come to love.

Is it possible to fall in love with a house, as you might with a person, if you are seventeen years old, a small-town boy waiting for the adventure of his life to begin? I knew only that every hidden shape in that house, every glint and glimmer, beckoned to me, soothed me and thrilled me, quickened me with a sense of something discovered. I'd been in many houses, without thinking much about them—nice porch, corny place mats—but this dark house awakened me, pierced me with something I hadn't known I longed for. It occurred to me that only once had I thought of the hanged wife. A death might have happened here, but this was no place of moans and sighs, of eerie whispers. Only people who knew joy could have lived in this house. I felt as if I had opened a secret door and come to the center of things.

I spent the night drifting from room to room, sitting on half-seen chairs and couches, lying on dim beds, running my hands along the tops and sides of unknown shapes. It was as if I wanted to memorize the house, to encourage its spirit to flow into me. I remembered how, as a child, I would ride with my parents to New York, to visit one of the grandmothers, and when I arrived home, after the long drive under the stone bridges of the parkway, I would walk into the house and feel it entering me: the fireplace with the bookcases on both sides, the stairway with the banister, my room upstairs with the two windows that looked down at the swing set, the two crabapple trees, and the hedge where bumblebees floated above white blossoms. The Harrington house stirred in me something that I felt I needed to take with me, as I prepared to set out for the wider world, though what it was I couldn't say, didn't have words for. The house—oh, who knew what it was doing to me, out here at the end of the road, the end of the world? I knew only that I wanted as much of it as I could bear.

So in the long night that was like no other I drifted through the house of a stranger, like someone who knows he has come to a place he may never find again.

IV

Light scalded my eyes. In the brightness I saw a wall, a strange window. I was leaning back on a couch I did not know. It came to me: morning, danger. I made my way toward the glare of the cupboard room. I climbed out through the window.

The sky blazed blue. Blades of grass flamed up at me. The edges of trees were sharp in the light.

I looked down at my sneakers. They were moving along, one after the other. I saw them pushing down on the grass, which sprang up a moment later.

In the shade of the woods my eyes felt cool. The house was far away. I heard a stirring of leaves and jerked my head around. A figure stood next to me. "Another minute and I was going in there. What the hell happened to you?" Lindberg's voice was harsh, mocking. Charley said, "It's late. Let's get out of here." The line of his jaw pressed through the skin of his face.

In the back of the car I sat hunched against a door. My face was turned from the shine of the windows. "I don't want to talk about it," I said.

"He doesn't want to talk about it," Lindberg said. "Keeps us up all night and doesn't want to talk about it."

"Tell us what you saw in there," Charley said. The muscles in his neck twisted as he turned his head.

"I'm sick of this town," Lindberg said.

When I opened the door above the three steps, my mother was looking hard at me. "Where've you been all night? Where? I almost called the police." A line of sun cut across the side of her neck. "You and those friends of yours."

"I need to sleep," I said. Upstairs in my room I closed the blinds and lay down on the bed. I could hear my mother on the telephone. The books lined up in my bookcase made me think of people standing with their backs to me.

One of my curtains moved a little. I heard dim sounds, whispers. I sat up suddenly, but no one was there.

When I opened my eyes, it was almost dark. A shape rose over me at the side of the bed. I could make out the sleeves of my father's shirt. "Where were you?" my father's voice said. The lenses of his glasses shut out his eyes. The circles looked down at me. "Not letting us know," the voice said. His hand moved against his leg. The hand looked larger than a hand. I turned my head away.

My arm lay across my face. When I moved my arm, I saw that the air was now black. I could see the dim outlines of my window blinds. A mutter of voices rose through the floor. From my closet I heard sounds that made me think of paper being folded.

Footsteps stopped outside my door. I could hear breaths going in and out.

The footsteps moved away. A rubbing sound came from behind a window. I understood that something had changed, that things would be different from now on. I sat up in bed. I waited.

THE SUMMER OF LADDERS

Then came the summer of ladders. I don't mean that the presence of ladders is in any way surprising, in our New England town. Every March or April, as soon as the last snow melts from the last strip of lawn, the first ladders appear. We see them leaning against the sides of houses, harbingers of spring as reliable as the unfolding petals of dogwood and forsythia. As the weather grows warmer, the ladders begin to multiply, as if nourished by the sun. Stepladders spread open beside high hedges and backyard fences. All summer long you can find us standing above our well-mown lawns, touching up our shingles and window frames, cleaning out our rain gutters. By summer's end the ladders have begun to grow scarcer, though you can still see them in a scattering of yards. Deep into autumn a few remain, disappearing at last with the coming of the first snow.

But that summer you could feel a difference. At first it was only the familiar sight of ladders poking above rooflines or resting next to second-floor windows, the sort of thing you notice and don't notice as you stroll along the tree-shaded sidewalk on a Saturday morning or drive out to the mall at the edge of town. But soon the ladders were displaying themselves as never before. You could see them tilted against gazebos and garden sheds, you could spot them disappearing into tall sugar maples and lindens, where pairs of arms were trimming branches or hanging ropes for swings. Stepladders stood beside porch posts and windowsills. They nestled into flowering shrubs, loomed in the doorways of open garages. In a single yard I saw one aluminum extension ladder leaning against the sunny front of the house, another leaning against the shady side of the house, a paint-stained wooden ladder rising over the garage roof, and a dark-blue stepladder standing under the branches of a Norway spruce.

This efflorescence of ladders was probably no more than one of those common accidents of town life, like the sudden appearance of basketball nets on all the garages of a random stretch of block, but I soon became aware of something else. The ladders were growing taller. Extension ladders leaning against roofs began to rise higher, sometimes reaching full length and stretching far into the air. Here and there you would see someone dangerously climbing a few rungs above the rain gutter, clutching the rails with both hands and looking around. In one yard I caught a glimpse of the top of a ladder sticking through the crown of a towering red maple. Moments later, a head appeared. The head looked around, nodded down at me, and continued rising, pulling up with it a tanned neck and a pair of shoulders in a checkered shirt. The head turned thoughtfully, gazing from side to side, and finally stared straight up at the blue sky.

In my spare time I had been climbing my own ladder, in order to touch up my window frames. One afternoon I carried the ladder around to the back of the house, where I set it in place next to the garbage cans. I pulled on the rope and watched as the rungs rose beside the second-floor bedroom window and came to a stop a few feet above the rain gutter. I climbed carefully toward the sunny window, holding my paint can and brush and sanding block in one hand. At the level of the sill I stopped, hung my paint can on the ladder hook, hesitated, and found myself climbing higher. Standing at last with my feet near the edge of the roof, clinging to the ladder rails, I looked down at the yards on both sides, at the dark-red hexagon that was the top of Jim Driscoll's table umbrella, at a white soccer ball casting a long black-green shadow, at the spray of a lawn sprinkler falling slowly toward glistening grass, and throwing my gaze over the top of my garage to the Benedicts' yard I saw a glass of lemonade shining with sunlight beside its trembling shadow on a wooden picnic table, I saw a blue sneaker lying on its side on the arm of a yellow slatted chair, and beyond the Benedicts' yard I could see green fragments of other yards with spots of red and purple flowers and, in the distance, a small car moving along a thin line of street. Up there on my ladder, standing with most of my body above the roofline, I had the sensation of looking down at a world I had scarcely noticed before, a world smaller and vaster than the one I knew, and suddenly turning my face upward I stared into the rich blue dizzying sky before clutching the ladder tightly and warning myself to be careful, careful.

The next day, leaving my brush and paint can on the grass, I climbed two rungs higher. I could feel a slight tremor in the rails, as if my excitement were passing through my palms into the aluminum, and for a long while I stood there, looking this way and that, not quite sure what I was doing, up there in the air, wondering how high it was possible to go.

Accidents, I suppose, were bound to happen. The first fall took place from a six-foot stepladder standing next to a back-yard hedge. A boy of seven climbed up, stood on the very top, peeked over the hedge into the next yard, and toppled sideways to the ground, fracturing a wrist and dislocating a shoulder. It was the sort of accident that we blamed on parental negligence rather than on the ladder itself, but two days later Bob Farrell, who coached our Little League team, plunged from a ladder on which he'd been standing far above the roofline and broke his right arm and three ribs.

News of the fall spread through every neighborhood. We were warned to climb carefully and to keep our feet four rungs below the point at which the ladder rested. Within two days the local hardware store was advertising a variety of new safety features. Ladder feet now came with heavy-duty antislip pads. Rungs were designed with special treads for superior traction. Fence-like supports, driven into the ground, stabilized the ladder base and permitted it to stand close to the house, so that the nearly erect ladder could reach higher than the old models, now called "leaners." You could even buy safety nets, which you suspended from ropes and spread out some dozen feet below the ladder top.

As if encouraged by these precautionary measures, ladders soared even higher. On every block you could see them, touching the roofline and reaching far above. People stood in the sky, looking down. One day the hardware store displayed a supply of newer ladders equipped with aluminum support poles that swung out from the side rails. The poles, slanting to the ground and fitted with extra-wide footpads, prevented the ladder from falling backward or to either side.

It was during the spread of safety ladders, in mid-July, that the third and fourth falls took place. On sidewalks and front porches you could hear people talking about Ed Harrison's broken neck, about Susan Meyer's injured spine. Would they ever walk again?

A few ladders were taken down and stored in garages, but others rose higher still. In the hardware store you could now buy extension ladders that came in three and even four sections, stretching to sixty feet, to seventy-two feet, to eighty feet. They were so heavy that they had to be delivered by truck and set up by three men. Additional poles could be fastened against the roof slope.

One night Tim Cullen, sixteen years old, was dared by friends to climb his father's new ladder at the back of the house. At the top he held out his arms in triumph, bent his head back to look up at the moon, and plummeted to his death. In a show of respect, no one set foot on a ladder rung on the day of the funeral. Three days later, you could see people in every neighborhood climbing high above the roof peaks.

I continued to climb my twenty-four-foot ladder, moving a rung or two higher each time. Not long after Tim Cullen's death, I found myself staring with impatience at the steep slope of my roof, which rose before me as if in mockery. Hardly aware of what I was doing, I stepped onto the roof shingles, crouched down on all fours, and made my way up to the chimney. There I sat awkwardly with my back against the bricks. As far as my eyes could see, ladders rose over the tops of red and gray and green roofs. Some were so far away that they quivered in sunlight. A few distant figures stood against the sky, like birds resting before continuing their flight.

The next morning I drove over to the hardware store and purchased one of the new four-section extension ladders, which was delivered that afternoon. The ladder included six ground poles and four roof poles. Workers in hard hats set it all up a few feet from my old ladder, which still leaned against the roof edge. They stood watching me make my way up before they returned to their truck. Climbing slowly, resting first one foot and then the other on each new rung, I rose far above my rooftop and stood looking down at rectangles of green yards stretching away, at the smaller and smaller roofs of distant neighborhoods, at a ripple of blue-green hills. As I turned my head to each side, the ladder rails trembled slightly. Shifting my feet so that I could look over my shoulder, I took in the sweep of roof peaks and treetops behind me, all the way out to the reservoir. I could feel again the old exhilaration, shot through now with a new restlessness, even a dissatisfaction, as if any height could never be enough.

The sixth and seventh falls happened toward the end of July. They proved to be serious: John Sorenson broke both legs and his collarbone, Theresa Mastrianni suffered head injuries and a fractured pelvis and remained in critical condition. In early August we learned that Dennis Holtzman, who managed a popular family restaurant, had tumbled from his three-section ladder and endured a traumatic brain injury. A few days later we heard about the second death. Richard Warren, a retired gym teacher, fell from a height of sixty-six feet and died on the way to the hospital. His ladder had been secured by support poles and equipped with a safety net, which apparently failed to extend far enough.

The ladders seemed to pause, as if listening. Warnings against the dangers of climbing appeared on signs displayed in front yards. One sign showed a demonic ladder rising from the flames of hell and toppling terrified people from its rungs. A minister addressing his congregation denounced our ladders as materialistic perversions of spiritual striving. By the third week of August, I was aware that a change had begun to take place. The great surge upward had tapered off. It may have been the shakiness of those uppermost extensions, the fear of falling, the screams of police and ambulance sirens on nearby streets. It may have been the exhaustion of a certain style of pleasure, or an end-of-summer tiredness. Whatever the reason, many of the new ladders now stood empty. Others were taken down and hidden away in cellars and garages.

Not everyone succumbed to the new caution. The remaining ladders continued to thrust their way higher. At times it seemed to me that they were trying to outdo one another, as if a passion for competition were vying with a sense of wonder. At the hardware store we discovered five-rung extensions that could be carried to the top of a ladder and fastened in place. One climber in particular, Henry Pulaski, a civil engineer, was expert in connecting the new extensions to each other and inventing intricate supports for his always lengthening ladder. Pulaski was a quiet, polite man who appeared with his wife at occasional town functions but otherwise kept to himself. People stopped on the sidewalk to gaze up as he climbed higher, day after day.

And day after day I mounted my own ladder, forcing myself to ascend a few more rungs each time, as the rails trembled and swayed. At the top I carefully attached and locked into place a five-rung extension. Always, in the near distance, I saw the Pulaski ladder, rising higher and higher.

One morning near the end of August I made my way up my ladder, determined to push myself farther than ever before. It was one of those brilliant blue days of late summer, with a narrow line of cloud low in the sky, as if a streak of white had been painted there in order to intensify the vividness of blue. As I stood near the top of my gently swaying ladder, holding tightly to the rails of the new extension, I saw Henry Pulaski climbing up into the sky, like a man determined to reach the sun. I noticed that the line of cloud at the horizon had grown broader and was edged with gray. More clouds began to spread across the blue. Soon a heavy layer had moved in, passing across the top of Pulaski's ladder and hiding it from sight. I saw Henry Pulaski stop and look up. Moments later he continued climbing. As his head disappeared into the cloud, I thought of a boy making his way into a tree thick with leaves. Did Henry Pulaski want to see what was inside that cloud? Did he imagine there might be some unknown world in there, as in a child's storybook? Did he want to burst through to the brightness on the other side? I watched his upper body rise into the darkening white. Soon there was nothing left of him but a single foot. The foot grew misty. It floated upward. Suddenly it vanished. My ladder shook in a stir of wind. Far off I could see slanting lines of rain. I began to make my way carefully down before it was too late, but a change had already set in, light was breaking through the clouds, the sun slid into a space of blue. Below, green yards glowed in a burn of light. Pulaski's ladder stood clear against the sky. But Henry Pulaski was no longer there.

I climbed down as quickly as I could, like a man running backward. At the bottom I stood clinging to the ladder with both hands, savoring the feel of my feet on solid ground. Then I set off in the direction of the Pulaski house, some five blocks away. When I arrived, three police cars were parked in the street. Rosa Pulaski was pointing up at her husband's ladder again and again as she spoke excitedly to two policemen. A few neighbors lingered nearby, looking up at the empty rungs. Pulaski had disappeared. No one had seen him climb down. No one had seen him fall, though the police were awaiting further reports. I imagined a body lying smashed on the roof of someone's back porch, one arm dangling over the edge.

In the course of the next few days, no trace of him was found. Police cars cruised the neighborhood. A dozen witnesses had seen Pulaski climb up into the cloud, but no one had seen him return. Was he lying dead in the middle of a rose bush? Nervous rumors, half joking, began to circulate. Pulaski had been carried off by an eagle to the top of a distant mountain. Pulaski had entered heaven. Pulaski had been abducted by aliens. Pulaski had stepped into the cloud and now lived among the cloud people. Pulaski had descended by means of a rope and sneaked away in order to escape his marriage and start a new life. The disappearance disturbed us far more than the injuries and deaths, as if an element of dark magic had come into our town. It proved to be the final blow to our ladder craze. On street after street you could see the ladders coming down, growing horizontal, vanishing into cellars and garages.

I stayed away from my sky-high ladder but left it standing there, the last one on the block. Neighbors threw me disapproving looks. In an effort to appease them, I took down my old two-part ladder and hung it sideways on hooks in the garage. One morning I woke with the sudden understanding that I had to make a final climb. Was I hoping to penetrate the mystery of disappearance, up there in the sky? I knew only that I wanted to be high over the rooftops once again.

I moved steadily from rung to rung, ascending past the rain gutter and continuing beyond the peak, climbing higher and higher until I reached the place where I had stopped the last time. As I looked out over the town, I could tell that something had changed. I realized that my eyes had become used to the spectacle of ladders rising high over housetops, but now I saw only chimneys and their slanted shadows. It was like returning to a garden from which all the flowers had been plucked away. Restless, unhappy, I climbed a few rungs higher and stood with my hands clasped over the tops of the quivering rails, my face turned up toward the sky. What was I expecting to find up there? Was I hoping to see the bottoms of celestial ladders, hanging down from above? Did I long to leave the familiar world for the sake of some other world that I didn't believe in? Lifting a leg carefully to make my way onto one more rung, I became aware of some slight shift of pressure in the sole of my lower foot, all at once I could feel myself slipping to one side, the weight of my body tore one hand from the rail, the other hand lost its grip, I was falling now, plunging to my death, thinking not of my life spread out before me from the moment of birth but only of a coffee cup that I had left in the sink, a cup that I regretted not having washed and placed in the rack, suddenly my body slammed against the slope of the roof, slid toward the rain gutter, knocked against the foot of a support pole, and stopped. My shoulder ached, my hip was throbbing. After a while I struggled over to the ladder and made my way down. A neighbor drove me to the ER.

Soreness, bruises, no bones broken, no head injuries: they called me a lucky man. The next morning I hired workers to take down the ladder and haul it away. One day in late September I took a walk in my neighborhood. It was one of those warm days of early autumn when the leaves are still green, when basketballs slap against driveways and squirrels scamper across telephone wires, and you can feel, in the drowsy air, a momentary chill. Bursts of grass flew out behind a lawn mower. Water from a hose splashed against a car. At the side of one house I saw a stepladder standing close to a kitchen window. A man wearing a baseball cap stood beside the dark-green windowsill. He waved to me and returned to his scraper. The doors of a yellow school bus opened and released two children with backpacks, who walked across the street and broke into a run. Already the summer of ladders seemed a dream from which the town had awakened, an uneasy dream that was changing and dissolving, a dream that we would have trouble remembering as we watched the snow falling outside our windows in the stillness of a winter night.

IV

THE CIRCLE OF PUNISHMENT

Your crime is grave. Your punishment will be terrible.

Look at me. I said: Look at me. There. That's better. That's much better. I see by various signs that despite your age you know a thing or two about punishment. Those scars on your neck, that missing finger on your left hand. You also think you know a thing or two about me. To you I'm bound to seem—mmm, how would you put it? An instrument of oppression? A complacent member of the ruling rich? Look at him!—funny old gent, with the power to crush me. Oh, we know how you think. We know. But enough of this. I'm not here to play games with you. I'm here to announce the result of our twenty-six days of deliberation. I plan to do so in just a moment. But first I'd like to say a few words to you about our system of punishment, so that you may be in a position to understand the nature of what we've decided to do to you. For if there's one thing you can be sure of, in this uncertain world of ours, it is this: we take our punishments seriously.

Is that a smirk? I advise you not to smirk. A smirk makes a bad impression. A smirk, I regret to say, makes a very bad impression. But more than that, a smirk is unworthy of your crime. You do understand, don't you, that the extreme loathing, the almost physical revulsion, that we feel for your crime suggests a certain, what shall I say . . . interest? esteem? It would distress me—seriously!—to find myself disappointed in you. And bear in mind, young man: by lifting my right index finger one-half inch, I can have you instantly removed from this court and taken to a punishing cell, where your lips will be cut from your face—a painful ordeal that won't prevent, but will only delay, your punishment.

Have I made myself clear? Good. But please. Please. Let me be clearer still. I'm not asking you to be humble. I'm not proposing that you grovel before me. That would be an embarrassment for both of us. I ask only that you bear yourself with dignity.

Shall I repeat it? We take our punishments seriously. And what better testimony to that seriousness than our *Book of Punishments*, with its many hundreds of volumes containing every actual and possible crime, along with the corresponding punishment. No one knows exactly how many volumes the book contains, since even as a new volume is printed, older volumes are being revised and expanded, to say nothing of the addenda and supplements that issue daily from the courts and are bound in small booklets of three or four or a dozen pages, which gradually find their way, often in modified form, into revised versions of earlier volumes.

You find it amusing? Of course you do. You find everything amusing. Let me ask you something. Is it amusing to have your hands chopped off at the wrist? Is it amusing to have your eyelids ripped from your face? But forgive me. I digress.

In addition to the always expanding *Book of Punishments*, with its daily addenda and supplements, you must also keep in mind the Commentaries, a much vaster compilation in which every crime and every punishment is subjected to analysis and interpretation by scholars and legal experts, who rarely agree and whose opinions are themselves open to analysis and interpretation by other scholars and legal experts, in an always growing series of refutations, counterarguments, and fresh considerations. The Commentaries, along with the *Book of Punishments,* are scrupulously studied by all of us, here in the Citizens' Court, before we decide upon a punishment that is satisfactory in every respect.

But why, you may wonder, should there be so great an emphasis on punishment, in our fair city? Even our children are made to memorize passages from the *Book of Punishments,* in their school readers. You yourself no doubt recall those lengthy recitations. Let me assure you that our belief in punishment, our concern for its precise application to particular acts, as well as for its larger meaning as a method of ensuring social harmony, is in no sense arbitrary. It is based on a philosophy of punishment that in its simplest terms may be expressed by this formula: every crime is the outward and visible sign of an inward and invisible guilt. This principle leads to a crucial corollary: all citizens are guilty. From these two principles a third inevitably follows: no punishment is a mistake.

Let me give you an example. Imagine that a man running from the scene of a crime is apprehended and punished, say by the loss of one or both arms. And say that afterward we discover he did not commit the crime of which he has been accused. Even so, he is justly punished. For although the particular crime expressing his guilt did not in this instance belong to him, nevertheless his failure to commit the crime in no way detracts from his essential guilt, which exists independently of the accidents that make it visible. For the crime was always within him, awaiting release. In this respect, it's worth mentioning that of the small number of citizens punished for crimes not their own, by far the greater proportion accept their punishment as just, in part because any protest is itself a crime that is immediately and severely punished, and in part because every citizen has been taught to understand that punishment need not attach itself to an actual crime, in order to be merited.

That said, it remains true that we make every effort to fit the punishment to the crime. Indeed, our *Book of Punishments* is the record of that endeavor. There you will find a scrupulous evaluation of the weight or seriousness of every crime, from the most trivial to the most heinous, and the calculation of the corresponding punishment. But in all such reckonings there is one important principle at work, which may be called the Principle of Imbalance. According to this principle, a punishment must always be greater than the crime to which it corresponds. And the reason is this, that the punishment is measured not only against the crime itself but against the additional crime of failing to do everything in one's power to prevent or impede the commission of a crime. In this sense, the apparent imbalance is in fact a balance, so that the Principle of Imbalance has also come to be known as the Principle of Balance.

I advise you to pay attention, young man. This speech is our only kindness to you.

In classifying and evaluating the vast array of crimes that may be committed by our citizens, and assigning to each its proper punishment, we must also take into account that body of laws known as the Hidden Laws. These are the not inconsiderable number of laws concealed from citizens, who, in addition to being guilty of committing crimes they know to be crimes, are also guilty of committing crimes they don't know to be crimes. The purpose behind our Hidden Laws is twofold. First, by concealing certain laws and rigorously punishing their infraction, we demonstrate to our citizens that any action, however innocent it appears to be, may, upon thorough investigation, turn out to be a crime. And second, we remind our citizens that everyone, at every moment of the day or night, stands on the brink of punishment.

From my remarks it should be clear to you that we are firm believers in what might be called the universal nature of punishment. No one is free of crime; no one goes unpunished. As you well know, our system of punishment begins in earliest childhood. Outsiders who visit our city are often disturbed by the sight of our children. We are accused not only of punishing them cruelly but of failing to make any distinction between the crimes of children and the crimes of adults. The accusers are mistaken on two counts. Our punishments are not cruel, but just; and although we apply the law impartially, we are fully aware that our punishments fall most weightily on our young. This is part of a deliberate and well-considered policy. Adult citizens are without the dangerous delusions of freedom that beset our children and lead to violations of law. The severity of our punishments is meant to curb childish impulses toward disorder, to impress upon the youngest members of our society the serious consequences of yielding to temptation. Thus it comes about that we see in our city many children whose fingers have been cut off at the knuckle, whose faces have been branded or burned, whose tongues have been torn out at the root. Indeed, it isn't too much to say that the great majority of our children bear upon their faces and bodies the signs of our watchfulness.

Now, if all citizens, sooner or later, require punishment, a problem might seem to arise. Shall the punishers, who themselves are citizens, be exempt from punishment? If not, how shall the punishers be punished? Our earliest records show that far back in our history the punishers were granted the privilege of exemption. For as instruments of the law, they were the incarnation of the act of punishment and therefore could not themselves be punished. There thus arose a division between two groups of citizens: those who punished and those who were punished.

This state of affairs led to a number of troubling incidents, culminating in the case of a punisher who scandalized citizens by his reckless flouting of the law. Various remedies were attempted, all of which proved unsatisfactory, until a brilliant solution was found, which remains in force to this day: the act of punishment was itself declared a crime. Thus those entrusted with the responsibility of punishment are themselves repeatedly punished and bear upon their bodies the signs that you know well. Observe this arm, this eye. Of the many advantages of such an arrangement, one in particular deserves your attention: the punishers bring to their task a peculiar ferocity born of the knowledge that, the moment their work is done, they themselves will be mercilessly punished.

We live, then, you and I, in a society of the punished. Punishment is our destiny, our way of life. It is woven into our sense of things as intimately as sight or touch. Without our punishments, we would scarcely know who we are. Would we even be human? Thus it comes about that among the punished, which is to say, among all of us, there exists a profound sense of kinship, a fierce bond that unites us beyond the claims of family or friendship. On every street corner, in every living room and coffee shop and school playground, the signs are visible: the missing hands, the severed arms, the shattered legs, the blinded eyes. Such signs remind us of our destiny, join us in a great brotherhood of punishment.

In the Commentaries there are found a number of illustrative tales, said to date from our prehistory, long before punishments began to be recorded. In one famous tale, a miller punishes his wife. The wife punishes the son. The son punishes the dog, who punishes the cat. The cat punishes a rat, who punishes a snake, who punishes a mouse. The punishments descend to smaller and smaller animals, until a fly punishes an ant. One night the ant crawls into the miller's ear and bites him deep inside his head. This tale, known as "The Circle of Punishment," has many interpretations, of which the most widely known is this: we are all connected to one another in a great harmony of punishment, a bright ring of pain. In this way we are all equal, however widely our wealth or social positions may differ.

And so I return to your crime, which I haven't for a moment forgotten, even as I seemed to speak of other things. For as I spoke of those things, I was speaking all along of you, and of your crime, and of your punishment. Your crime is a daring one, young man. By this I mean that it is an uncommon crime, a dangerous crime, one that we are bound to consider with the greatest seriousness. For your crime, by its very nature, strikes at the heart of punishment itself. It is a crime directed against punishment, against the very idea of punishment. We of the Citizens' Court have spent many days considering your case. We have studied the *Book of Punishments* and the Commentaries, we have debated among ourselves late into the night. Breaking, branding, cutting, stoning, blinding, all seemed to us to fall far short of the high gravity of your offense. Only gradually, over the course of weeks, did the necessary punishment reveal itself to us—at first slowly, as if it were reluctant to be known, and then more swiftly and surely, presenting itself to us, in the end, as inevitable.

Look at me, young man. Stand straight. Concentrate your attention.

Young man, your punishment is this: we forgive you. We don't of course forgive you in the sense of excusing your crime. Your crime fills us with contempt and disgust. Rather, we forgive you in the sense of excusing you from punishment, of withholding from you the high privilege of being punished.

You look surprised. Are you surprised? You also seem relieved. Let me be frank with you. At first, yes, you may feel a certain relief. You may even feel pleasure. It will never last. In a world of the punished, you will walk as an outcast. Your fellow citizens will withdraw from you as from a man covered with excrement. But quite apart from that, you will feel in yourself, day by day, a growing absence, a terrible lack. That lack will spread in you like a disease of the nervous system. You will lie awake in the dark. You will walk the night streets in search of ease, but there will be no ease, only an unrest, like the gnawing of an inner animal. You will seek to hurt yourself, at first in small ways, then in larger ones, always to no avail. For even if you slice off your thumb with the blow of an ax, even if you slash open your cheek with the thrust of a knife, you will continue to feel, inside the pain, an abiding emptiness. Disgraced, haunted, shunned, alone, you will drag yourself through the long vacancy of your days, yearning for something that can never come.

In comparison, how content the man with a sawed-off leg! How carefree the woman with a missing eye! For they are filled with the peace that comes from a knowledge of crimes well punished. It may be that you will seek to commit lesser crimes, in order to join the ranks of the peaceful. But although your new crimes will be punished as befits their nature, those punishments will in no sense fill the lack within you, which will grow larger and ever larger, until it consumes you utterly.

But you are young. You are clever. You believe in hope. I can see what you must be thinking, behind those shrewd eyes of yours. You're thinking that if I am right—if, that is to say, the absence of punishment is in truth the harshest of punishments—then, by a merciful paradox, you are destined to find yourself at last among the brotherhood of the punished. I'm afraid you are terribly mistaken. It is the nature of this punishment to be unlike all others. For the suffering it causes is the suffering of unpunishment, which produces the lack of which I've spoken; and whereas the suffering of all other punishments lasts for a time, diminishes, and at length is replaced by a sensation of peacefulness, the suffering of unpunishment remains undiminished and even increases with time, feeding upon you and growing stronger as you sicken.

Young man! Listen to me. For you there can be no peace. There can be no rest, no relief, no recovery, no inner harmony. For you there is only nothing. Do you understand?

So. We are done. You're free to go. Please remember to sign the form on the desk to your right, through those doors. By the authority vested in me by the Citizens' Court and the High Council, I hereby forgive you. Go.

GREEN

One morning toward the middle of April, John D. Ewing, a retired investment banker who lived in one of the better neighborhoods of our town, decided to solve his backyard problem of patches of dead grass by hiring a local firm, Backyard Answers, to pull up his lawn and replace it with flat-topped cobblestones in brown and red, arranged in a pattern of intersecting arcs. To celebrate his new yard, Ewing invited some dozen friends and neighbors to a grilling party, where guests praised his handsome cobblestones, inquired about cost and upkeep, and turned their attention to local politics. Two days later, one of the invited couples, the Hathaways, hired Backyard Answers to replace their weed-grown back lawn with porcelain tiles on a base of mortar. When another couple, Alan and Rose Perlstein, converted their backyard to alternating squares of dark and light granite, people in the neighborhood began to take notice. Was there something to be said for the new style? In a different part of town, on a street of older houses behind high hedges, two sisters replaced their back lawn with hexagonal tiles and rows of pebbles. After three more backyards—in less prosperous neighborhoods—were transformed into tile and stone, it was clear to us that something had begun to happen in our town, something that appeared to be more than a mere inclination to imitate one's neighbor.

I observed it all with the mixture of amused interest and vague disapproval that is my habitual response to changes in fashion, but when my fifteen-year-old daughter began pleading for backyard cobblestones, I gave way without protest. No more weeds springing up between the back porch and fence, no yellowing grass requiring my anxious attention, no mowing, no edging, no seeding, no raking, no fiddling with the sprinkler and shifting it from place to place: the benefits readily justified the expense and far outweighed the loss of green in one small part of our quarter-acre property. Up and down our street, neighbors were replacing back lawns with tile and cobblestone and brick. You could feel an excitement in the air.

As the fad for grassless backyards swept across town, many of us were struck by an event that took place toward the middle of May. In the front yard of a Victorian home not far from the town library, a broad lawn shaded by two ancient sycamores was torn up and replaced by three colors of travertine tile on both sides of the flagstone walk. The sycamores remained, surrounded by curved wooden benches. By the end of the week, patterns of brick and tile had sprung up in the front yards of some two dozen homes in different parts of town.

When my daughter and her friends expressed enthusiasm for the new look, I found myself stirred into opposition. Lawns, I pointed out, were refreshing spaces of green, welcome contrasts to sidewalks and streets. Their loss was something to be taken seriously. But more than that, any lawn, however trim and orderly, was an expression of natural growth within the artifice known as a town. A town without lawns was like a city without parks. The teenagers would have none of it. Lawns, they argued, were all alike. The new yards had different kinds of stone, different designs and patterns. And besides, there were still trees, bushes, hedges, flowers. Nature was everywhere, if you wanted nature. And what about water? Lawns needed a lot of water. Wasn't it eco-friendly to save water? Surprised by their passion, I became thoughtful but held firm. Within two weeks, front yards all over our neighborhood were being transformed. Under protest, sighing mightily and shaking my head, I gave way. We chose brick in three shades of red, reaching to the front sidewalk and around both sides of the house to the cobblestoned back.

By the end of May, more than half the yards in our town had done away with lawns, including those narrow stretches of grass between sidewalk and curb. By mid-June, only a scattering of green yards remained. Homeowners unable to afford the expense were sought out and generously aided by the recently formed Society for the Yards of Tomorrow, which raised funds vigorously for that purpose. One stubborn owner, who ran his own plumbing business and loved taking care of his yard, refused to give up his lawn for any reason. He was paid a visit by twelve concerned neighbors, who after three hours of discussion were able to persuade him to sell his house to all twelve of them for double its market value. The new owners quickly transformed the grass into elaborate patterns of many-colored tile and sold the property at a substantial profit to the assistant manager of a software-development firm, who had been searching for the ideal home in the suburbs.

Even as our lawns were disappearing, we became aware of other changes. Many of the new yards still retained borders of soil along the base of the house or the bottom of a fence, where rows of bushes and flowers flourished in sun and shade. Owners now began pulling up their plants and filling in the strips of earth with brick and tile. Hedges vanished; window boxes stood empty. Stalks and leaves once visible in the latticework spaces of porch aprons were cleared away, leaving only darkness. You would have thought our town was ridding itself of some harmful invasive species. Flowerpots on porch steps sat upside down or held nothing but a squeegee or a paintbrush. On the dark-red walls of the public library, green vines no longer climbed along the bricks.

One morning toward the middle of July, as I stepped out of my house to drive to work, I saw at the end of the block a section of beech tree moving slowly through the air, clasped by metal arms at the back of a transport truck. I learned that a neighbor had hired a tree-removal company to cut down his beech tree and extract the roots from their circle of earth in his tiled front yard. It was no exception. All over town, trees were beginning to disappear. It was as if their green-leaved branches were perceived as upper lawns, hovering above our heads. We were scarcely surprised when the Department of Public Works voted in August to send out crews to our curbsides to cut down town-owned trees and extract the roots. This official elimination of our street trees seemed to me the definitive sign of the destructive passion that had overtaken our town, though at the same time I recognized the chain saws as the logical culmination of a desire for change that had begun innocently enough.

By Labor Day, our town had been stripped of green. No leafy branches shaded our sidewalks, our yards, our paved-over park with its picnic tables and duck pond. No blades of grass thrust up between cracks of stone. In what might have been a touch of nostalgia for our absent trees, statues began to appear in front yards. Rodin's *Thinker* rose up in various neighborhoods, along with Greek gods and goddesses, an occasional Abraham Lincoln or P. T. Barnum, and twisting abstract sculptures in steel and stone. On a property near the town hall, a massive oak tree of granite was erected in a tiled front yard, with precisely carved leaves and hundreds of elegantly sculpted acorns. After numerous protests and a visit from the Town Planning Commissioner, the owner ordered the oak to be removed and replaced by a twenty-foot granite Statue of Liberty, with a winding inner stairway leading into the torch. Window boxes once filled with petunias and snapdragons now contained colored glass pellets, playful elves, or rows of pinwheels. People swept and washed their tiled yards, wiped bird droppings from the faces of statues. Was I the only one who missed the turning of the leaves?

Snow fell, covering our yards in the old way. The question of Christmas trees was addressed at a town meeting, where it was decided that banished conifers would be replaced by locally built structures reminiscent of hat stands, with arms that lengthened as they descended the central post. On New Year's Eve we clinked our glasses, resolved to lead better lives, and wondered what the coming year would bring.

Spring came, and with it the familiar sense of awakening, of a world of hidden things about to burst into life. The absence of green confused many of us, as if we had expected the melting snow to reveal the old springtime hidden underneath. In the warm air, no green-leaved forsythias thrilled us with their promise of yellow blossoms, no green leaf-tips sprouted at the twig ends of sugar maples. The few remaining birds poured out their song from the heads of statues, before returning to old nests crumbling in roof gutters or under eaves. As I walked the streets of my neighborhood, on treeless sidewalks exposed to relentless sunlight, I waved hello to neighbors kneeling beside soapy buckets and scrubbing their tiles with stiff-bristled brushes or repairing cracks that had formed under ice and snow. At home, my daughter and I took turns hosing off our cobblestones and bricks, while I dreamed of showers of grass thrown up by the lawn mower. Behind the garbage cans at the side of the house, I discovered an empty flowerpot, which had once overflowed with fern fronds, deep green.

The turn came quietly, a few days later. Mark and Carol Ackerman were next-door neighbors of Alan and Rose Perlstein, up on the hill. He was a cardiologist, she a dental surgeon. A year ago, they had made a point of displaying originality by selecting brightly colored tiles and overseeing their arrangement in artful designs, such as mosaic images of heraldic lions, intertwined serpents, and spread-winged falcons enclosed in borders of white and red stone. They now employed Yard Makeovers Inc. to extract two square feet of tiling and mortar on each side of the front porch steps. In each empty space they planted an evergreen shrub, purchased at a garden shop in a nearby town.

Was it nothing more than an aesthetic whim? An act of showy self-assertion on the part of a couple who liked to draw attention to themselves? Was it perhaps a medical decision reached by thoughtful doctors concerned about the quality of our air? Whatever it was, neighbors gathered on the sidewalk in front of the Ackerman house to stare. People from other parts of town drove over to see what the fuss was all about. By the end of the week, you could see green bushes rising here and there in the stone yards of our town.

Within two weeks it was difficult to find a yard without some touch of green: a bush beneath a living-room window, a bed of ferns enclosed in a rim of stone, a breast-high sapling casting its thin shadow over tiles. It might have ended there, a minor variation introduced to bring out the subtle qualities of arranged stone, but one day a waist-high hedge appeared along the border of a front yard near the high school. In another part of town, a flowering dogwood stood suddenly in a small circle of grass. Three days later Alan and Rose Perlstein, with an eye on the Ackermans, hired Yard Makeovers Inc. to remove all of their granite tiles and to cover their entire property with fresh sod.

There was no stopping it now. Yard after yard was turned into new grass or richly seeded soil. Hedges and bushes took root again. Young maples and hemlocks appeared on sunny lawns. One afternoon my daughter sat me down for a serious talk and offered to contribute her weekly babysitting income to the uprooting of our cobblestones and bricks. In another part of town, the twenty-foot Statue of Liberty was carried off on a flatbed truck and replaced by a massive oak tree rumored to have come from a forest in Maine. The town board, responding to public pressure, ordered the Department of Public Works to begin planting young trees along curbsides: red maples, sugar maples, lindens, sycamores, beech.

By the end of June our town had returned to the old world of tree-lined streets and green lawns. Under new branches, strips of fresh grass rose up between sidewalk and curb. I hummed as I gripped the rubber handles of my power mower and guided the blades across the yard. My daughter and I planted a vegetable garden in back, with rows of sticks for tomato vines and corn. Together we tended the flower boxes on the front porch. When all is said and done, I'm the kind of man who embraces the normal without apology. I woke each morning happy to greet the smell of cut grass. After a brief diversion, a playful experiment, things had returned to normal in our quiet town.

Or had they? As the days passed, I became aware of a slight difference. People were working away in their yards, a familiar enough sight in the middle of summer, but what drew my attention was the uninterrupted planting of new bushes and young trees, even in yards well supplied with both. A crowding seemed to be taking place. It was as if households had made up their minds to prevent any future assault on their little worlds of green.

Large hedges, higher than my head, were replacing smaller ones. Tall shrubs overshadowed low bushes. In the neighborhood of John D. Ewing and friends, it was common enough for houses to be set back from the road behind lofty hedges and thick-branched trees, which prevented passersby from peering in. But now, in more modest neighborhoods, such as my own, porches were disappearing behind high rows of honeysuckle and azalea. Ivy vines wrapped themselves around porch posts. Wisteria and lavender-flowered hydrangea climbed past living-room windows and made their way up toward bedroom windows on second floors. From the sills of the same windows, lush vines spilled down. Chimneys vanished within swirls of green.

I could feel it myself, this restlessness, this desire to push beyond carefully defined limits toward unknown lands. I had longed deeply for the restoration of our green yards, but the return no longer seemed enough. Our neat lawns and clipped hedges now struck me as tame and meek, mere imitations of manufactured items for the home, like wool rugs and mahogany sideboards. At best they were decorative touches in a world aggressively dedicated to the eradication of natural things. I applauded the desire to fill yards with growing forms, with life. One July day, in a burst of energy, I lined both sides of my narrow front walk with ten-foot shrubs purchased at a recently opened garden center. My daughter and I laughed as we pushed our way through thick leaves and springy branches to the hidden front porch.

In the same spirit, people in many parts of town had become impatient with the slow growth of saplings. They began buying trees that were nearly full-grown. On street after street you could see transport trucks carrying great horizontal oaks and beeches and firs, the roots wrapped in burlap. In every neighborhood you could watch as metal arms tightened around trunks and lowered great trees into prepared holes.

Small forests, extending to the property line, were becoming popular. Homeowners refinanced to cover the cost. On my block alone, one backyard was filled with freshly planted Norway pine, which pressed against every window and rose above the roof, while a nearby front yard was given over to a dense growth of birch and beech. Driveways became woodland paths. Caught up in the fever, I took out a loan and hired workers to turn our vegetable garden into a copse of hemlock.

One Saturday toward the middle of August, a work crew in yellow helmets stood in the middle of the street not far from my house. A group of us gathered to watch as the men drilled into the center of the road, tore out chunks of blacktop, and left a broad hole surrounded by dirt. Soon a long truck arrived, bearing an immense sugar maple tilted on its side. The heavy tree rose slowly before being lowered into the ground. When we asked what was happening, we were informed that crews were at work in every neighborhood, tearing up streets and planting trees. Paved roads had been condemned by the Department of Public Works as undesirable throwbacks to our earlier town, old-fashioned obstructions to natural growth.

By early September, dense groves had sprung up in many of our streets. Despite some expressions of concern, the decision of the DPW was enthusiastically embraced by most of our citizens. Those of us who could no longer drive through the forested roads now rode bicycles or walked to the one remaining bus stop in town.

Though I vigorously supported all efforts to increase the number of trees in our town, I was startled at times by the sheer swiftness of our accomplishment, the daily evidence of lushness and rapid growth. It was as if the energy of our desire had entered the roots and branches themselves, filling them with extravagant life.

As late summer passed into autumn, there were no signs of letting up. In our tree-crowded yards, we stood on branch-pierced ladders and trained leafy tendrils to spread across bare window-panes. Many of us took to covering our front and back porches with strips of sod. Indoor walls became sites for climbing vines. A few enthusiasts went so far as to carry buckets of loam into their living rooms in order to replace an end table with a cone of soil supporting an evergreen bush. Meanwhile, on block after block, town crews worked tirelessly to tear out any remaining sections of paved street and fill them with thickets of pine and spruce.

Extremists urged the destruction of all public buildings, those masses of brick and stone that did nothing but interrupt the designs of nature, but more reasonable minds prevailed: all school corridors, all town-hall offices, and the main room of the post office were lined with bushes and trees in terra-cotta planters concealed beneath slopes of imported soil. In alternate aisles of the town library, rows of tall shrubs pressed against the spines of books. When we stepped into privately owned buildings open to the public, such as churches, banks, downtown stores, and car dealerships, we found ourselves pushing aside branches heavy with leaves.

Sometimes, in the deep hours of the night, a doubt came over some of us, but in the morning we were swept up once again in our desire to carry on with what we had so passionately begun.

Now, as the ground hardens and the air grows colder, we understand one thing: there can be no turning back. Our town is slowly being transformed into a deep forest. Some of our citizens, defeated at last, have abandoned their homes and moved to nearby towns, with the vague hope of returning someday soon. The rest of us remain in our mossy houses, where branches occasionally break in through upper windows. We spend hours each day exploring the surrounding woods, learning to identify and gather edible leaves, fruit, and mushrooms, though we can also purchase meals from food trucks that park behind the deserted mall at the edge of town. Half-hidden among trees, our schools, our library, our post office, and our downtown businesses have sharply reduced their hours. All are in danger of shutting down completely as they fill with foliage and small, scurrying animals.

My daughter and her friends spend most afternoons in the woods, returning with pine cones and sprigs of berries arranged in their hair. Owls sit on the edges of our roofs. Raccoons thump and scratch in our attics. There are rumors of prowling wolves, though that is nothing but ignorant gossip. It's true enough that some dogs and cats have left their homes to roam in feral packs. Far more worrisome are the notices posted on tree trunks by our diminished police department, warning us to guard our homes against break-ins.

When we try to recall our earlier town, with its neat rows of houses seated in little rectangles of green, the image seems to be that of a colored drawing made by a kindergartener with a box of new crayons. Some say that if we don't change direction, our town is destined to disappear entirely. They prophesy a time of smashed and decaying houses, with mighty trees thrusting through floors and bursting through roofs. Others feel that just as we once turned from green to stone and back again to green, so another change is imminent, though what that change might be, no one can say. In the meantime, we can only get ready for the long winter, storing supplies in our cellars and reinforcing our windows and doors. Already we find ourselves dreaming, at times uneasily, of the coming spring.

THANK YOU FOR YOUR PATIENCE

Thank you for calling customer service. All agents are currently assisting other customers. Please stay on the line and your call will be answered in the order in which it was received. *Pause.* Thank you for your patience. Please stay on the line and a representative will be with you shortly. *Pause.* Your call is very important to us and we appreciate your patience. Assistance is just a moment away. You don't have to keep saying the same thing over and over again. I'm not an idiot. *Pause.* Thank you for calling. Please be assured that your call will be answered as soon as possible. Just pick up the phone. I've got better things to do than stand around all day waiting for you to pick up. Yoo-hoo! I'm right here! Stuck in the kitchen. Dropped off my daughter at preschool ten minutes ago. It's my free time. Sun's out. You need my account number? It's here in front of me. Just pick up. Pick up. We're sorry to keep you waiting. Please do not hang up and redial, as this will only further delay your call. Oh, you're good. Is that what you do? Read people's minds? Fine, I'll give it another minute. Whatever it takes. You want me to be patient? Is that what this is all about? Patience? Don't talk to me about patience. I'll give you patience. I've got patience coming out of my ears. But hey, you know that. We're good at waiting, you and me. It's what we do. Me and you, girls. It's what women do. Boys take, girls wait. Put *that* on your bumper. Thank you for calling customer service. All agents are currently assisting other customers. Please stay on the line and your call will be answered in the order in which it was received. You'll make me scream. I swear you will. Is that the plan? Make her wait? Make her scream? The waiting room or the nuthouse? Oh, right: patience. A little practice is all it takes. Waiting. Waiting. Waiting for Tommy Edstrom. God, Tommy Edstrom. Does that ever happen to you? Standing around minding your own business and look out, you're back in the old neighborhood. Fifth grade. I wasn't thinking of boys yet, not in that way. But I was aware of them. There was this one boy in my class, Tommy Edstrom. I'd see him looking over at me sometimes. Tommy Edstrom. Thank you for your patience. Please stay on the line and a representative will be with you shortly. Blue eyes, and these blond lashes, even though his hair was brown. He hung out with boys on the playground, but he'd look over at us girls. In class he was always polite, friendly. So what happened is this. On the last day of school, he comes up to me and asks if he can walk home with me. No boy had ever asked me that before. At first I couldn't understand why he wanted to walk home with me. Why would Tommy Edstrom want to do that? It didn't make sense. But I—Your call is very important to us and we appreciate your patience. Assistance is just a moment away. I could feel something inside me, an excitement. We walked home. The same walk I took every day, past the same old houses, but now they all looked different, like I'd never seen them before. They looked, oh, I don't know. Alive. Every shingle, every window, alive in the sun. I remember a baseball lying in the grass. The creamy whiteness of the leather, the red stitching. Grass stain like wet paint. At my house he followed me into the living room. Shook my mother's hand. I could tell she liked that. He stood talking to her a little before we headed upstairs to my room. You know what we did in my room? Thank you for calling. Please be assured that your call will be answered as soon as possible. You know what we did? Try and guess. You'll never guess. No, not that. We set up my folding table and began working on a five-hundred-piece puzzle. Big old ship with sails on a choppy sea. He was very good at puzzles, Tommy Edstrom was. He asked me about the books in my bookcase, right above my favorite stuffed animals left over from when I was a little kid. *Anne of Green Gables*. I loved that book. He said he liked to read. Asked me if I ever went to the movies. At five o'clock he said he had to go home. My mother gave him a ride. Me sitting in back hoping he'd turn around. At the door of his house—We're sorry to keep you waiting. Please do not hang up and redial, as this will only further delay your call. At the door of his house he turned and waved. That was the beginning of summer. Tommy Edstrom. Each day I waited. God, did I wait. I don't know whether I was waiting for Tommy Edstrom to call me up on the phone or just show up one morning in my backyard. Like a squirrel or a blue jay. Or maybe I'd bump into him when I walked to the bakery down by the stream to pick up a sliced rye for my mom or some blueberry muffins hot out of the oven. Can you fall in love in fifth grade? Did you? Age ten going on eleven? I don't know if I was in love with Tommy Edstrom. Maybe I was in love with the houses in the sun. The baseball in the grass. All I know is that I wanted to walk home with him again. Thank you for calling customer service. All agents are currently assisting other customers. Please stay on the line and your call will be answered in the order in which it was received. That sentence doesn't sound right. Do you even know what you're saying? Tommy Edstrom. I kept waiting for him that summer. One evening I rode my bicycle out to his neighborhood, way across town. When I got to his street I saw an old woman sitting on a porch, looking at me. She had a bony white cat on her lap. The whole thing gave me a funny feeling. I turned back. All summer long I waited. I knew, but I kept waiting anyway. End of August I was already thinking about the first day of school. What if Tommy Edstrom had moved away to another town? What if Tommy Edstrom—Thank you for your patience. Please stay on the line and a representative will be with you shortly. The first day of school, there he was. He was friendly, polite, just like before, but something was different. His hair was combed back in a new way and his eyes had a hardness to them. On the playground he hung out with a crowd of tough sixth-graders. Collars up. Belt buckles on the hip. He didn't ask me to walk home with him that day. He never did again. I could tell he'd swerved off in some other direction. And though I knew it, the way you know things like that, I still waited for him to come up to me after school and ask if he could walk home with me, the way he'd done back then, a long time ago, in the fifth grade, when I was young and innocent. If you know what I mean. Are you still there? Are you listening? Your call is very important to us and we appreciate your patience. Assistance is just a moment away. Assistance is ten years away. Doesn't it make you sick? A job like this? How about getting a real job? What are there, three of you? Two? Hard to tell you apart. The Patience Sisters. You know what you could do? You could put out a CD. The Patience Sisters, singing "Assistance Is Just a Moment Away." Hit the charts big time. But watch it, girls. Someday somebody won't be able to take it anymore. They'll sneak up behind you: a hand on your mouth, knife across the throat. Blood soaking through your blouse. Onto your sports bra. Or how about a needle in the arm? Wake up in a dark place. Hands tied behind your back. Duct tape over your mouth. Jeans around your ankles. You'll see. Just keep it up. Just you keep making me wait. Thank you for calling. Please be assured that your call will be answered as soon as possible. Spring Dance, junior year. Maplewood High. I wasn't one of the popular girls, but I wasn't unpopular either. I had friends. We went shopping in town, hung out together on our back porches. Rode our bikes to the beach, played badminton in our backyards. I wasn't what you'd call pretty, but I wasn't bad-looking. Good eyes, straight teeth. No cheekbones, but what can you do. I had friends who were boys, but no boyfriends. It was all right. I didn't worry about it. Did you worry about it? Then came Spring Dance, junior year. I was invited by—We're sorry to keep you waiting. Please do not hang up and redial, as this will only further delay your call. Invited by a boy in my history class, Gary Pearson. It was the first time a boy had wanted to be with me since Tommy Edstrom. Do you know what I felt? Relief so strong I didn't know what to do with it. It bothered me, that relief. Had I been standing around waiting, all this time? One of those tight-sweater girls who spend all day doing nothing but thinking about boys? Another dumb blond, and I wasn't even blond? More of a you've-got-to-be-kidding-me brown. I began looking at Gary Pearson in a new way. I don't mean at his body. Though you know, he did have a nice body. I liked the way he'd roll back the sleeves of his shirt twice and push them up a little, so you could see his wrists and the beginning of the muscly part of his forearms. But looking at him was more about figuring out who he was, this boy I'd known in Maplewood High for almost three years, this boy who for some reason—Thank you for calling customer service. All agents are currently assisting other customers. Please stay on the line and your call will be answered in the order in which it was received. This boy who for some reason had made up his mind to invite me to the Spring Dance. What did he see in me? He must've been trying to decide. Picturing me in his mind. What excited me wasn't what you think. Not kisses, touches, naked bodies. What got my heart going was the thought of some connection between me and this boy, this Gary Pearson, some closeness that had nothing to do with skin but with something deeper, untouchable, something that—listen to me! Can you believe it? I don't know what's gotten into me. Talking away a mile a minute. But it was like I'd been missing something all this time and now, at sixteen, I was walking home again with Tommy Edstrom, who'd been keeping me waiting all these years. Or something like that. I don't know. Something like that. Something like that. Thank you for your patience. Please stay on the line and a representative will be with you shortly. God, do you ever listen to yourselves? Do you? Same old song, over and over. Round and around and around we go, where we stop, nobody knows. And what's the message? Shut up and wait. I'll wait, all right, but I sure as hell won't shut up. I'm good at waiting. I waited for the Spring Dance. I saw him every day, Gary Pearson. He was friendly, an easygoing smile, but it was never more than that. Sometimes we talked about the dance. He'd just gotten his driver's license, he'd pick me up at quarter to eight. That was it. He was always rushing off to track practice, tennis practice, this practice, that practice. The night of the dance he drove up to the house in his father's Buick. Walked up to the front door and handed me a red rose. Complimented my dress. Your call is very important to us and we appreciate your patience. Assistance is just a moment away. The Spring Dance. Who knows what I was waiting for, the night of the Spring Dance? It wasn't what you're thinking. Oh, maybe off to one side of my mind. But in the center I was waiting for something to happen in my life, something that would push me away from what I was. That baseball in the grass. The sort of push you'd want if you were unhappy, but here's the thing: I wasn't unhappy. Can you want something, even if you're happy? How does that make sense? At the dance we danced close, but not closer. When we sat, we talked. I was having a good time. But I was also waiting for something. Waiting for what? Maybe for the night to show me what it was. The dance ended at midnight. He asked me if I'd like to—Thank you for calling. Please be assured that your call will be answered as soon as possible. He asked me if I'd like to take a ride in the car. I said yes. He drove us one town over, where there was a small parking lot looking down over a lake. You could see the lights on the other side of the water. I realized the night had been leading up to this moment. Here I was, alone in a car with Gary Pearson, the night of the Spring Dance. He started talking. He was tired of this town, he said. He wanted something bigger. He was planning to go to college in a big city. Manhattan, Chicago. Sometimes, driving around with friends at night, he'd think: there's got to be more. He felt I was someone he could talk to. We're sorry to keep you waiting. Please do not hang up and redial, as this will only further delay your call. He told me about his plans, his dreams. He said he liked talking to me. Said I was a good listener. And then something happened, in that car. It's not what you're thinking. It's never what you're thinking. What happened was this. As Gary Pearson talked, I felt a little shift inside me. I'd been feeling a kind of closeness to him and then I wasn't feeling it anymore. He was talking about himself. He was talking and talking about himself. He was like somebody studying his chin in a mirror, turning his head this way, that way, every which way. It would've been better if he'd stuck out his hand and grabbed a handful of breast. Oh, I'd've knocked his arm away. But it would have been *something*. I just wasn't there, in that car. You know what he did? You know what Gary Pearson did? Thank you for calling customer service. All agents are currently assisting other customers. Please stay on the line and your call will be answered in the order in which it was received. He pointed through the windshield at the moon. I looked at the moon. It looked like a moon. He said the moon didn't even know he was alive. He said the moon would still be there when he was dead. I tried not to glance at my watch. When he was done talking he turned to me and said he guessed it was time to head home. There was a question in his eyes. I said I guessed so. At my house he walked me to the front door, thanked me for the evening, and bent toward me. I turned my face and he kissed me on the cheek. In school he—Thank you for your patience. Please stay on the line and a representative will be with you shortly. In school he was the same as always, friendly and busy. Sometimes we talked in the halls. Never about the dance. He was always rushing off somewhere. I didn't want him to call, but I waited anyway. Even when we don't wait, we wait. That summer he sent me a postcard from Wyoming. He said he liked seeing a different part of the country. In a PS he wrote: "I'll never forget the Spring Dance." At the end of summer his parents shipped him off to some prep school in Massachusetts. He called me once and talked for an hour. I never saw him again. I know what you're thinking. I know exactly what you're thinking. Your call is very important to us and we appreciate your patience. Assistance is just a moment away. You're thinking, Poor girl! Nobody loves her! Boo-hoo! You're idiots. This isn't about boys. You think everything is about boys? I don't even know why I'm talking to you. I know you. I went to school with you. Small-town girls with small-town ambitions: hook your man, make a baby, grab that house. Split-level ranch on a quarter acre. Maple tree out front. Waiting for your hubby to get home from work. And what about me? You want to know my story? Is that what you're after? The story of my life? My life doesn't have a story. Or maybe it's a story everyone's heard before. Small-town girl graduates from high school, goes on to college, finds work, ho-hum. It's not what you want. You want pain. You want glamour. You want failure. You want death. I can't give you that. I can give you just one thing. Just one little thing. A little secret. Thank you for calling. Please be assured that your call will be answered as soon as possible. As soon as possible? Really? As soon as possible? I wanted to be done with high school as soon as possible. All senior year I waited for college. I was tired of popular girls and unpopular girls and Spring Dances and Gary Pearsons. I wanted something new. Have you ever wanted something new? College. There's not much to say about it. I slept with a few boys, read a few books. More books than boys. Another one for your bumper: **More Books than Boys.** That about sums it up. That doesn't sum it up. Listen, college was all right. I grew up a little. But all the time I was still waiting for something. Not for a man. That would take care of itself. But something. Sometimes I found myself thinking about Gary Pearson, talking in the car. There's got to be more, he said. There's got—We're sorry to keep you waiting. Please do not hang up and redial as this will only further delay your call. There's got to be more. Was I turning into Gary Pearson? Maybe I needed to hitch a ride out to Wyoming, jump on a plane to Paris, join the Peace Corps and save lives in Africa. I didn't do anything. Don't get me wrong. I wasn't unhappy. But I wasn't exactly happy either. An in-betweener. That's what I was: an in-betweener. The good thing about college? I met people who had passion. Not that kind of passion. I mean passion for theater, passion for math. Only a few, but still. You could see it. You could smell it. Was that what was wrong with me? Not that anything was wrong with me. But I wanted something. I was waiting for something. Not unhappy. Not one of those. But short of the real thing, if you know what I—Thank you for calling customer service. All agents are currently assisting other customers. Please stay on the line and your call will be answered in the order in which it was received. But why would you know what I mean? You've got it all figured out, haven't you. Here's a question for you. Have you ever thought of killing yourself? It's not that hard. A rope around the neck. They'll have to cut you down. Be sure and comb your hair carefully. And take your time choosing the right dress. Oh, and don't forget: fresh underpants. That's very important: fresh underpants. You don't like rope marks on your neck? There's always the bottle of sleeping pills. Easy as pie. Car in the closed garage. Breathe deep. I'm getting tired now. My ear hurts, even though I keep shifting to the other one. I want to tell you something. One more thing, before you pick up. Because you will pick up, won't you? I've been waiting a long time. It's a little secret I have. Just one. Thank you for your patience. Please stay on the line and a representative will be with you shortly. Not that kind of secret. How come that's all you ever think of? Is that your own little secret, out there in your house with the baby and the bird feeder and the sunshine coming in through the kitchen window? Your husband's probably doing it. Why not you? Is that what you want from me? Well, give a listen. After college I lived at home for a year, temping at a nonprofit. Then I took a job on a newspaper, rented an apartment in town. I liked my work. I learned a few things, dated a few men. Then it happened. Are you ready? Are you ready for this? I met someone. A good man. I loved him and he loved me back. I married him at thirty-two. And you know what? I'm still in love with him, after six years. Are you disappointed? Of course you're disappointed. A story with a happy ending. I've let you down. I can feel it. Your call is very important to us and we appreciate your patience. Assistance is just a moment away. Not even a juicy tidbit you can sink your teeth into. No red-hot affair with the guy next door in his black nylon running shorts and sleeveless T. No arguing over who does the dishes. No troubles in the ol' bedroom. Talk. Laughter. Things feeling right. No, I'm happy with the way things turned out, happy as a lark. Are larks happy? Only sometimes, when I'm walking downtown on a sunny day, or say I'm sitting on the back porch, when the sun's gone down and the sky is that shade of blue you only see just before night, there ought to be a name for it, a feeling comes. Do you know that feeling? It's like a shadow falling across your heart. Or say it's like finding something in a drawer. It's something you haven't seen before. Thank you for calling. Please be assured that your call will be answered as soon as possible. A small wooden thingamajig, a little larger than a thimble. Set on a small block of wood. You don't know what it is, that thingamajig. If you could just figure it out, something would calm down inside you. You could stop waiting. Does that sound crazy? It's hard to say what I'm trying to say. It would be nice to lie down and close my eyes. But then I might not hear you, when you pick up. Something happened to me, two months ago. I've never told anyone about it before. It's my little secret. It won't take long. Are you still there? Hello? We're sorry to keep you waiting. Please do not hang up and redial, as this will only further delay your call. It was the middle of the morning. My daughter was at preschool. I drove to the supermarket. We needed a few things, a half gallon of milk, fresh veggies for dinner, a can of spray for a stuck window. I like supermarkets. They give me a sense of freedom, you know? Everything changes, aisle after aisle. It's like being in one of those big-city zoos: here come the polar bears, right after the monkeys. Of course, I know every aisle by heart. But you keep seeing things. Shouldn't I get those cherries, two dollars off, today only? What about that package of macaroons? Do I want a package of macaroons? When was the last time I had a macaroon? Do I even like macaroons? I always go up and down every aisle, just to make sure. There were plenty of people around, pushing their carts, stopping, reaching up. And then, who knows why, I put some things in my cart that I didn't really want. Maybe it was because my cart looked a little empty. Have you ever done that? Just a few things. Thank you for calling customer service. All agents are currently assisting other customers. Please stay on the line and your call will be answered in the order in which it was received. The sight of those extra boxes in my cart, I don't know, gave me a good feeling. Who knows why? I began pushing my cart down the aisle, stopping along the way, reaching out for cans of soup, jars of mustard and relish, boxes of cereal. Dropping them all in. By the time I was done with two aisles, my cart was almost full. Who knows why you do what you do? Do you know why you do what you do? My cart had one of those wobbly wheels, so it wasn't all that easy to push. I didn't care. I just wanted to keep doing what I was doing. Thank you for your patience. Please stay on the line and a representative will be with you shortly. I was feeling excited. I wanted to see how much the cart could hold. I told myself I'd put it all back the second I was done. I kept sticking things in, shoving a jar of salted peanuts between two boxes of pancake mix, adding bottles of cranberry juice and packages of tortilla chips. The fuller it got the more excited I felt. One aisle later, my cart was heaped over the top. I mean way over. Something fell onto the floor. I scooped it up and jammed it back in. I knew it was time to stop but I also knew that if I stopped now I would never forgive myself. Your call is very important to us and we appreciate your patience. Assistance is just a moment away. I was in the next aisle. I began taking down packages of English muffins, fitting them in. Whole-wheat multigrain bread, packages of seeded rye. I came to boxes of crackers and began putting them on top. Cheddar-cheese crackers, sea-salt crackers, heart-healthy crackers with those little red hearts on the box. The pile was up to my chest, my neck. Some lady at the end of the aisle had stopped and was looking over at me. I wasn't pushing the cart anymore. I was just piling things on. Higher and higher. Have you ever done that? A man in a green uniform was walking toward me. I could see his pants flapping against his legs. I began pushing the cart away. Thank you for your patience. Please be assured that your call will be answered as soon as possible. The cart was too full for pushing, but what could I do? The man was coming toward me. I could see the high pile shaking a little. Do you know what that's like, the shake before the crash? You hardly notice it at first, but you can see it growing, like there's a living thing inside. And then it all came down, boxes and jars and cans and bottles, smashing against the floor, rolling along, splitting open. A lovely avalanche. It was horrible but lovely, lovely. The man in the green uniform was coming closer. I've never told this to anyone, not even my husband. And you know what? We're sorry to keep you waiting. Please do not hang up and redial, as this will only further delay your call. You know what? I didn't care. Isn't that the strangest thing? I didn't care. Let them arrest me and throw me in jail. Let it all come crashing down. But you know what? Nothing happened. I offered to pay for it all, but the manager said no no, it's all right, not a problem. They didn't want any trouble. Just get her out of here and clean up the mess. They thought I was crazy. Do you think I'm crazy? Who does a thing like that? My life is good. I have what I want. Not many people can say that. Can you say that? All you can say is please be patient, please be patient, please be patient. I'm as patient as they come, but sometimes. Sometimes. I'm tired now. I'm not angry at you anymore. For keeping me waiting. You can't help it. It's who you are. But you know, I'm done talking to you. If you pick up, I'm not saying anything. Not another word. Thank you for calling customer service. All agents are currently assisting other customers. Please stay on the line and your call will be answered in the order in which it was received.

A TIRED TOWN

At first it was nothing, really. One morning toward the middle of July, as I set off on my daily walk along the tree-shaded sidewalk, I gave a little wave to my neighbor, old Mrs. Schumacher, seated on her porch in the cushioned rocker beside the white wicker table. Even as I waved, I noticed that her eyes were closing, her hands slipping from the book that lay open in her lap. Across the street, Jim Garrity started to wave to me from behind his lawn mower and broke off with a yawn. A few houses down, one of the Hollister boys lay on his back on the grass, his arms stretched out and his head resting on a skateboard, and later that morning, as I stood in line at the supermarket, the woman in front of me raised the back of a hand to her mouth and burst into a long, shuddering yawn, while behind me a teenager in low-slung jogging pants and a half-tucked T-shirt began to open his mouth, shook his head, and yawned again. It was nothing, nothing at all—the sort of thing you expect to see, on a hot day in a small town in summer. But the next morning I saw old Mrs. Schumacher leaning sideways in her chair as her book lay open on the floor, I saw Garrity's eighth-grade daughter sitting on the top step of her porch with her cheek pressed against the iron banister and her eyes shut tight, and farther down the street a painter in bib overalls stood at the foot of his stepladder, his head bowed against the pail shelf, his arms hanging at his sides, his paintbrush lying near his feet.

That was how it started: a yawn here, a droop there. It might have been the midsummer doldrums, or some germ floating in the atmosphere, or maybe a toxic chemical that had worked its way into our water supply and was now moving through our bodies. Whatever it was, I'd begun to feel the effects myself. I struggled to get out of bed each morning, yawned as I brushed my teeth, became sluggish during the day. I found myself putting off small tasks, like mowing the lawn or touching up the front porch steps. I'm an energetic man in my late fifties, recently retired from guidance counseling at the local high school, a man who has always loved his summer vacations, and I struggled to throw off the tiredness even as I felt myself succumbing to its power.

You could sense it in other neighborhoods. All over town you could see them, the yawners and droopers. They walked along sunny sidewalks with their mouths wide open, they nodded off as they sat weeding their lawns. On a residential street near one of the elementary schools, a man stood in his driveway with his head bowed and his eyes closed, holding in one hand a hose that was squirting water past his dusty car. Even on Main Street, which always attracted lively crowds of summer visitors, things had changed. People sat drowsily at café tables or stood with slumped shoulders in front of shop windows, as if trying not to fall forward against the glass. In the mall at the edge of town, you could see them dozing on slatted benches or sitting on the floor with their backs against the bottoms of store windows. One man, seated on a low wall surrounding a display of ferns, was bent far forward, his fingers on his shoelaces. Only after observing him for a while did I realize that he was fast asleep. A weariness was coming over our town. You could feel it spreading like an infection.

I resisted every step of the way. I forced myself to get up early every morning, I took cold showers, I strode along the sidewalk swinging my arms in an exaggerated way. Toward the middle of the second week I made an appointment with my doctor, who kept yawning as he looked into my ears and listened to my heart. Rubbing his eyes with the knuckles of both hands, he assured me that I wasn't the first to come to him with this complaint. He and his colleagues were advising rest and caution until the source of the problem was determined.

Meanwhile, the town council acknowledged what it called a "possible health hazard" by ordering an inspection of our reservoir and our supply pipes, as well as dispatching a group of health inspectors to local restaurants, child-care facilities, and public pools. Citizens were urged to stay at home or avoid driving whenever possible. Only the other day, the police had been called to a traffic light in the center of town, where the driver had fallen asleep at a red light and sat slumped over the wheel.

Apart from all such questions of health and safety, I felt an instinctive rebellion against this outbreak of tiredness. It was as if premature old age were sweeping over our town. The lack of energy, the desire to remain quiet, to stay indoors, to move as little as possible—all this struck me as a withdrawal from the wider world, a retreat from the life of the community into a narrow preoccupation with self. And what about the practical consequences? Yards and houses were showing signs of neglect. Town services like garbage collection and street repair had grown erratic. Workers in stores and gas stations kept coming in late or failing to show up at all.

In the midst of our deepening crisis, a number of voices rose up in support of the new order of things. Tiredness, it was said, was a deliberate challenge to the unfair demands of everyday life. One group, calling itself the New Way, claimed that our town had chosen to protest against a social arrangement driven by greed, consumerism, and conspicuous consumption. Tiredness, in their view, was an expression of moral resistance. A few voices fought back, mine among them, arguing that moral behavior had nothing to do with the weariness afflicting our town, and that in any case an ethical response to life demanded more than falling asleep all day. Another group maintained that just as the individual body needed periods of rest, so a flourishing communal body could only benefit by retreating now and then from the stresses of normal life into peaceful quietude. In that claim I heard nothing less than the sound of exhaustion itself.

As the summer advanced, signs of decline were visible everywhere. Knee-high grass and seed-heavy stalks grew in front yards; long blades leaned over the walks. Cans of paint hung from the rungs of abandoned ladders resting against house sides. Newspapers in plastic wrappers lay on sidewalks and porches, garbage containers and recycling bins remained between house and drive with their lids pushed up by bulging bags. Downtown, a scattering of customers sat at the outdoor cafés, leaning their heads on crossed arms or staring dully at stripes of sun on sugar packets in wire holders. A police car without a policeman was parked in front of a closed hat shop. A few people strolled slowly along the sidewalks, as if making their way through a thick mist, though sunlight glittered on the store windows and the windshields of parked cars.

Toward the middle of August a town meeting was held in the high-school auditorium to address issues pertaining to public health. Only one of the seven members of the Public Safety and Health Committee appeared, apologizing for his lateness and fanning himself with an envelope. A man introduced as deputy moderator rose slowly and stood with both forearms resting heavily on the podium as he spoke in a barely audible murmur and seemed to have difficulty reading his notes. In the sparse audience people leaned back against their seats with their legs stretched out, their eyes half closed, their shoulders slack.

One Saturday afternoon I forced myself into my car and drove through deteriorating neighborhoods to visit a friend of mine, a math teacher who lived on the other side of town. In the high grass of his front yard a power mower sat next to a can of gasoline, on the front porch a window screen in an aluminum frame leaned against the side of a white plastic chair, and in his darkened living room he lay on the couch with a magazine on his chest as he slowly opened his eyes and asked me what day it was.

I could feel it in myself, this draining away of attention to things. How nice it would be, I said to myself, to stop what I was doing, to lie down, to take a little nap, to forget whatever it was that was on my mind. Every morning I forced myself out of bed, I pushed myself out into the day. One morning I noticed that a cellar window at the side of the house had developed a crack. I told myself it would probably be a good idea to remove the window, lay it on a towel in the back seat of the car, and drive over to Stan's Glass, one of these days. Another time, returning home from a walk, I sat down to rest for a moment on the chaise on my front porch. The lawn was definitely in need of mowing. I felt my eyes beginning to close, my head tipping to one side, and like someone escaping the embrace of a demon I lunged to my feet and began pacing up and down the porch, turning my head back and forth and shaking my hands rapidly, as if any lack of movement were a form of capitulation.

One afternoon I was walking along a familiar street in my neighborhood. Patiently I noted the details of decline, as if I were assembling evidence to present before an investigative committee exploring the decay of our town. The blades of grass on most lawns were more than a foot high, though here and there an abandoned lawn mower had left a trail of shorter grass. A shutter hung crookedly beside a front window. On one driveway a toppled recycling bin lay on its side before a scattering of plastic bottles and cardboard boxes. It was a brilliantly sunny day, near summer's end. The houses themselves looked tired, as if they had closed their eyes and fallen asleep. As I walked along, I became aware of something, without knowing what it was. I stopped and looked around. Everything was still. It was the stillness, I realized, that had drawn my attention. No lawn mower or power saw sounded in the summer air. No hammer knocked against a nail. No car door slammed. I heard no sound of bicycle tires in roadside gravel, no hum of distant traffic, no squawk, no yap, no laugh, no whisper. It was a moment of silence so absolute that I felt as if I were hearing silence itself. As I stood bound by that silence, I felt a strange calm coming over me, a calm that had nothing to do with tiredness. The silence seeped through my skin, entered my blood. It flowed through me, washing me clean of what I was. The town and all its familiar, well-loved sounds seemed only a distraction from something deeper or richer that

I could not name. I felt that my whole life had been an evasion, though of what I couldn't say. In the silence I could feel another way rising within me. It seemed to me that at any second I would understand something of immense importance. Somewhere a chair scraped. I tried to shut out the sound, but now I was aware of a dish clinking, a yawn rising from someone on a nearby porch. I could feel my skin and bones taking shape again. All at once I realized that I was standing motionless in the middle of a sidewalk, on a summer afternoon.

Back at my house I looked without interest at the porch steps and the lawn, thinking only of the silence that had seemed to summon me to something higher or better. When the tiredness came over me, I no longer felt the need to struggle against it. Was tiredness really so different from busyness? Upstairs in bed I lay down and closed my eyes.

I woke to a roar of lawn mowers and power saws, of cars driving by and children shouting in the street. I dressed quickly, rushed downstairs, and flung open the front door. In every yard, neighbors were pushing lawn mowers, digging up weeds, sweeping off porches and front walks. Old Mrs. Schumacher was standing at her porch rail, vigorously shaking out a small rug. Turning to me she called out cheerfully, "Better late than never!" I wondered whether she was referring to herself or me. Green recycling bins and trash cans stood at the curb, a recycling truck with a side lift was raising a container and turning it upside down, and near the end of the block a man in a white hardhat and orange nylon vest stood high in the air, in a bucket at the end of a boom, working on a utility line. Hammers rang out, hoses shot streams of water at cars in driveways. Two boys passed, each bouncing a basketball. A jogger with earbuds ran along the side of the street. Three girls walked by, talking and laughing. My lawn startled me: the grass was even higher than I'd remembered. Without a thought of breakfast, I hurried around to the back, dragged my mower out of the shed, and set to work.

Later that morning, I learned from Mrs. Schumacher that everyone in our town had fallen asleep for three days—could you believe it? Three whole days. It was all over the news. Word on the street had it that we'd all caught some kind of bug, though officials were still investigating. This morning the entire town had woken up feeling refreshed and full of life, ready to tackle whatever needed doing. Her handyman was on his way to check for squirrels in the attic and change an O-ring on a dripping faucet, but that was nothing compared to Barbara Leitkowski on East Maple, who had mice in her kitchen and was standing on a chair waiting for the exterminator to get on over there and rescue her. Three days? I ran my hand along my prickly cheek.

Inside, I showered, shaved myself smooth, and devoured an egg-and-bacon sandwich on rye toast. Outside, I set to work on the peeling porch steps. I scraped off big chips of old paint, sanded thoroughly, applied the primer in even strokes. Even as I worked I knew that as soon as I finished I would sand and prime the porch rail. Later I'd tackle the porch posts and the floor. The backyard hedge needed trimming. The concrete foundation along the sides of the house could use some patching up.

When I finished priming the rail, I had no desire to rest. Instead, I set off to see what was happening in the neighborhood. In yard after yard, people were trimming hedges, tilting watering cans over bushes, slapping paint on shingles. Through open windows I could hear the whine of vacuum cleaners and the tumble of washing machines.

Downtown, the outdoor cafés were so full that waiters were carrying extra chairs outside. On the broad sidewalks between rows of storefronts and bumper-to-bumper parked cars, the crowd moved eagerly, trembling in sun and shade. Now and then people ducked into an ice-cream shop or a furniture store or a handbag boutique, or stopped to examine the jackets and skirts hanging on outdoor racks. Hands clutching smartphones rose up to take pictures. Wakened from its sleep, the town was surging with energy. I could feel it streaming within me.

As I returned to my block and swung onto my front walk, I observed with pleasure the freshly primed steps and porch rail. A brush soaked in turpentine lay on a sheet of newspaper. Tomorrow I'd apply a coat of gray latex paint and set to work sanding the porch floor and the cobwebbed posts. After lunch today I would touch up the window trim, replace the cracked cellar window, clean out the rain gutters. Avoiding the front steps, I went around back and entered the kitchen. I passed through the living room and out onto the porch, where I flung myself onto my chaise in order to listen to the sounds of the neighborhood. I sensed in myself a pleasant tiredness, which had nothing to do with the recent plague of exhaustion. It was more like a brief pause before the next burst of energy. As I listened, I was able to distinguish three separate power mowers, two chain saws, an edger, two hammers, the cry of a grackle, the crunch of bicycle tires on gravel, music from two car radios, a hose, a sprinkler, a rattling dish, a barking dog—on and on it went, the sounds of life, until gradually they blended together in a deep rumbling hum. Sitting there in the warm shade of late summer, I tried to recall that earlier walk, with its sudden moment of silence, when I seemed on the verge of understanding something that would change my life forever, but it all felt vague and far away, as if I had imagined it long ago, on a summer afternoon in childhood, and with a new burst of attention I listened to the clatter of a skateboard, a nearby shout, a shut door.

V

KAFKA IN HIGH SCHOOL, 1959

Kafka in English Class

Kafka is sitting in AP English class, two desks from the back, second row from the door. It's a mild day in early June, 1959; through the partly open windows, one of which is supported by an empty glass jar, he can see the end of the athletic field, a strip of railroad track, and distant roofs with prickly TV antennas. On his desk *The Macmillan Handbook* lies open to the section on restrictive and nonrestrictive clauses. With one hand he holds open a library book on his lap: *Four Great Russian Short Novels*. Kafka has slid down in an attempt to make himself less visible. The small of his back is resting near the front edge of the seat, and his left leg is fully extended, with the anklebone pressing against a chair leg of the desk in front of him, where Barbara Henderson sits erect with her knees together and her brown loafers flat on the floor. Behind him Mike Lorenzo shifts in his seat. In the row by the windows Bonnie Wilcox, in her white blouse and pleated plaid skirt, sits leaning forward with her chin resting on the back of her hand. Her short blond hair, in sunlight, is shot through with darker shades of blond. Kafka is good at grammar and understands without difficulty the distinction between restrictive and nonrestrictive clauses. He therefore sees no compelling reason to pay extreme attention to Miss Saunders as she stands with her back to the class writing examples of restrictive and nonrestrictive clauses on the green blackboard. The knock of the chalk against slate reminds him of a Ping-Pong ball striking a paddle. He lowers his eyes and returns to *First Love*, by Turgenev. The classroom windows, the far roofs, the sunny white blouse and glowing arms of Bonnie Wilcox, all waver and grow dim. In the princess's drawing-room, Kafka sits beside the beautiful Zinaida. Their faces are almost touching, under the silk handkerchief that she has playfully placed over their heads. He can feel the ends of her hair tickling and burning his cheek. He becomes aware of a disturbance of some kind—a sudden sound, he thinks, or is it the opposite of sound? He looks up from under the silk handkerchief and sees Miss Saunders staring directly at him. Her expression is one of disapproval, disappointment, and stern patience. Heads are turned his way. Kafka can feel the color rising in his neck. He imagines getting up from his desk, walking over to the windows, and hurling himself through the glass. He doesn't know whether Miss Saunders has asked him a question about restrictive and nonrestrictive clauses and is waiting for an answer, or whether she has stopped suddenly in the middle of a sentence in order to draw shocked attention to the book that one member of the class has rudely attempted to conceal on his lap. Splinters of glass tingle in the skin of his face. Whatever the reason for her silence, it's clear that she is waiting for him to say something. The class is waiting. Zinaida is waiting. Bonnie Wilcox is waiting. The jar on the windowsill is waiting. The blue sky is waiting. The expanding universe is waiting. Kafka knows that he has to say something. It isn't possible to sit there and say nothing. He sits there. He says nothing.

Kafka in the Living Room

In the lamplit living room, at ten o'clock at night, Kafka's mother is reading on the couch. His father is in the bedroom, behind the closed door, watching television. His sisters are in their room. "I'm going out," Kafka says. His mother looks up. "Where?" "I don't know." "You don't know? You're going out and you don't know? How can you not know?" Kafka considers it. "I don't know," he says. His mother closes the book and holds the place with a finger. "You don't know. So tell me, Mister I Don't Know. What *do* you know?" Kafka thinks hard about it. "I don't know," he says.

Kafka on the Beach at Night

Kafka is walking on the beach at night, wondering what he knows. He knows that he is walking on a beach at night. But how does he know that he is walking on a beach at night? Can he say with any certainty that he's not in his room, imagining that he is walking on a beach at night? To his right, low waves fall and scrape back, leaving a shine on the wet hard sand at the water's edge. Out on the water he can see a lighthouse and, farther away, a strip of dark land, sprinkled with a few lights, that he knows or thinks he knows is the northern shore of Long Island but that he prefers to think of as the coast of an unknown country. On his left is the slightly sloping beach, with its irregular tide line of seaweed and mussel shells. An upside-down rowboat lies beside the first of the three lifeguard stands. The sky is dark blue, with half a brilliant moon. Kafka wonders, as he looks at the tipped-back moon, whether it might be possible to arrange his mind so that he has no thoughts at all, only sense impressions. At the top of the beach, above the fence of the parking lot, a dim yellowish glow is visible from the distant lights of downtown. Here, on the beach at night, Kafka feels almost free. His body, instead of thrusting itself in front of him and blocking his way, is quietly accompanying him as he walks along the shore, and his mind, instead of perching on his shoulder and whispering in his ear, is now skimming along the tops of the waves. He is headed toward the jetty far down the beach, past the closed refreshment stand and the bathroom pavilion. When he arrives at the jetty, he'll climb onto the flat-topped boulders and walk out to the end, where the water washes over the stone and where, standing with his hands in his pockets, he can stare off at the dark water with its shimmer of moon-ripples and think about what he knows. Does he know anything? If he knows anything, how does he know he knows? Is knowledge nothing but a form of belief? But for now, as he walks along the low waves that break at his feet, it's enough just to be out here, under the night sky, away from himself, away from the sounds of the bathroom and the closing of bedroom doors, thinking, when he wants to, of flirtatious and mocking Zinaida, whose name, whenever it appears on the page, or in his mind, refuses to reveal how it ought to be pronounced, so that he hears conflicting whispers every time, and of Bonnie Wilcox, whose wide leather belt, when she bends forward, creaks like the rope of a ship in a movie, and who now, with her chin resting on the back of her hand, is surely staring through the window of her bedroom at this very same sky, shining and indifferent, in the long night that will never end.

Memory #1

I remember him but not all that well. A nice kid, didn't talk much. You had the feeling he knew a lot more than he was saying.

Kafka Looks at Himself in the Mirror

In the bathroom, the next morning, Kafka examines his face in the mirror. He has been studying his face intensely since seventh grade and has grown skillful in appraising it without mercy. Although his sisters are waiting their turn, they are good to him and will allow him to remain behind the door a little while longer. Kafka looks with distaste at his thick hair, which catches in the teeth of his comb and resists easy shaping. He would like to have the kind of hair that shows the lines of the comb and can be swept up in a wave. He dislikes his low hairline, which gives him the look of a member of an early anthropoid tribe that gradually branched away from *Homo sapiens*. His eyebrows are too thick and hang over his eyes like weed-grown ledges. His eyes are so dark that they seem to be glaring out at the world like the eyes of someone hiding under a bed. He dislikes the bony ridge of his nose. He dislikes the shape of each nostril. He dislikes the notch in his upper lip. He dislikes his cheeks, which succeed in being puffy and thin at the same time. His ears are the ears of elves. He has begun to shave recently, and he dislikes, along his jaw, the black prickles that are like the bristles of a stiff brush. He dislikes the color of his skin, which is neither pale nor dark but shadowy and yellowish. His chin sticks out like an unclosed drawer in a lamp table. In addition to disliking each part of his face, and each part of each part of his face, Kafka also dislikes his face as a whole. The skull has a flattened look, as if a weight has been placed on something soft. His face reminds him of an overripe piece of fruit. Kafka, who prides himself on being scrupulously fair, asks himself whether he is being scrupulously fair to his face. He considers this question, without reaching a conclusion, and begins, carefully, to brush his teeth.

Kafka at the Library Steps

On Saturday morning, after mowing the lawn and emptying the grass into the trash barrel at the side of the house, Kafka sets off for the library, where he will first renew *Four Great Russian Short Novels* and then wait for Mike Lorenzo at the top of the flight of stone steps. Together they'll walk into town to have cheeseburgers and cherry Cokes at a booth in Lillian's Luncheonette. Carrying his book against his hip, Kafka walks past the ranch houses of his neighborhood, where wives in wide-brimmed straw hats are weeding in the soil around flowering bushes while husbands are steering mowers across lawns or standing on ladders to paint window frames or touch up shingles. Soon he enters a quieter neighborhood, where older houses stand back from the side-walks. He passes the Presbyterian church, turns onto a road with still older and larger houses, turns again, and comes at last to the reddish stone library, which stands on the corner of Main Street. As Kafka is about to climb the steps, he sees, across the sun-pierced shady road, Bonnie Wilcox and Janet Pearson, walking side by side toward town. They're not wearing skirts or dresses, as the school dress code requires, but instead have changed to dungarees, with the bottoms rolled halfway up their calves. For a moment they seem to Kafka strange, mythical creatures, displaying exotic legs that rise higher and higher, unlike the legs of school, which are cut off above the knee and continue their mysterious upward journey unseen, like the legs of actresses glimpsed at the bottom of a slightly raised curtain. Although Kafka's sisters wear shorts or pedal pushers around the house, they are still in elementary school, and in any case his sisters have nothing to do with the likes of Bonnie Wilcox and Janet Pearson, who exist only in hallways and classrooms before vanishing into distant neighborhoods. Bonnie, glancing toward the library, shouts "Hi!" and gives a wave. Kafka, taken by surprise, hesitates. He begins to raise his right hand in a wave but notices with dismay that his hand is holding a book. He immediately lowers his arm and thrusts the book into his left hand. As the fingers of his left hand close around *Four Great Russian Short Novels*, Kafka realizes that his wave has been interrupted, if not eliminated, so that instead of simply waving back in the casual, friendly spirit of the greeting, he is now standing motionless on the sidewalk, staring at Bonnie Wilcox and Janet Pearson like a savage from a dark-haired country wondering whether he's allowed to remain in the presence of these pale-haired goddesses who have descended from the sky. The girls have stopped and are looking across at him, as he begins to remove his right hand from the book that is now in his left hand and asks himself whether it is too late to take up the wave where he left off. Bonnie Wilcox is wearing a blue-and-white checked blouse he hasn't seen before, with the collar turned up and the sleeves rolled high on her forearms. On her feet are low white sneakers without socks. With sudden decisiveness he squats down, places the book on the sidewalk in front of his feet, and straightens up. He hurls up his right arm in preparation for a wave, but realizes that, in his eagerness, he has lifted his arm to full length in what must look less like a wave than a military salute. Bonnie Wilcox laughs and says, "See ya later, alligator." Kafka watches the girls continue to the corner and turn left onto Main. With terror, with sorrow, he notices, in the air beside him, his raised right arm, which he has forgotten to lower to his side.

Memory #2

He was shy, but kind of cute. You never saw him with a girl, except maybe at the lockers. I'd catch him looking at me sometimes. I kept wishing he would ask me out.

Kafka Plays Ping-Pong

Kafka and Mike Lorenzo are playing Ping-Pong in the garage. Although Kafka doesn't yet have his driver's license, which he plans to get at the end of the summer, he is allowed to back the Chevy onto the drive, in order to make room for the Ping-Pong table. When not in use, the table with fold-up legs leans against the garage wall, where it hides the horizontal ladder on its hooks, the upright rake, the tilted shovel, and the pail filled with gardening tools. Kafka has a steady backhand and an erratic forehand. He therefore has acquired the habit, which he acknowledges to be a logical but inadequate solution to the problem, of using his backhand to cover both sides of the table. As a result, he often finds himself standing so far to the left or right that Mike

Lorenzo, master of the forehand smash, has no trouble slamming the ball out of his reach. Kafka considers himself a defensive player, with chopping or spinning returns that bounce low, but every once in a while he's able to let loose an aggressive backhand topspin that takes Mike Lorenzo by surprise and causes the return shot to sail off the table or smash harmlessly into the net. Both ends of the table present disadvantages. The end facing the door to the back porch is only a few steps from the wall, so that you can't step far enough back to answer a hard return; the end facing the open garage door allows a missed ball to bounce onto the driveway and under the car, from where it can roll all the way out to the street. The garage is hot, the overhead bulb produces a dull glare on the green table, and the sounds of lawn mowers and radios are a continual distraction, but Kafka loves many things about this game: the knock of the ball against the pimpled rubber paddle; the sharp satisfaction of a well-executed shot; the possibility, at all times, of not only losing; the sense, now and then, of sudden grace in his body.

Kafka Attends a Party

In Neil Conley's basement playroom, Kafka sits alone in the corner of an old couch. He bends forward to take a handful of Potato Frills from a blue glass bowl before settling back to sip his Coke and listen to the sounds of rock and roll blasting from a hi-fi stereo set that changes 45s automatically. On chairs and couches, Neil Conley's friends are talking and laughing. A few people sit in a circle on the rug; a girl in a pleated white skirt and black nylons is sitting sideways on someone's lap with her arm around his neck; a senior he's seen in the halls is sitting at the old piano banging out chords with both hands to accompany the songs; the girl in the white skirt suddenly falls backward and kicks up her legs, revealing, for a moment, a pair of brilliant red underpants, like a burst of blood; the smoke of cigarettes twists in the dim lamplight. Someone sits down next to Kafka, leans back, says a few words, and leaves for another part of the room. Now and then people disappear behind a far door. Although Kafka understands that Neil Conley is not his friend and has invited him to the party only as a favor to Mike Lorenzo, he is less tense and sorrowful than he expected to be, as he sits in the corner and crunches on Potato Frills while watching the party and wondering why Bonnie Wilcox is no longer in the room. He becomes aware that someone is standing close to him. The peg pants, the silky lavender shirt, and the wavy blond hair belong to Neil Conley, who looks like a crooner making a guest appearance on *The Ed Sullivan Show*. Leaning down a little, he points his thumb over his shoulder and says, "We need you in there, daddy-o. Just follow me." Kafka sets down his Coke on the table, pushes himself to his feet, and makes his way behind Neil Conley as a new record drops down: *Well all ah want is a party doll / To come along with me when ah'm feelin' wild*. Someone turns up the sound. A couple get up and start jitterbugging to whistles and cheers. Kafka steps over ankles and glasses of punch as he follows Neil Conley to the far end of the room, where three stairs lead up to a door. With a sweep of his hand, Neil Conley ushers him in. From behind he hears: *Come along and be mah party doll / Come along and be mah party doll / Come along and be mah party doll / And ah'll may love to you, to you, ah'll may love*—the door shuts. In the new room, people from the party are sitting in folding chairs along all four walls. In one chair Kafka sees Bonnie Wilcox, who looks at him and lowers her eyes. In the middle of the room stands an empty chair. Neil Conley leads Kafka over to the chair and motions for him to sit down. He places a hand heavily on Kafka's shoulder. "Welcome to the train station, my friend," he announces, in the deliberately artificial voice of a host on a TV game show. "We've got one heck of a trip planned out for you, all the way across this great country of ours. You'll never forget it—give you my word on that. Last stop: Salt Lake City! Everybody wants to party in Salt Lake City. Whaddya say, guys 'n' gals?" A cheer goes up from the room; someone whistles. "First, just let me get this thingama-hoochie on you—hang on a sec—there we go—" Neil Conley pulls a cloth tightly across Kafka's eyes and ties it at the back of his head. "Don't you try 'n' cheat now, y'hear, or you'll be sorry." The crowd laughs. "Ready? Sit tight, hang on, and off we go! *Ch*-ch-ch-ch, *ch*-ch-ch-ch, wooo-wooo! First stop, Philadelphia! Here we are, in the City of Brotherly Love. A great town, Philly, where the girls sure ain't chilly." Kafka hears the sound of footsteps moving lightly across the floor. Something presses against his mouth. He doesn't know what they're doing to him, but as the pressure continues he begins to understand that he is being kissed. Faint smell of perfume, a touch of shampoo: a girl has kissed him on the mouth. The footsteps move away. "Now how about that! Ain't that somethin'! Hold on to your hat, we're off again! Next stop: Cincinnati! *Ch*-ch-ch-ch, *ch*-ch-ch-ch, wooo-wooo! Oh, those babes from Cincinnati, they'll break your heart and drive you batty!" Again the sound of footsteps, from another direction. The lips are fuller, wetter; they kiss him hard once and pull away. In Chicago-go-go, where the chicks get their kicks and never say no, he is kissed by smaller lips, which linger and push, linger and push. At Kansas City, where the music rocks and the girls are real pretty, he feels, or thinks he feels, the tip of a tongue. "And here we are, folks, at Salt Lake City! Last stop! End o' the line and you're doin' just fine! It never gets better than this! Get yourself ready, man. Here she comes!" Kafka, who is still wondering whether it was a tongue, hears footsteps and tries to prepare his mouth. "Hey hey now," Neil Conley cries, "you really wanna pucker up for this one!" Kafka slightly parts his lips. "Welcome to Salt Lake City!" Something heavy slams against his mouth. People are cheering; his lips hurt. A sharp taste of salt is on his tongue. Neil Conley removes the cloth. Kafka sees him standing with a handful of salt in his open palm. Beside him stands Neil Conley's tenth-grade sister in a shimmery blouse, smiling and holding a box of Morton salt. People are applauding and laughing. Salt drips from Kafka's mouth onto his shirt. As he rises from the chair to take his place against the wall, he glances over at Bonnie Wilcox, who is looking for something in her pocketbook.

Memory #3

The kind of kid you'd think would've been made fun of, but no one did. The hoods left him alone. He was lucky that way.

Kafka Laughs

Kafka is sitting in the auditorium during an all-school assembly, listening to a speech by the principal, Mr. Upjohn. In the fifth grade, during a spelling bee, Mrs. Krementz told Nick Bassick

that you can always remember how to spell the word "principal" when it means the head of a school because the principal is
your pal. Although Kafka is listening to Mr. Upjohn's speech, the
meaning of the words eludes him, in part because Mr. Upjohn is
wearing a dark-blue suit so carefully fitted and pressed that each
motion of his body is expressed by a new line in the cloth, and
in part because the speech itself is so carefully tailored that the
words have become an immaterial extension of the suit. Although
Kafka is sitting with his homeroom class, the students, when they
assemble in the auditorium, are not required to sit in alphabetical
order, so that he finds himself seated between Jim Currey, captain of the swim team, and Joanna Marsiglia, who is wearing,
under her tight pink blouse, a bra with outthrust funnel cups that
remind him of sideways-turned party hats, with tips so pointed
that they look sharp enough to slice open a finger. Kafka hears
the word "pride" and the word "generation," separated by a series
of words that are meant to connect them in some way. The bottoms of his feet have begun to itch, as sometimes happens when
he is restless, and, as he pushes down on each foot, in order to
stop the itching, he can't help feeling that he is walking briskly
along, like a soldier in a parade, to the tune of Mr. Upjohn's
words, which issue from his mouth like the beats of a drum.
The tensing and untensing of the muscles in his thighs, as he
marches to the tune of Mr. Upjohn's solemn words, has caused
his legs to begin to tremble, a sensation that passes upward into
his abdomen and chest. Something is rising in him, like a wind
before a thunderstorm. His shoulders are tingling, his throat is
rippling, and he hears, escaping from his mouth, a faint sound
that fills him with fear, for it is the sound of a laugh that is
about to erupt. With a fierce effort of compression he clenches

both fists, clenches his entire body, in an attempt to suppress the laugh that is rising in him like a flock of birds, like a handful of flung confetti, his chest is aching, his fingernails are pressing into the skin of his hands, his eyes are burning, Joanna Marsiglia has turned her head in his direction, with a shudder of despair he bursts into a laugh that he tries to crush down, but it's too late, the laugh tears through him like a shout in the night, and as if strengthened by release it continues to break forth, it rolls through him and shakes him in the sudden stillness of the auditorium, for Mr. Upjohn has stopped talking, Joanna Marsiglia is leaning away from him, tears of anguish burn in his eyes as he laughs and fiercely laughs, feeling, as the sounds roar out of him, the dreadful freedom of someone who has jumped from a building and changed his mind.

Kafka on the Back Porch

On a weekday afternoon in mid-June, Kafka finds himself on the screened back porch, sitting in the cushioned wicker chair beside the green wicker table. His father is at the office in New York, and his mother and sisters are at the beach. He is alone in the house. On the table a glass of lemonade stands beside a closed trigonometry textbook and the open, facedown copy of *Four Great Russian Short Novels,* which he is reading again but in a different order. He has been walking slowly up and down the shore of the Black Sea, thinking of abandoning Nadezhda and returning alone to St. Petersburg, where he will start a new life, but now he is far from the Black Sea, from the lies he has told Nadezhda, from the coming duel with Von Koren, just as he is far from the screened back porch, the green yard with its high fence, and the street of ranch houses two blocks from the beach, as he sits with half-closed eyes in the warmth that asks nothing of him, not even gratitude. The warmth has a weight he can feel. The heat is a great cat lying against him, preventing him from raising a single finger of the hand lying on his leg. But even as his body has become heavy it has also become light, it has become transparent, it is penetrated by sunlight, and in the wavering heavy lightness he remembers himself at the age of ten. He is sitting at his desk in his upstairs room in the other house, the house of his childhood. He is writing with a pencil in a notebook. He is an earnest child and has decided that morning to write a story about a boy who runs away from home. With excitement he describes the boy leaving the room, which is the very room he's writing in. He describes the familiar stairway with the carpet and banister, the living room, the wooden door beside the high record player. He sees very clearly the front walk leading to the sidewalk and the maple tree. He knows that it is better to write "maple tree" than "tree." He describes the boy walking up Canaan Road to the White Walk Market, where he himself often walks to buy an ice-cream cone or a package of red pistachio nuts that leave red smudges on his fingertips. At the White Walk Market the adventure begins, because he has never walked or ridden his bike beyond that corner. His plan is to show the boy entering a new neighborhood, passing down street after street, arriving at the train station that the boy writing in the notebook likes to visit with his father when they drive to Bridgeport to pick up the grandmothers. The boy in the story will jump onto a moving train and travel west, across America, until he leaps off and the true adventure of his life begins. But that is far away, and the

boy writing in the notebook has paused after the White Walk
Market. He cannot, in his mind, see the unknown streets of the
nearby neighborhood, he doesn't know the look of the houses or
the names of the trees, his pencil will not move, he tries desperately to write more words, but he sees nothing, and there at the
edge of the known world he stops forever. On the back porch,
as the memory dissolves into circles of light, Kafka waits for an
illumination that does not come. He feels, as he waits, that he has
been shown something that he is meant to understand, if only
he knew what it was.

Memory #4

What I remember is bumping into some guy in the hall and
there go my books crashing to the floor. Papers flying all over the
place. This clown looks at me and stands there doing nothing.
At the end of the hall I see some other guy running toward me
like my hair's on fire. He comes right up to me and right there in
the middle of everybody he bends down and starts picking up all
my books and papers and handing them to me. When he's done
I try to thank him but he says "Sorry, late for class" and takes off
down the hall. I ask somebody if they knew who it was. They
said: "Oh, that's Kafka."

Kafka Downtown

One afternoon a few days before the start of summer vacation,
Kafka steps out of Cullen's Drugstore, clutching in one hand a

small white paper bag containing a bottle of allergy pills pre-scribed for his sister Ottla, and begins to walk along the plateglass windows of Main Street, past Luigi's Barber Shop, the Ice Cream Scoope, Buds 'n' Blossoms, and Mario's Pizza, where he happens to glance across the street and see Bonnie Wilcox standing at the curb. She's wearing white shorts and a light-blue blouse, with a dark pocketbook slung over one shoulder. From one hand hangs a pink shopping bag. She waves at him, steps from the curb, and begins crossing over to his side, even though the light is green and two lanes of cars are passing in both directions. Kafka, who never crosses when the light is green, immediately begins to cross, as if to rescue Bonnie Wilcox from death. At the double yellow lines in the middle of Main Street they meet, while cars pass close to them on both sides. Bonnie Wilcox gives him a quick smile as she studies the traffic, holds up her shopping bag, and rolls her eyes. A moment later she continues across the street toward Kafka's starting point, glancing at him for a moment over her shoulder. Cars in two lanes pass between her and Kafka, who, unable to follow her, sees a break in traffic on the other side of the yellow lines and hurries to the far side of the street, where he turns to see Bonnie Wilcox standing on the opposite sidewalk, looking across at him with a puzzled expression. Kafka realizes that he has somehow managed to change places with Bonnie Wilcox, instead of joining her, as he planned to do. He needs to get to her with-out delay, but he can't possibly cross the street through four lanes of steadily moving cars. In both directions, half a block away, a stoplight hangs above a crosswalk. Kafka hesitates between the two crosswalks, wondering which one will enable him to reach Bonnie Wilcox sooner. He turns toward the slightly closer light, guarding the crosswalk that leads to Cullen's Drugstore. When he arrives across from Cullen's, he sees that the slightly farther light has turned red, allowing people to walk to the side of the street where Bonnie Wilcox is waiting, while he remains stuck at the wrong place staring at a green light that refuses to change and has probably been broken for the last fifty years. In the spaces between passing cars he can see pieces of Bonnie Wilcox, who is still standing on the sidewalk, holding her pink shopping bag. When the light turns red, Kafka walks quickly across the street. He notices that he's holding in one hand a small white bag containing a bottle of allergy pills. At the sidewalk he turns in the direction of Bonnie Wilcox, but Bonnie Wilcox is no longer there. Kafka wonders whether she has stepped into a store, maybe the very store she'd been thinking of when he first saw her standing on the curb, or whether, because she believes he's no longer on this side of the street, she has crossed back to the other side in order to look for him, unless of course she has crossed back to the other side only in order to continue shopping along the original sidewalk, as she was doing before she interrupted and probably ruined her day to be with him, if in fact she crossed over to be with him. As he again walks past Luigi's Barber Shop, the Ice Cream Scoope, and Buds 'n' Blossoms, he looks in the windows and sees himself staring back with an expression of ferocity. At Mario's Pizza he wonders whether, if he looks across the street, he will see Bonnie Wilcox standing on the curb again, waiting for him to notice her, as if no time has passed and he's being given a chance to do it all over again, and turning his head sharply he sees, standing on the opposite curb, a woman in a white straw hat and yellow dress, who, catching his sudden look, draws her hands toward her throat, as if to protect herself from harm.

Kafka Works on His Tan

On his dark-blue beach towel, Kafka is sitting straight up with his legs stretched out before him. At one corner of the towel lie a folded white T-shirt, a squeeze bottle of suntan lotion, a pair of rolled-up dungarees with a black comb in the back pocket, a scuffed sandal that rests at a slant against a second scuffed sandal, and a copy of *All the King's Men* with a scrap of paper as a bookmark. With his right forefinger he applies small dabs of lotion to his nose, his throat, his shoulders, his chest, his thighs, his bumpy knees, his sharp shins, his wrist-thin ankles, and the tops of his veiny feet, before leaning back on his elbows and watching the life of the beach. Close to his towel lies the striped yellow-and-white towel of Mike Lorenzo, who is standing down by the water talking to Neil Conley and Richie Barbone. Mike Lorenzo has a perfect tan, to go with a muscular body that lacks, according to Mike Lorenzo, three inches in height, a defect that he can partly but never entirely overcome by lifting weights in his basement. He admires Kafka's height and urges him to work out, but Kafka, who knows that nothing will save his body, limits himself to a modest regimen of sit-ups, knee bends, and curls with ten-pound weights. Mike Lorenzo wears a short tight aquamarine bathing suit that makes his buttocks resemble two baseballs. Kafka's suit is dark blue, neither tight nor floppy, and reaches partway down his thighs. Kafka knows that he can never have a satisfactory tan, much less a perfect one, because his skin has a yellowish hue shading toward olive that no amount of sun and lotion can transform into the desirable darkness of whiteness tanned, but he is hopeful that he'll be able to conceal his true color beneath a plausible imitation of tan and thereby achieve what he desperately desires above all else: the ability to pass unnoticed at the beach. Although his shoulders are too narrow, his chest too thin, and his legs too bony, they are not so narrow, so thin, and so bony as to attract hostile attention at the beach, despite the occasional glare of a passing hoodlum with hair slicked back on both sides and cold angry eyes that say "I could break you in half, you skinny piece of shit, but you're not worth my time," but for the most part he's able to get away with the affliction that is his body and concentrate on his tan. Despite everything, Kafka likes the beach. Now, as he leans back on his elbows while the sun works its way through the lotion into his incurable skin, he looks around at the red and yellow and blue beach umbrellas casting their half circles of shade, at the low waves falling and sliding back, at a girl with a black ponytail strolling along the shore in a tight white one-piece that makes her look entirely naked and entirely hidden at the same time, at the brilliant green Coke bottles lying tilted in the sand beside towels and blankets, at the sandbar glistening in sunlight, at the folding chairs that older people have brought with them to sit in as they face the water, at the wide straw hats, the sunglasses, the wicker picnic baskets, the red and silver radios, the two boys playing catch with leather baseball gloves and a pink rubber ball, the yellow helicopter against the burning blue sky, and as he looks around and listens to a shout, a cry, a splash, he can feel the tension of his body almost begin to subside, in the warm air, with its smell of wet sand, saltwater, and suntan lotion, on this day in late June, 1959, as if there were only this.

Kafka at the Railroad Station

Kafka is walking with his father across the parking lot of the Bridgeport railroad station, where they will meet Grandma Lena on the train from Manhattan. Kafka's father walks swiftly, with long strides, swinging his arms. Although Kafka's own strides are long, they are not as long as his father's, and he is aware of his arms held tensely at his sides, a little away from his body, like someone prepared to draw a gun. His father wears a jaunty fedora, light brown with a dark brown band, pulled low over his forehead. In the station his father swings over to the newsstand, purchases a paper, and surveys the rows of crowded wooden seats that face the windows overlooking the tracks. Kafka, seeing a single empty seat, points it out to his father and heads over to the viewing machines. His father strides to the seat, flings himself down, shakes open the paper, and begins to read. The machines are the old ones that Kafka has loved since childhood. When you put in a nickel and turn the crank, the man raises the chair jerkily over his head and the woman widens her eyes, places the back of her wrist over her mouth, and steps away. In the bright room the machines look worn and tired; a few have signs that say Out of Order. Kafka remembers his visits as a child, when the machines rose over him like corner mailboxes and he had to stand on a little stool. His childhood took place so long ago that it's like a story told by Grandma Lena about her early life in Manhattan or the time she rode the roller coaster at Coney Island. He is old, he is old. He leaves the machines, passes the lunch counter, and steps through the glass doors onto the waiting platform, where he remembers the train wheels rising higher than his head. In the distance he hears the train whistle, like the sound of a ship at sea. He returns inside and calls to his father, who folds the paper, tucks it under an arm, leaps to his feet, and begins walking toward him with one swinging arm. Kafka thinks: I am old. I am older than my father, I am older than Grandma Lena, I am older than Jehovah with his long beard on the cover of *Old Testament Tales*. He has passed from childhood directly into old age. He can feel the tiredness in his ancient bones. It's all he can do to turn his weary body halfway around and drag himself back through the doors onto the platform, as his youthful father rushes out behind him.

Memory #5

I hardly knew him, but I remember those eyes. They were the darkest eyes I've ever seen. But that's not it. It was when he looked at you. Even if it was only for a few seconds, you had the feeling he was looking straight into the middle of your brain. He knew everything about you, all your secrets, things you didn't even know about yourself. It sounds crazy, I know. How could he? But that's what I remember.

Kafka Answers the Telephone

In early July, at ten o'clock on a Saturday morning, Kafka is sitting alone at the kitchen table, eating his breakfast. The rest of the family have eaten two hours ago. Now his mother is weeding at the far side of the house, his father is standing on a ladder at the front of the house cleaning out the rain gutter, and his sisters are working on their tans at the beach. In a semicircle behind his cereal bowl are a box of Raisin Bran, a quart of milk, a glass of orange juice, and a bowl of sugar with a slanting spoon and a tilted top. To the right of his bowl lies a library copy of *The Wayward Bus* by John Steinbeck, held open by the edge of a pot cover. Kafka contemplates the day before him without pleasure. He does not want to mow the lawn. He does not want to go to the beach. He does not want to play Ping-Pong in the garage. He does not want to stroll into town. He doesn't want to go over to Mike Lorenzo's house, he doesn't want to lie on his bed all day and read, he doesn't want to go to the movies, he doesn't want to hang around the house doing nothing, he doesn't want to think about what he doesn't want to do. He asks himself what he does want to do. He decides that he wants to be a stowaway on a cargo ship headed for an unknown island in a distant ocean. At this moment the telephone rings. The phone sits on the kitchen counter, beside the door that opens onto the back porch. Kafka doesn't want to answer the telephone, an act that would require him to speak the first words of the day. At the same time he doesn't want the ringing of the phone to force his father to climb down the ladder and rush into the house, or his mother to rise from the cushion and make her way urgently toward the kitchen, perhaps at the same moment that his father is bursting through the front door, while he himself remains sitting at the table five feet from the ringing phone. With a sigh that strikes him as false and exaggerated, he rises from the table and walks over to the telephone as he slowly chews a mouthful of Raisin Bran. He thinks: the phone is ringing, life is impossible, death is inevitable. He carefully swallows the Raisin Bran, clears his throat, and picks up the receiver. "H'lo," he says, in a mumble so dim that he wonders whether he has spoken at all or whether he has only imagined the crushed word emerging from his throat. The voice says, "I was hoping it would be you." He recognizes the voice of Bonnie Wilcox. Kafka wipes his mouth with his hand, as if she can see his wet lips through the little holes in the receiver, opens the door to the porch, sits down on the steps, and leans back against the doorframe. Bonnie Wilcox says she has started her part-time summer job on the town paper and has been asked to conduct a survey. It concerns the four-way stop at the corner of Beach Road and the Old Post Road. Does Kafka support those who are asking the town to put up a traffic light at this intersection, or is he on the side of those who believe that the four stop signs are adequate? Kafka, who has never considered this question before, tries to imagine, without success, the arguments on both sides. He explains to Bonnie Wilcox that he doesn't have a strong opinion one way or the other and asks whether the survey has room for such a position, if in fact the absence of an opinion can be thought of as a position. Bonnie Wilcox says that she can put him down as "undecided." He is about to say that "undecided" is misleading, because it implies that he is carefully considering both sides of a difficult question without being able to reach a decision, whereas in fact he is not considering any side, although if he had more time—say, a few days or a week—he might be able to compare the strengths and weaknesses of each side in turn and then, when he arrives at a conclusion—but before he starts to speak he is overcome by the understanding that this is not helpful and is certainly of no interest to Bonnie Wilcox. He agrees to be listed as undecided. In the silence he can sense that the conversation is about to end. He hears the words "Do you" coming from his mouth, and stops. He has almost said "Do you ever go to the beach?" but finds it impossible to continue. For one thing, the question sounds so much like an invitation that he might seem to be taking for granted an interest on the part of Bonnie Wilcox that he has no right to take for granted. For another thing, the question sounds so little like an invitation that it would almost certainly require an explanation of some kind, after which he would probably have to ask another question, and maybe even a third. "Do I what?" Bonnie Wilcox says, in a different voice. Kafka tries to imagine how to complete the sentence. "I don't know," he says. Bonnie Wilcox bursts into a laugh. "That makes two of us," she says, laughs again, and hangs up.

Kafka Asks Himself What He Knows

Leaning back against the orange-and-white webbing of an aluminum lawn chair in the side yard, in the warm shade of the three Scotch pines, an open copy of *The Grapes of Wrath* resting facedown across his thigh, Kafka asks himself what he knows. He must know something. Everyone knows something. He knows the capitals of all the countries of Central America, a list that he memorized for a test in sixth grade. He knows the names, colors, and monetary values of all the properties on the Monopoly board, from Mediterranean Avenue to Boardwalk. He knows that the word "mayor" in the sentence "They elected him mayor" is called an objective complement. He knows that Mel Ott hit a lifetime total of 511 home runs. He knows that a red maple is named for its red flowers and a silver maple is named for the silvery sheen on the underside of the leaves. He knows the order of the ten minerals in the Mohs hardness scale: talc, gypsum, calcite, fluorite, apatite, feldspar, quartz, topaz, corundum, and diamond. He knows that Tippecanoe in "Tippecanoe and Tyler too" is William Henry Harrison. He knows that the state of Connecticut takes its name from an Algonquian word meaning "beside the long tidal river." He knows that in the duel between Laevsky and Von Koren in Chekhov's *The Duel,* Laevsky fires into the air and Von Koren fires at Laevsky. He knows how to work the clutch on the Chevy. He knows how to play canasta. He knows how to print a photograph in a darkroom. He knows that the nicknames of Babe Ruth, Walter Johnson, Ty Cobb, Joe DiMaggio, and Willie Mays are the Sultan of Swat, the Big Train, the Georgia Peach, the Yankee Clipper, and the Say Hey Kid. He knows the internal structure of a paramecium. He knows that the last three piano sonatas of Beethoven are op. 109 in E major, op. 110 in A-flat major, and op. 111 in C minor. He knows that the winged red horse on the Mobilgas sign is Pegasus. He knows what a shmoo is. He knows what a schmo is. He knows who Curly is. He knows who Moe is. He knows the five main arguments for the existence of God and the major argument against each position. He knows the words of the Buster Brown ad: "That's my dog Tige, he lives in a shoe / I'm Buster Brown, look for me in there too." He knows the words of the Robert Hall ad: "When the values go up, up, up, and the prices go down, down, down, / Robert Hall this season will show you the reason: / Low overhead, low overhead." He knows what a hippogriff is. He knows what a Heffalump is. He knows that the Louisiana Purchase took place in 1803. He knows that P. T. Barnum was the mayor of East Bridgeport. He knows that P. T. Barnum once built an Oriental mansion in Bridgeport and named it Iranistan. He knows that P. T. Barnum never said "There's a sucker born every minute" but did say something even better: "Every crowd has a silver lining." He knows that if White opens with P-K4 and Black replies with P-QB4, Black is playing the Sicilian Defense. He knows that rock-and-roll chord changes are based on the twelve-bar blues. He knows that Ralph Kramden drives a bus and Ed Norton works in the sewer. He knows the names of every character in *My Little Margie, Father Knows Best, I Love Lucy, Gunsmoke, The Life of Riley, The Honeymooners, Our Miss Brooks, Have Gun—Will Travel, Private Secretary, The Lone Ranger,* and *Dragnet.* He knows how to calculate the area of an isosceles triangle. He knows that the words "This is the ship of pearl, which, poets feign, / Sails the unshadowed main" are the opening lines of "The Chambered Nautilus," a poem by Oliver Wendell Holmes that he had to memorize in seventh grade and recite in front of the entire class. He knows that "Winston tastes good like a cigarette should" represents a common grammatical error. He knows that in German the word *Hafendampfsschiffartsgesellschaftskapitän* means "captain of the harbor steamship line." He knows that the illusion of motion in flipbooks, movies, and the hand-cranked machines in the Bridgeport railroad station is made possible by the optical phenomenon known as persistence of vision. He knows that "See ya later, alligator" comes from a hit song by Bill Haley and the Comets. He knows that the Yalu River separates North Korea from Manchuria. He knows that he is growing tired. He knows that he knows nothing.

Memory #6

I remember one time walking home with him and Mike Lorenzo. There was this high-school kid across the street, standing there on the sidewalk near a hedge—big kid, maybe fifteen, sixteen, fat, but with big shoulders, big arms. He's beating this little dog with a branch. The dog's sitting there whimpering, hardly moving at all. Me and Mike Lorenzo stop walking, but Kafka? Kafka puts his books down on the sidewalk and runs across the street. He rips the branch out of the guy's hand and throws it over the hedge. What surprised me was what happened next. What happened next was, Kafka grabs him by the throat with one hand and holds him like that. Stands there holding him by the neck and staring him in the eye. When he lowers his hand, Big Guy starts coughing and rubbing his neck. Says it's a free fucking country, but he walks away. That was the only time I saw Kafka do a thing like that. It made an impression on me.

Kafka and His Sisters Play Monopoly

Kafka and his sisters are seated around the green card table, on the back porch, playing Monopoly. For years all four have sat down together to do jigsaw puzzles and play simple board games, but last summer, when Gabriele was about to enter fifth grade, she asked whether she could play Monopoly with him, after watching a game between Kafka and Mike Lorenzo that lasted three hours. The younger sisters begged to join in. Gabriele always chooses the steamship, which she says will take her on a trip across the ocean to Holland. There she'll get on a train and go to Amsterdam, in order to see the house where Anne Frank hid for two years. She's been reading Anne Frank's *Diary of a Young Girl* and has begun a diary of her own, which she keeps hidden in a box under her bed. Gabriele's unvarying strategy is to buy two sets of properties on different parts of the board, in order to increase her chances of collecting rent; her favorite monopolies are the pinkish-purple group (St. Charles Place, States Avenue, Virginia Avenue), which remind her of grapes, and the yellow group (Atlantic Avenue, Ventnor Avenue, Marvin Gardens), which remind her of lemon-flavored cough drops. Valerie, a year younger than Gabriele, always chooses the racing car. She says her car can go faster than the old steamship and can get to any place in the world. It even knows how to race along the ocean floor. Her strategy is to try for Boardwalk and Park Place so that she can wipe out her opponents in one blow. Ottla, who will turn eight in the fall, insists that she understands the rules and doesn't need to be anyone's partner. She loves the iron, which she says is the best-looking piece. When Gabriele teases her about getting ready to spend the rest of her life ironing shirts for her hubby, Ottla replies that her iron will flatten anyone who gets in its way. It has a secret button that allows it to fly through the air over ships and racing cars. She buys whatever property she lands on and will take advice from no one except her brother, who knows everything. Kafka always chooses the hat. As a child he liked to try on his father's hats, and now, at sixteen, he says that the hat is necessary because when you're descended in a direct line from Miles and Prudence Kafka, who sailed over on the *Mayflower* and settled in Plymouth Colony, the least you can do is show a proper respect for the memory of your distinguished ancestors. His strategy is to build hotels on the first two sets of properties, which have the lowest rents but give him control of one entire side of the board. As Ottla rolls the dice, Kafka remembers reading to all three sisters when they were small. He read, over and over again, *And to Think That I Saw It on Mulberry Street*, asking each of them which was her favorite picture, and a few years later he read *Pippi Longstocking*, as his sisters sat or lay on the floor of their room. Now Gabriele and Valerie read to themselves and he reads only to Ottla. He recalls the long afternoons of Wiffle ball in the yard of the other house, the excited cries of hide-and-seek, games they no longer play. Since Gabriele entered fifth grade, she and Valerie spend more time together, have their own TV programs, and share secrets. But still they look forward to playing Monopoly, with a sense, as they begin, of sophisticated superiority to their old childhood games and then, as they continue, with a resurgence of the old passion. "Trade you Pacific Ave for Illinois Ave, if you throw in a railroad and five hundred," Valerie proposes to Gabriele, who replies, "You've got to be kidding," and turning to Kafka adds, "Can you believe her?" "Not a bad deal," Kafka says, "since she's handing you a monopoly and then—" "But how can I buy houses if I don't have any money?" Gabriele says. Through the screened windows, a smell of cut grass mingles with a faint scent of low tide.

Kafka Rings a Bell

One Saturday afternoon toward the middle of July, Kafka returns two books to the library and takes a walk through town, glancing at the window displays and imagining what it might be like to be a pair of polished cordovan shoes with little holes in the toes, or a

yellow-and-green beach umbrella that can tilt in different directions. After three blocks, when the gas stations and body shops
begin, he turns right. The road dips under the railroad tracks and
soon runs under the throughway overpass, with its concrete walls
painted with names and initials (J.C. LUVS D.R.). On the other
side of the throughway embankment he comes to a small park.
Beyond the park, large houses stand back from the road behind
broad lawns with high hedges. Under the sun-flecked shade of
elms and sycamores, Kafka strolls along a wide sidewalk until he
comes to a red slate walk. The walk leads to a house with five windows on the second floor and two windows on each side of the
front door. He's passed this house before but has never stopped
to look at it closely. All the windows are flanked by black shutters. Over the door is a half circle of multicolored glass. Encouraged by the thought that no one is likely to be home, because
who would be home on a sunny afternoon in the middle of July,
Kafka considers turning onto the walk and making his way to
the front door. He rejects the idea as dangerous and insane, and
continues along the shaded sidewalk. Moments later he stops. He
returns to the red slate walk. The house is very still. He begins to
stride along the pieces of slate, passing two thick elm trees that
lean a little away from him. At the end of the path he climbs the
two front steps. On both sides of the door are tall, thin strips of
glass with a design that reminds him of long petals. He tries to
remember what he planned to say but can't get beyond "I was in
the neighborhood and I." He observes his finger pressing against
the button in the silver disk beside the screen door. He hears
two loud tones, a high and a low, which make him think of the
woman with the big pocketbook standing at the door in the TV
ad: "Avon calling." He glances over his shoulder and estimates

that he can turn back along the slate path and disappear from view in three and a half seconds. Inside the house, footsteps are coming closer. As the inner door begins to open, Kafka imagines reaching over the top of the frame, removing a piece of colored glass, and plunging it into his neck. Behind the screen door stands a woman he has never seen before. She is wearing khaki slacks and a white halter top. Kafka clears his throat and says, "Is Bonnie home? I was in the neighborhood and I." The woman, one of whose tanned shoulders glows in sunlight, says, "Oh, I'm sorry, the Wilcoxes are away on vacation. I'm afraid they won't be back till the end of August. Are you a friend of Bonnie's?" Kafka considers it. "An acquaintance," he says. Before he knows what he's doing, he places a hand on his stomach and lightly bows. "Aren't you the gentleman!" the woman exclaims. "I'm Bonnie's aunt, by the way. Jane. And you are?" Kafka, rising appalled from his bow, gives a strained smile. "No one," he says. He turns and walks swiftly away along the red slate path, while he imagines Aunt Jane watching him with a mixture of amusement, irritation, and stern judgment. "Dear Bonnie," she will write. "You simply won't believe what happened the other day." He turns onto the main sidewalk, but only when the house disappears around a bend in the road does it come over him that Bonnie Wilcox has vanished for the entire summer. She won't be back until almost the start of senior year. Her hair will be different. Her life will be different. She'll barely remember the muddleheaded admirer who crossed over to the wrong side of the street. His shock of disappointment is so great that he stops for a moment to lean against a tree and contemplate the history of his failure, and as the bark presses sharply into his shoulder, he detects, at the very center of his disappointment, a stillness that might or might not be relief.

Kafka Rows a Boat

Kafka is walking on the beach at night. Because it's late, nearly half past twelve, the couples on blankets have already left. He is alone with the crescent moon and the low waves breaking in uneven lines. Never will he lie down at night on a blanket on the beach with Bonnie Wilcox. Along the stretch of sand leading to the jetty, the three dark lifeguard stands are gazing out at the water like stern kings. As Kafka approaches the second stand, which casts a long shadow broken by irregular rectangles of dim moonlight, he sees a rowboat resting nearby. The lifeguard boats that he sometimes sees on the beach at night are always turned upside down, but this one, for reasons unknown, sits right side up on the sand. The oars lie neatly across the seats. It's as if someone has rowed high up on the beach, pulled in the oars, and walked away. Kafka stands next to the boat, which is tilted a little to one side, the bow facing away from the water. He hasn't been in a rowboat since the summer after sixth grade, when his scoutmaster gave rowing lessons in a lake with an island. He remembers the feel of the oars against the palms of his hands. Kafka glances up at the lifeguard stand, as if to ask permission. He looks around and quickly steps into the boat. He sits on the middle seat, facing the low waves and the distant black line that is the coast of Long Island. He picks up one of the heavy oars and lowers the shaft between the prongs of an oarlock. He picks up the second oar and settles the shaft in the second oarlock. The two oars slant down so that the blades rest on the sand. Kafka grips the oar handles, raises the blades, and begins to row. The blades scrape lightly forward across the top of the sand, sweep up before him, and move backward through the air to land again in the sand. As he rows, the metal oarlocks rattle, sand flies from the oars like spray. The boat remains motionless in the sand, but Kafka has no desire to move the boat. His desire is to row. He pulls the oars hard, faster and faster, on the beach that stretches away on both sides. His upper arms ache, he can feel a vein pressing through the side of his neck, the oars are flinging sand into the night sky, while the moon, alarmed, takes cover behind a cloud, and still he goes on rowing, he will never stop, he imagines the boat moving backward across the sand, making its way into the streets, passing the ranch houses of his neighborhood, gliding under the throughway overpass, moving along the red slate walk, slipping through the front door, passing into the unknown living room, where Aunt Jane looks up in alarm, sliding out the back door, moving swiftly through yard after yard, through openings in hedges, between lawn chairs and under badminton nets, into the sunny backyard of the other house, the house of his childhood, then through the pricker hedge and out onto Canaan Road, past the White Walk Market, along streets lined by two-story houses with gliders and tricycles on the front porches, past boys shooting hoops at the ends of driveways, past a girl with a blond ponytail who watches him with her hands on her hips, all the way to the Bridgeport railroad station, where he rows past the old viewing machines and bursts through the glass doors onto the tracks and continues along the rails, bumping over the wooden ties, rowing fiercely out, out, out into the heart of the country. In a small western town, with a sheriff's office and a saloon, Kafka stops rowing. A horse snorts in the street. His shoulders ache. The blades of the oars rest on the sand. He's breathing hard. After a while he pulls in one oar and lays it across the seats. He pulls in the other oar and lays it across the seats. He steps out of the rowboat and continues walking along the beach.

Memory #7

He was in some of my classes. A smart kid, straight-A type. Quiet, polite. Kept to himself. I think he was in the chess club. I figured he'd be successful in whatever line of work he took up.

Kafka on a Summer Morning

On a Saturday morning in August, Kafka is walking along a tree-shaded sidewalk. He is on his way to the library, where he'll shelve books for two hours as part of his ten-hour-a-week summer job. Later, he and Mike Lorenzo will play Ping-Pong in the garage and then head over to the beach. Kafka likes the old houses on this street, with their front porches close to the sidewalk and their big chimneys on steep-sloping roofs. As he walks through leaf shadows trembling with spots of sun, he takes it all in: the green hose hanging over a porch rail, the open garbage can filled with bush branches, the ladder leaning against the side of a garage. On a driveway an old man in paint-stained dungarees and a short-sleeved T-shirt is washing his car with a soapy sponge that he keeps dipping into a bucket of dark water. In a side yard a woman wearing Bermuda shorts and a strapless top is kneeling on a tasseled cushion next to an azalea bush and turning over the soil with a trowel. Kafka is pleasurably aware that he is seeing these things, on this summer morning, instead of thinking thoughts that separate him from what he is seeing, but it's also true, he can't help thinking, that his awareness that he is seeing these things is itself an act that separates him from the act of seeing. This thought, which at some other time might have seemed interesting and worth pursuing, irritates him. He attempts to return to pure seeing, but he has become aware of a slight shift in things, a subtle alteration. The porches, the roofs, the branches, the sky itself, have changed in some way. They are penetrated by strangeness. He has never seen this street before. He has never walked in this town. Windows glitter like the blades of knives. White shingles blaze at him. It's all trembling with something he cannot name. At any moment the mask of the world will be ripped from its face. And then? In the spaces between tremors of light, Kafka sees. A dark plain stretches away. Figures are kneeling on the plain. Men with lashes stand over them. Sounds of weeping rise up and blow through Kafka like a wind. The toe of his shoe knocks against something hard. He sees: a slab of sidewalk tilted up by a tree root. On a white-painted porch rail, a glass of water shines in the sun. A jump rope with red wooden handles lies half in sun and half in shade. The world, unstoppable, streams in on him. He is here. He is breathing. He is on his way to the library. It's a peaceful August morning. Somewhere a laugh rings out. On a nearby porch a woman on a cushioned chair looks up at him with a frown. Kafka turns up his palms, as if to apologize for the world's laughter, and continues along the sidewalk. Things are here, on this side of seeing. And on the other side? A bottlecap gleams in the grass by the roadside. It's a Saturday morning in summer. He is on his way to the library, on this summer day.

VI

A COMMON PREDICAMENT

She's the one, the only one for me, after all these years I've finally found her, so why should I allow a little habit of hers to destroy my happiness? Isn't it better to look on the bright side? We're perfect for each other in almost every way. What difference does it make, all things considered? Does it really matter, in the long run? At first I thought her behavior was a temporary oddity, a sign of preoccupation, probably nothing more than a fit of absentmindedness, or say a nervous habit, one of those accidents that can easily happen when two people are getting to know each other. I soon came to understand that it was a deliberate and unwavering choice. If you love someone, you don't make a fuss over every little thing.

When I arrive at her house in the evening, on a quiet street lined with sycamores and sugar maples, I ring the bell and wait to hear her warm welcome. At the sound of her voice I step into the front hall and find her standing across the living room, facing the fireplace, with her back to me. I cross the room slowly, but not so slowly as to puzzle or alarm her. I place my hands on her shoulders, I kiss the back of her head. She makes a kissing sound but does not move. I return to the other side of the room, slip off my coat, and sink into the armchair that looks toward the fireplace. On the lamp table stands the white wine she has poured for me, in the slender glass with the twisted blue stem. We fall into easy talk, sharing with each other the events of the day, the small dramas of our lives. We laugh, she and I, we're serious, I feel soothed and exhilarated by her company, I'm grateful for her very existence. Why then should I mind that she chooses to keep her back to me? Is it up to me to dictate the movements of women? Whenever we go out to dinner we take separate cars, she first, then I, and as I enter the restaurant I find her sitting at a small table, studying the menu, with her back to me. I sit in my usual place, at the table directly behind hers. We order from the same waiter, she first, then I, all the time talking and laughing easily. Why on earth should I envy the couples who sit across from each other, face-to-face, often in deadly silence? To love someone is to desire that person's happiness. If such an arrangement makes her happy, shouldn't I be happy, too? I don't mean that I'm not happy. I've never been so happy. I am deliriously happy. It's only that I can't help feeling, from time to time, a slight uneasiness.

Once, at the beginning, when I asked her why she liked to stay that way, her back became a little straighter and assumed what seemed to me a thoughtful expression. At last her voice said, from the other side: "I don't want to rush things." I think of myself as a patient man, the kind of man who doesn't assume the world is his for the asking, and I dared to hope, as she spoke, that she was searching for someone who could exercise restraint, who could wait for things, especially important things, instead of reaching out greedily to grab whatever happened to please him.

In the meantime, it's almost enough to look at her from behind. I love the way her hair, with its three shades of brown, falls just below her shoulders and gives back the light of lamps or sun. I love the way it collects on one shoulder more than the other, depending on how she moves her head. When she speaks, her hands appear suddenly from the other side as she gestures in the midst of animated talk, like visible flashes of her spirited mind. And always I lose myself in admiration of her long skirts and shimmering blouses, her belted dresses, her jeans with the back pockets at subtly different heights, determined by the weight she places on one leg or the other, the sandals that reveal the reddish backs of her heels, her furry slippers with slightly crushed sides, her flowy and twisty scarves, and of course her hats, especially the ones with the swooping brims, but also the wool knit hat with the tassel, the white beret, the red felt cloche. In truth, it isn't always easy for me. There are times when I'd like nothing better than to stare into her eyes, to admire the exact shade and brilliance of her blue, or brown, or gray-green irises, to be drawn into her quiet or intense gaze, to see her seeing me. Instead I see the back of her head, with a bit of ear showing through her hair. I see the tops of her shoulders, curving away out of sight. But you can't have everything you want in this world, just because you happen to want it.

Still, though she faces the other way, I'm never banished to a corner. That's not how it is at all. When the mood is right, I walk up to her and wait until I'm sure that she welcomes my closeness. Slowly I draw my hands through her hair. I stroke the backs of her arms, I run my fingertips along her shoulder blades. Never do I have the sense that she's in any way skittish, wary, or resistant to touch. Sometimes she leans back against me, so that her head fits snugly between my shoulder and cheek, and we stand that way for a long time. Sometimes she reaches behind her, always with the back of the hand facing up. With gratitude I bend to kiss the soft pouch of skin between her thumb and forefinger, with joy I brush my lips across her knuckles, all the while being careful not to graze her palm with a careless touch or to move her outstretched arm in a way that might make her gasp with pain. Later I follow her up the stairs and into her room. In the light of a small lamp she undresses, still with her back to me. She lingers for a few moments, as if to refute the charge of demureness, before slipping sideways into her bed, while I remove my clothes eagerly and then lie down behind her. Our sexual pleasure is mutual and intense, and rendered only slightly disquieting, for me, by the understanding that no part of my body may cross an invisible line that divides her back from her front. Before she falls asleep I take my leave, in order to make it absolutely clear that I have no intention of spying on her. Gratefully I place a drawn-out kiss on the back of her neck. Of course I can't help wanting a little more, I'm a man like other men, the back of a woman can never satisfy me entirely, and if I don't insist that she turn around and face me, even for the briefest of moments, it isn't from lack of longing but because I know, insofar as it's possible to know anything about the woman you love, that a rash act would ruin everything.

What I don't know is why she persists in behaving as she does. Can it really be a matter of *rushing* things if we've been together for nearly two years? It's more reasonable, isn't it, to suppose that she is extremely shy—so shy that she can't bear to be seen directly. But there's nothing remotely shy about her manner of speaking, her easy laughter, her wit, her walk, her bearing; on the contrary, she seems sure of herself, playful, high-spirited, unconstrained.

It seems more likely, taking everything into consideration, that her refusal to turn around derives from some other source. Can it be that she's worried about my response to the way she looks? Does she fear that I'll be so disappointed in her face that my love for her will suddenly vanish? Is it conceivable that she thinks of herself as an unattractive woman? An ugly woman? Did she grow up hating her large, bulbous nose, with gaping nostrils the size of nickels? Do her shaggy eyebrows grow together? Are her teeth thrust out like tusks? Even as I ask myself these atrocious questions, which fill me with shame, I realize that there are plenty of reasons why a woman of pride or sensitivity might want to hide her face from a man. What if she once suffered a terrible injury? Years ago, in the supermarket, I was standing behind an elegant woman who turned around to reveal a tight knot of wrinkles instead of an eye. Can the woman I love be hiding a long, jagged scar from an old bicycle accident? Has the flesh of her face been burned away by fire, leaving ridges of naked bone? Was she once attacked on her way home from work by a robber with a vial of acid? Then again, maybe it isn't her face at all, but some other part of her body, that causes her to turn away—a goiter, say, like a tennis ball, bulging from her throat. But these are the kinds of monstrous thoughts I despise myself for having, however excusable they might be, under the circumstances. Then I assure myself that if I love her seriously, and I do, I do, I would never permit a mere physical imperfection to come between us. Shouldn't she trust me, after all this time? Doesn't she know the kind of man I am?

And how certain is it, really, that she's acting out of fear or shame? Consider: she's no recluse. She holds a job, doing research for a nonprofit cancer foundation, and I met her at a Christmas

party at the home of a business acquaintance. In the overcrowded
room it wasn't especially surprising that this lively, intelligent
woman didn't turn to me when I addressed her from behind.
Nor was I shocked, but only amused, when she passed me a slip
of paper over her left shoulder, with a message that read "Call
me." Also: ever since she and I have grown close, she has spoken
in great detail about all phases of her life, including episodes of
unhappiness in childhood and adolescence, and never once has
she hinted at the kinds of sadness or bitterness that come to those
who feel cursed with plainness or who have suffered the torments
of disfigurement.

Isn't it therefore possible, taking into account everything I
know of her, isn't it more than likely, when I evaluate the situ-
ation carefully, that she is, in fact, a woman of extreme beauty?
I try to imagine the shadows of her lower lashes on her high
cheekbones, the perfectly chiseled groove between her narrow
nostrils and her upper lip. But why should a beautiful woman
remain with her back to me? Maybe she's so beautiful that beauty
has become a burden to her. There are women who attract men
so powerfully through the sheer perfection of their loveliness that
they come to distrust their outward appearance and long to be
admired for qualities less accidental and superficial. If this is so,
if she wants me to love her without succumbing to her beauty,
then her plan is a disaster, for I'm helplessly drawn to the luster
of her hair, to her shoulder blades moving beneath her blouses. It
might even be said that I'm physically attracted to her precisely to
the extent that she remains unrevealed in the completeness of her
being, so that her behavior, far from drawing attention away from
her face and body, might be called an act of seductiveness. After

all, I've seen the faces of many women; only her face remains
unknown, mysterious, and impossible to ignore.

And yet, however rational such speculations may be, I'm well
aware that they all share the same assumption: that the reason for
her behavior concerns her sense of her own looks. But isn't this a
terribly self-regarding way of accounting for things? Isn't it possible, isn't it more than possible, that she's not worried at all about
whether or not her features happen to meet with my approval?
Isn't it just as likely that she faces the other way because she's
troubled by what she might find if she looks at *me*? It may be that
she has imagined a particular face for me, based on my voice and
touch, and fears disillusionment if she discovers that my actual
face bears no resemblance to the imagined one. Or perhaps she
has so strict and exacting a sense of male attractiveness that she
knows I'm bound to disappoint her. When I try to imagine what
she might wish me to look like, an anxiety comes over me. Then
I feel a powerful desire to hide my own face, even though she's
standing across the room, with her back to me. I would say that
I'm a reasonably decent-looking man, with nothing striking or
memorable about my face. My features are well formed, my skin
good, my eyes large and clear, my teeth straight, my chin firm,
though it's also true that my face displeases me in various ways.
My eyebrows are thinner than I'd like, my nose is too small, as if
it has never achieved full growth, and my cheekbones are without
strong definition. I wear eyeglasses only when I read, but I read
a great deal, and when I remove my glasses there are raw, red,
shiny patches on the bridge of my nose that are very unpleasant
to look at, in my opinion. My shoulders, though not narrow, are
narrower than I want them to be. My left index finger is slightly

crooked. I could go on. It's of course impossible for me to know how she might feel about my appearance, even if I have no reason to believe that she would draw back in horror. Naturally I want to please her, and the fact that she remains facing away makes me acutely aware of what it is about me that might prove unpleasant or disappointing, if she should happen to turn around, for unknown reasons, one of these days. As a result, I often feel awkward in her presence, as if she were standing directly in front of me and studying me with a hostile glare, instead of remaining considerately on the other side of the room, with her back to me.

But what if her reason for not turning around has nothing to do with the way either of us looks? Why should I take it for granted that the woman I deeply love is obsessed with appearance? Doesn't such a conjecture imply that she's a shallow person, with trivial concerns? Aren't there many excellent reasons why any woman might desire to keep her back to a man? Maybe she's waiting for me to say the right words, the words she's been hoping for from the beginning, after which she'll turn around with a tender smile. Or maybe she's testing my loyalty by imposing a difficult and enigmatic rule that I must obey without question. It's possible, of course, that she's a person of fixed habit, who began, for obscure reasons, to behave a certain way, and now has settled into an unalterable routine. But isn't it more likely that she's a protective woman, watching carefully over our future? Foreseeing the almost inevitable diminution of passion between lovers over the course of time, she has found a way to preserve our love by the perpetual reminder of a secret she will never disclose. Then again, she may be a woman of uncompromising honesty, who wishes to demonstrate, by turning her back to me, that all lovers, in the end, remain unknown to each other.

Still, even as I rack my brains to solve her riddle, I understand perfectly well that it lies within my power, at any instant, to put an end to all such questions. I simply have to stride across the room and step in front of her. This I will never do. It isn't that I feel helpless before her silent prohibition. Rather, when I imagine walking to the other side of her, or when I'm tempted to place my hand decisively on her shoulder and spin her around, I sense within myself a fierce resistance. How to account for it? I think the answer is this, that I resist the introduction of a change so great that nothing will ever be the same. For my love has taken this form and no other. If I should ever step in front of her, I would discover some other woman, a stranger who has nothing to do with me. It may be, of course, that I'm only a timid man who fears change, a coward who avoids risk at all costs. I'm not afraid to charge myself with that weakness, but in the end I find it isn't true. After all, I welcome new intimacies, new discoveries; I love it when we embark on new adventures together, such as our recent outing on the lake. She sat with her back to me as I rowed across the still water to the wooded shore. There, on the picnic blanket streaked with shade, she sat with her back to me while spots of sun trembled on her shoulders and hair. Later she lay down on her side and invited me to lie down behind her. We lay there a long time, side by side, my left arm stretched out beneath my cheek, my right arm bent so that the forearm leaned along her back and my palm rested on her shoulder blade. These are the moments of serene tenderness, of ecstatic peacefulness, for which I would exchange nothing on this earth. It's at such times that I understand one other thing: she loves me because she knows I will never ask her to turn around. If this is so, then what I love includes the very hiddenness that troubles my nights. And here is the farthest I can see into the darkness of my love: that it rests on an unshakable foundation of uncertainty, anxiety, and deep unknowing, which promises at any moment to disappear, if only she would face me, as I know she never will. Then I feel a fresh burst of love for her, even as I wonder, not for the first time, whether there might be some other way.

THE CHANGE

It's not the most brilliant idea she's ever had, walking alone at night, headed home after the party. Nearly one in the morning, later than she thought, too late to be walking home alone, though how late is late. Blame the party itself, not a bad party as parties go, even if you can't stand parties, but Sarah had begged her, pretty please, it wasn't exactly a party, more a bunch of friends getting together, but something about the shut-in feel of things, the rattle of the AC, the look of the night through the closed windows, she needed to breathe free, out there in the summer night. Sometimes you just have to breathe a little. Fifteen years old and she shouldn't be walking home alone at night, even if you're less than a mile from your own neighborhood, where everything's safe as can be, nothing to watch out for except the chestnuts hitting you in the head every fall. But this whole part of town is the safe part, trimmed hedges, slate front walks, houses set back a little from the road, just be sure and keep your doors locked, maybe a bike stolen from a porch, a beer can tossed onto a lawn from a passing car. Not her neighborhood but sidewalks that have a familiar feel to them, the big trees by the curb, branches touching in the middle of the street, orange streetlamps that seem part of the dark, the two-story houses with porches like hers, a few lights still on, one porch with the handle of an upright broom throwing a slanted shadow, and over it all the dark-blue night sky, a blue glow like no other, it makes her think of a lampshade with the bulb on. Half a moon up there, leaning back with a little swelling on the straight part, the moon pregnant tonight, clack of her block-heel sandals on the sidewalk. How she loves being out here, making her way home in the warm summer night, somewhere the slam of a car door, good thing she doesn't see anyone in the dark up ahead, coming in her direction, she'd have to cross over, because let's face it you're not supposed to be out walking the streets at night, even on the safe side of town, not if you're fifteen years old wearing clingy pants and your new block-heel sandals, low heels clacking on the sidewalk. Not that anything's ever happened to her that way, boys glancing at her in the halls, the creep in the mall who brushed against her leg, no shootings in her neighborhood, no stabbings, murders, corpses, maybe a break-in or two, a policeman ringing the bell. Her mother told her to call when the party was over, but who wants a ride on a night like this, sometimes you need to walk outside under the blue lampshade of night, or call it an umbrella, a great blue umbrella, walking home under the big blue umbrella of night, watching her shadow stretching out under the streetlamps, breathing deep in the freedom of the open air. The houses dark, everyone fast asleep, it's already Monday morning, people have to get up and go to work, even she works, if you can call it that, babysitting for neighbors a few nights a week, she's not a kid anymore, not at fifteen, though she still keeps a few of her old stuffed animals at one end of the top shelf in her bookcase, old Billybear leaning up against the dictionary her father gave her when she graduated from eighth grade. As she walks past a dark house a sudden light goes on in an upstairs window, a blurred shape behind a yellow shade, she walks a little faster. Slows herself down, don't be an idiot. She's already at the corner, an old house with gables and tall windows, a pointy tower, the kind of house that scared her when she was little, watch out for ghosts and witches, hooooo. Left turn onto a darker street, everything dead except for a few streetlamps, one porch with a dim glow up ahead. Voices on the porch, now she sees it's a group of boys, older boys, better to cross the street, but what if it draws attention, anyway what's the big problem, she's walking home from a party on a warm night in summer and the only amazing thing is that there aren't more people out walking, on a night like this.

Four of them there on the porch, she can see them from a few houses away, a collegey look to them, no interest in little fifteen-year-old girls walking by in the dead of night. Not that she's so little, five six in her stocking feet when last measured against the wall next to the refrigerator, the ladder of little pencil lines starting from when she was six, a figure to be proud of, according to her mom, stomach flat as a tight-stretched towel, good curve to her behind, breasts nothing to write home about but she can live with that, four guys hanging out on the porch on a summer night, and as she comes closer she tries to deaden the sound of her heels clackety clacking against the sidewalk. She sees it now, the light of the porch coming not from the ceiling but from a yellow glass lantern on a table, and there on the wooden top of the porch rail two partly crushed silver-and-blue cans, one bent in one direction, the other in the other, like two actors bowing to an audience. Just walking home from a party, nothing wrong with that, the porch coming closer, too late to cross over, look straight ahead, she's in the dark and they're in the light, but somehow it feels the other way around. Walk on by, mind your own business, just minding my own beeswax, as whatsisface says, and as she comes up to the porch she feels a tensing-up in her arms, she's walking across a stage in a white blouse and black leggings and clackety-clack sandals. She can sense something changing as she walks past, maybe the talk has stopped, or maybe the faces have turned toward her, but it's not till she reaches the other end of the porch that a voice calls out, "Going somewhere?" A voice sure of itself, friendly, a hint of challenge. Of course she's *going* somewhere, why else would she be out walking at one in the morning, just keep going, don't say anything, walk a little faster but not too fast, no reason to draw attention to yourself walking along in skintight leggings that hug your legs and push up your behind, not that it's anybody's beeswax. She can feel her shoulder bag knocking against her hip, hear her heels knocking against the sidewalk, and now he's standing at the top of the steps calling "Come on up and say hello." A voice shouts "Hello there," bursts of laughter, footsteps on the stairs. From two houses away she glances back quickly and sees him standing on the middle step, low-hung jogging shorts, running shoes without socks, a tight white T, she already knows everything about him, wise guy in seventh grade, swim team and basketball in high school, king of the hallways, the blond hair falling carelessly over his forehead, the sharp-cut features, thinks he's a young god, on to college and a new world of frat parties and girls, always girls, and she's not one of them, doesn't want to be one of them, no boyfriend yet, she could but not yet, plenty of time for all that, she's in no hurry, and if she did it wouldn't be a chisel-face boy-man with a pretty smile and hard blue eyes drinking beer with his buds on a porch at night. "That's not polite," he says, more laughter, and as she passes the next house she hears him step onto the bottom stair and begin to walk after her along the sidewalk.

She walks a little faster, hesitates, breaks into a run. Maybe not the smartest thing to do, sandals with heels, the dark sidewalk, but her body has made up its mind and all she can do is follow. She runs as if her life depends on it, and maybe it does, because now he's running, too, and what's he going to do if he catches up to her—hit her? murder her?—on this quiet street with its tall old trees and dark houses not so many blocks from her own neighborhood. He's running hard, she hears the laces flapping on his shoes, feels fear like a thumb pressing against her neck, and as she runs she wonders whether she's the one to blame for it all, sashaying past the lit-up porch in her look-at-me pants, her blouse coming down only a little over the waistband. Not that she was sashaying, just walking past on her way home from the party, no big deal, the pants are what everyone's wearing, wrapping themselves around your legs like spray paint and lifting up your butt with a line down the middle, displaying it to the world, all of it going on behind your own back. Maybe all he wants to do is talk to her, come sit on the steps and talk for a while, just spend a little time with me and talk on this summer night. She's running as fast as she can in her block-heel sandals, easy to trip on these tilted sidewalks, even in daylight they can knock you down, the tree roots pushing up the slabs of concrete, she'll trip and break her arm, smash her face. No house lights on, no one's up at this hour, maybe she can rush along a front walk and pound on a door for help, please let me in, but she doesn't dare stop, maybe he's only chasing her down to the end of the street, he'll break off and return to his friends and they'll all have a good laugh about it, the girl who ran away. She remembers

Jimmy Santino chasing her down the street in second grade, he wasn't planning to kill her, or rip off her clothes, it was a boy thing, chase girls down the street and then go home and feel good about yourself. But this is no Jimmy Santino chasing her home from school, this is something else, her chest hurts, her legs burn, suddenly she sees herself sitting on her father's lap in the armchair by the lamp table, he's reading to her and pointing to each word, her mother is sitting on the couch, reading a book, they all read in her house, she's five years old and nothing will ever change, the lamp on the lamp table, the rocking chair by the fireplace, Billybear waiting for her on her bed, in the long summer of childhood that never ends. No way of knowing about the pain in the nipples, the blood between the legs, your hip bone pushing against your jeans, Ron Harding stepping off the school bus with his arm around Janet Winthrop's shoulders and his fingers resting on the edge of her low-cut bra. Boys standing around in groups and suddenly looking you over as you walk by, checking you out, just like you checking yourself out over your shoulder in the mirror every morning to make sure everything's in place back there. Always the A student, always raising her hand in class, memorizing French verbs, the conditional, the subjunctive, trying to get the accent right, *je suis enchantée de faire votre connaissance*, aware of her body, aware of boys, but putting it off till later, not impatient like some girls, the lamp on the lamp table, the rocking chair by the fireplace, he's gaining on her, she's afraid to look around, blood beating in her ears, and as she runs she pulls off her shoulder bag and flings it onto a lawn, take it and leave me alone, take everything, my wallet, my credit card, iPhone, gift card, key chain, compact, lip gloss, no lipstick, not yet, take it, all of it, just let me go, I swear I won't say anything to anybody ever. She turns onto a dark block but he's still running after her, bag or no bag, she should've stopped at his porch and talked a little, no girl says no to Chisel-Jaw Joe, close to her now on this dark street, the houses quiet, the trees thick, the branches high, safe from it all, up there under the moon. After this night things will never be the same, even if he turns back like Jimmy Santino it won't be the same, he's right on her heels, his breath on her neck, or is it only a breeze, a little breeze on this summer night. His fingers touching her back, even her father can't save her now, her teachers can't save her, she feels his fingers gripping her sides, trying to pull her to a stop, there's a wetness on her face, tears or maybe the wind of her running blowing against her eyes, she can't do it anymore, save me, kill me, save me.

His hands on her waist, the press of fingers. She tries to twist away but he's got hold of her, she's beating at his hands, she yanks her body sideways, thrusts herself from the sidewalk onto the curbside grass, but he's there with her, fingers tugging at her waistband. No way out, none, a desperate tiredness coming over her. She feels a hardness on her hips, her back. She needs to fight but the fight is going out of her, something is happening, the hardness spreading. She feels it in her knees, her neck. Her blood is thickening. She can't move but she's growing, expanding, her arms over her head, her breasts hardening, her feet plunging into the ground, her shoulders rising, her branches lifting and spreading, higher and higher, smaller branches angling out from larger ones, leaves bursting forth, her bark thick and hard, her branches stretching, up and up, high over everything. She's safe from him, safe, nothing can hurt her now. She thinks of her room on the second floor, the bars of sunlight slanting in through the venetian blinds, the windows looking down at the side of the garage and the hedge with white blossoms, the sun shining on the white shingles. Her father reading to her in the light of the table lamp, summer trips to the bank of the river. Never again the mussel shells on the beach, the sandbars glistening, never the other side of things, the girl of sixteen bent over the birthday candles, the woman of twenty-one, the stranger of thirty-five, all gone, even regret is gone, think of the branches stretching, rising up lovely above the housetops, reaching high overhead, safe at last, up into the night sky, away from it all, under the light of the moon. A warm night in summer, touch of coolness in the air.

HE TAKES, SHE TAKES

He takes the dish rack, she takes the hat rack, he takes the table, she takes the chairs, he takes the upstairs, she takes the downstairs, he takes the front yard, she takes the back, he takes the storm door, she takes the screen door, he takes the downspout, she takes the rain, he takes the summer, she takes the winter, he takes the weekend, she takes the week, he takes the flathead, she takes the Phillips, he takes the ballpeen, she takes the claw, he takes the inside, she takes the outside, he takes the upside, she takes the downside, he takes the grandma, she takes the grandpa, he takes the cradle, she takes the trike, he takes the horsey, she takes the moo-moo, he takes the wee-wee, she takes the doo-doo, he takes the chichi, she takes the froufrou, he takes the hoo-ha, she takes the boo-hoo, he takes the oak tree, she takes the ash tree, he takes the coat tree, she takes the shoe tree, he takes the headboard, she takes the breadboard, he takes the outboard, she takes the floorboard, he takes the backboard, she takes the washboard, he takes the drainboard, she takes the dashboard, he takes the duct tape, she takes the Scotch tape, he takes the sheetrock, she takes the sheets, he takes the stemware, she takes the stoneware, he takes the hardware, she takes the flatware, he takes the tinwear, she takes the swimware, he takes the cookware, she takes the cake, he takes Broadway, she takes Park Place, he takes the lead pipe, she takes the wrench, he takes anguish, she takes heartache, he takes fire, she takes the heat, he takes her fancy, she takes his breath away, he takes her measure, she takes his eye, he takes shelter, she takes pleasure, he takes umbrage, she takes flight, he takes a back seat, she takes a powder, he takes a chill pill, she takes a hike, he takes a look-see, she takes a dim view, he takes a gander, she takes a goose, he takes a snapshot, she takes a potshot, he takes amiss, she takes amister, he takes exception, she takes correction, he takes instruction, she takes possession, he takes over, she takes after, he takes up with, she takes off, he takes her down a peg, she takes him for all he's worth, he takes it on the chin, she takes it lying down, he takes her for a ride, she takes him to the cleaners, he takes the wind out of her sails, she takes the words right out of his ever-lovin' mouth.

THE COLUMN DWELLERS
OF OUR TOWN

The Columns

The columns of our town range in height from 60 to 140 feet. Most are constructed of stone and mortar, though recent years have seen a turn toward concrete reinforced with ribbed steel. All columns have four sides of equal length, not less than four feet or more than five. The stones are supplied by a local masonry contractor and may be rough or smooth. Evidence of wooden columns in earlier centuries comes from correspondence studied by town historians, but no trace of any wooden structure has survived. Our columns rise from a scattering of back and side yards, from the wooded slope of the park by the river, from the thicket behind the parking lot of the mall, from the strip of lawn that borders the town graveyard. All columns are equipped with a system of ropes and pulleys to assist with the delivery of food and occasional changes of clothing, as well as the daily bucket for waste. At present there are forty-one columns in our town, of which thirty-seven are in use, and one stone-and-mortar column under construction in the backyard of a split-level ranch house on Crommelin Road.

The Dwellers

At the top of each column, a dweller lives alone. Ascent is voluntary, as is the decision never to return to the earth below. Although it is tempting for us to think of the dwellers as members of a fanatical sect, they belong to no church and there is no evidence of communication among them. Whether we stroll along the sidewalk of a shady residential street, or drive to a restaurant in the center of town, or shop at the mall beyond the post office, we are aware of them, up there above us, like a species of bird that has landed and will not fly away. They are in fact our sons and daughters, our friends and neighbors. They have left us and will never return. We do not really know what they are doing up there.

Visitors

Sometimes at the base of a towering column you see a group of visitors from other towns, who talk among themselves, point up at the distant top, and hold up their phones in an effort to capture something glimpsed above. We are of two minds about the visitors. We feel pride that our pleasant but rather ordinary town contains unusual elements worthy of the attention of strangers, while at the same time we resent that very attention, which feels like the kind of curiosity directed at freaks in a sideshow. Our columns, as they are stared at by visitors, become a form of entertainment that makes them part of the familiar world. They are slowly drained of the very sense of strangeness that drew the visitors in the first place.

The Column Top

The column top is a flat square of stone or concrete no wider than the base. In this small space, ranging in area from four by four feet to five by five, a dweller remains until death. The earliest dwellers are believed to have sat motionless on the hard surface, with legs crossed and each foot resting on the thigh of the opposite leg. They are said to have trained themselves to sleep in the same position. The first overhead cover for protection against the weather is recorded in the late nineteenth century, though several of our historians believe that temporary protective structures date back at least another hundred years. All column tops are now supplied with flat-roofed huts of stone or concrete, which leave room beyond one wall for standing, sitting, or walking. One of the four walls is open but contains a panel that slides up and down, to permit exposure to fresh air during good weather. All concrete columns, as well as newer columns of stone, enclose a central pipe for the delivery of heated air during the cold nights of winter. The little evidence we possess suggests that today's dwellers spend long hours seated inside their huts, emerging at irregular intervals to stand still or to walk back and forth slowly. Each hut contains nothing but a rubber mat. The waste bucket, with its roll of toilet paper, may stand inside or out.

Ellen Olshan

At the age of forty-six, Ellen Olshan had been married happily for twenty years. She was the mother of two loving daughters, one a junior in high school and one a sophomore away at college.

Ellen worked part-time in our library, a job she liked in a building she loved. Exactly when things began to trouble her remains
unclear. She described it to one close friend as a slight restlessness, though she immediately questioned the word "restlessness"
and said the feeling was more like wanting something you didn't
have, without knowing what that something was. When she discussed it with her husband, he listened carefully and suggested
that they take time off from work and go on a vacation, just the
two of them. Ellen embraced the idea but within a week begged
off, realizing that what she needed wasn't a change of scene or a
pleasurable distraction but something else, something else. That
summer she began taking long walks. She had always been an
energetic walker, refusing to drive the ten blocks from her house
to the library, but now she walked all over town, looking around
at every porch and parked car as if she were searching for something she had lost. One day she found herself standing near a
column in a vacant lot out past the auto-parts shop. In the past
she had accepted the columns the way we all more or less did,
as odd but familiar features of our town. Now she began to seek
them out. She would stand in the near distance and stare up at
the simple hut high above, which sometimes seemed to quiver
in bright sunlight and at other times to grow darker than the
column itself. Sometimes she walked over to the base of a column
and placed her hand against the hardness. She especially liked the
many patterns of different-sized stone, which reminded her of
old walls in farmers' fields. Ellen had never seen a dweller ascend
to the top and tried to imagine what it might be like. One day
she returned home long after dark from the columns in the park
by the river. Her husband and high-school daughter, greeting her
with worried looks that changed to immense relief, said they had

first called the library and finally the police. An impatience came over Ellen. Didn't these people understand? When the decision to live above came to her, it was accompanied by a ripple of alarm, which gradually grew quiet and left only a settled calm. The night she told her husband, his mouth trembled and his eyes brightened with tears. Why? he wanted to know. Why? Ellen answered that she didn't know why. She knew only that she could no longer continue in the old way.

History

Although detailed historical records go back only to the early nineteenth century, bits of evidence from a variety of sources have persuaded most of our historians that columns were present as far back as the late seventeenth century, some hundred years before our village was incorporated into a town. There is no agreement about what purpose the first columns served. We begin to hear of citizens mounting to the tops and living there only in the early years of the eighteenth century, at which time there appear to have been no more than six or seven columns. The custom may have had some connection with a fiery preacher. The oldest of our present-day columns is believed to date back to those years. The first significant expansion in the number of columns took place soon after the Civil War, perhaps as a sign of the town's resistance to the Industrial Revolution. Other notable increases occurred between the two world wars and in our present era. Nothing whatever is known about the first column of all, but one attempt to account for its origin is a tale that is said to have survived for three hundred years.

The Tale

The tale tells us that the first column was built by a young man unhappy in love, who ascended in order to spend the remainder of his days alone and in sorrow. The woman he loved, passing the column every day, slowly came to fall in love with the young man seated above, whose love she had rejected. Now she could no longer bear a life without him. Stone by stone she erected a column of her own, not far from the young man's, and ascended to the top. There they sat facing each other day after day, never speaking but delighting in each other's company high above the village. As the months turned into years, their bodies weakened but their love grew stronger. They died within moments of each other, bending forward in farewell, and were buried side by side. Historians agree that the tale has no verifiable basis in fact and cannot be relied upon to provide any knowledge whatever concerning the origin of our columns, but none of this prevents us from reciting it to our children. Even as we do so, an uneasiness comes over us, for the story reduces the mystery of the columns to a series of easily grasped romantic feelings that cannot account for what drives the dwellers to ascend, never to return.

What They Do

What do they do up there? We know that the dwellers spend most of their time sitting motionless, but exactly what they do while sitting motionless is a matter of dispute. Some say that the dwellers have given up on life and ascend for the sole purpose of dying. It's true enough that they have abandoned life on earth, our life, but it is entirely misleading to claim that they are seeking death, since all dwellers take nourishment precisely in order to keep themselves alive, often for decades. Others say that the dwellers are misfits who are unable to face the difficult choices of everyday life and ascend in order to escape. There is little doubt that the ascent represents a refusal of everyday life, but the suggestion that the dwellers have chosen an easier path is impossible to sustain, since most of us can imagine nothing more difficult than a life spent alone on top of a column. It is far more likely, as many of us believe, that the dwellers have chosen a life of contemplation, though exactly what is meant by "contemplation" remains unclear. Are they attempting to break free of the world of sensory delusion into a universe of spiritual transcendence? Are they searching for the true meaning of life, by removing their minds and bodies from the diversions of the material world? Are they waiting for something they believe will come to them, if only they are able to practice sufficient patience and discipline? Many of us think that any interpretation of their purpose limits them unfairly, for it implies that all dwellers have a straightforward and definable goal, of the kind we know all too well, down here in the world below.

Awareness

We are aware of them, of course, our towering columns, with their sometimes half-visible dwellers at the top, whether we take a stroll in our neighborhoods, or go on a picnic with our families in the park by the river, or step from the hardware store onto the parking lot. Even if we pay no attention to them, we know they are there. They form a familiar and accepted part of our town, like the seven church steeples or the rows of transmission towers in the field behind the shopping center. They may even be said to offer a kind of comfort, the way all familiar objects do. At the same time, we know perfectly well that our columns are strange and disturbing objects, unknown in other towns. What are they doing there, as they reach into the sky? And what are you doing down there, they seem to whisper, with your predictable lives? When thoughts of the dwellers pass through our minds, we wonder sometimes whether they are as aware of us as we are of them. Do they catch glimpses of us far below, pushing mowers across our lawns or blowing snow from our driveways? Do they hear our buzz saws, our car radios? Do they ever wish to join us, in our world of backyard barbecues and family birthday parties? Do they feel pity for us, down there in the little world, without the courage to break free?

Opposition

Some argue that our columns should be torn down and hauled away. Such structures, they claim, serve no purpose other than to lure weak-minded citizens to their death, while at the same time they cause tremendous suffering to families and friends below. As if that weren't enough, they are perpetual distractions from the business of real life. They are unsightly blemishes that render our town ugly and grotesque. From a practical standpoint, they take up small but valuable pieces of public land that might be put to better use: a flagpole, a gazebo, a memorial commemorating the loss of our heroic young in World War II, a statue of our one Revolutionary War general. The opposers constitute a small minority of our citizens and are regularly outvoted at town meetings, but their voices persist. We who are in favor of preserving the columns, we who cannot imagine our town without them, sometimes ask ourselves, in the small hours of the night, what it is that we are defending.

Daniel Friedman

The summer after law school, Daniel Friedman returned to our town to be with his family before undertaking an internship at a major firm in a nearby city. Although he looked forward to leading an independent life as an adult, Daniel loved his home and was determined to throw himself into the old routines before moving away. He remembered fondly everything about the old house where he'd spent his first seventeen years: the faded living-room rug that had once belonged to his grandmother, the piano by the fireplace, the wooden handrail on the carpeted stairs, the view of the backyard beneath the raised blinds of his two bedroom windows. As in the old days, he went with his parents to the park by the river for weekend picnics, turned over hamburgers on the charcoal grill out back, went shopping in town with his mother for summer shirts and a bathing suit, talked with his father late at night. He took up again with a few old friends from high school, who now lived in town and had started families of their own. Sometimes it seemed to Daniel that he had returned to the strange summer before college, when he felt suspended between the life he had always known and the new life awaiting him. Was he still that boy of seventeen? Things were on hold with his law-school girlfriend, who had taken a job halfway across the country and seemed never to be home. Daniel began setting out on walks all over town, savoring the details of familiar neighborhoods and venturing into new ones. He loved walking under thick-leaved branches, stepping into the sun, staring down at velvety clusters of dark-green moss in the spaces between rectangles of sidewalk. One day he found himself standing not far from one of the stone columns out by the reservoir. He stood with his hands in his pockets, staring up with his head bent back. As a child he had asked his mother and father many questions about the columns and the people on top, the same kind of questions he had asked about Eskimos and alligators. At the base of the column a teenager in ripped jeans and a T-shirt sat on the ground with his back curved against the stone as he bent over his phone. Daniel removed his hands from his pockets, kicked at a dandelion, turned away. Later that afternoon he walked up to another column and drew his palm slowly across the uneven stone. He now made it his business, during his daily wanderings, to visit every one of our columns, the older ones of stone and the newer ones of stone or smooth concrete, until they were all as familiar to him as the wooden posts and sloping roofs of the porches of his street. Exactly when he knew what he was going to do, he couldn't say for sure. It was as if his preparation for a new life had taken an unexpected and irrevocable turn. His parents, terrified, begged him to reconsider. When it became apparent that his mind would not bend, his father accepted the decision and made a final request of his son: he begged Daniel to permit the column to be erected at the side of the house, between the strip of hollyhock and the high hedge. Daniel, who was indifferent to the location of the column, agreed with a shrug. The masonry

contractor required permission from the town hall before starting work, in order to ensure that all safety regulations would be
complied with. As the blocks of stone and layers of mortar began
to rise, surrounded by wooden scaffolding, Daniel prepared to
take leave of his house from cellar to attic, room by room, wall
by wall, until it came over him that he had spent the entire summer taking leave of everything he had once loved. His real life
was about to begin.

Finances

The earliest columns for which records exist were paid for privately. All were constructed by local masons, with the aid of
one or more assistants. An additional fee was charged for the
rope-and-pulley system attached to the completed column, while
a monthly rental cost for the use of public land could be avoided
by building on one's own property. By far the greatest expense
was the food itself, which was provided twice daily and might be
required not simply for months but for years. Evidence suggests
that charitable institutions, usually associated with a church, con-
tributed what they could to the maintenance of the diet. Despite
the charities, the system clearly favored the well-connected and
well-to-do, thereby creating the paradox of a life of constriction
and deprivation affordable only by the upper levels of our society.
A remedy began in the middle of the nineteenth century, when
an association called Citizens Above was founded by the wealthy
father of a daughter who spent her last fifteen years at the top of
a column. The money, skillfully invested, produced income used
exclusively for the support of column dwellers. Citizens Above,

now known as the Community Service Association, or CSA, today provides all expenses necessary for the construction and maintenance of a column, as well as for twice-yearly inspections and all repairs required of older columns. A number of local institutions, as well as private citizens, regularly contribute to the CSA, which has become one of the most profitable organizations in our town. Those who oppose the columns are particularly angered by the Association, which, they say, not only encourages antisocial behavior but squanders money better spent on low-income housing, an expanded teaching staff in our middle school, and additional downtown parking.

Descent

All dwellers ascend with the fixed intention of never returning. In this they have been remarkably successful throughout the course of our history. Nevertheless, exceptions have occurred. Records show that in the year 1902, on the occasion of his fortieth birthday, Charles Vanderberg ascended a column in a field owned by his grandfather. Vanderberg was the successful owner of a local business that sold farming supplies and equipment. His startling decision devastated his wife and two sons, his numerous aunts and uncles and cousins, his many friends, and the community at large, for he was a respected and well-liked man eagerly sought after for every kind of social occasion. After two years seated at the top of his column, during which his wife and sons operated the business, Vanderberg one day descended on the platform used for delivering food. For six months he returned to his old life, never speaking of his two years up above. Soon he began to show a new interest in town affairs. He ran for Commissioner of Public Safety and won by a landslide. Three years later he was appointed by the Board of Selectmen to the position of Town Manager. Vanderberg devoted the remaining years of his life to the welfare of our town, throwing himself passionately into everything from building construction to education to the personal concerns of private citizens. At his funeral, one of his sons said that his father's two years up above had somehow had the effect of drawing him closer to the affairs of the town below, though how or why that happened he couldn't say. A more recent example is that of Mary DelSanto, whom many of us knew from school. She was a lively girl who loved to party. She also loved to lie alone in her room and read long nineteenth-century novels. As early as sophomore year in high school, Mary began telling us that her goal in life was to join the column dwellers. We laughed, rolled our eyes, and slammed our lockers shut. After high school she worked part-time in the post office while applying to colleges. It was shortly after her first acceptance letter that she announced her decision to ascend. A group of us watched as she rose slowly on the platform along the side of the column. We continued to watch as the empty platform came back down. Shaken, we agreed to meet once a week to honor her memory. Three days later someone reported seeing Mary DelSanto at night through her second-floor bedroom window. It turned out that she had descended from her column on the food platform early that morning. Mary shut herself indoors for the rest of the summer, refusing to reply to phone messages or answer the door. That fall she left for college but returned home after a few months, where she resumed her indoor life and shunned her friends. Rumor had it that she was suffering from depression, from drink, from drugs. Sometimes we glimpsed her at night, walking with her head down. None of us tried to speak to her. Some said she had never recovered from her journey up above, others said she was so ashamed of her return to the world below that she was unable to adjust to her old life. One day she and her parents moved to another town. We never saw her again.

O You Who Dwell

O you who dwell high above us, you who have left us for another world, tell us what it's like up there! Is it like being in our town, without the town? Do you ever grow bored? Do you ever feel joy? Have you passed beyond boredom and joy? What are you thinking? *Are* you thinking? Are you searching for something that has no name? Do we have no name? Are we nothing to you? Are you so far above us that you are filled with a glory we can never imagine? Do we embarrass you? Do we disgust you? Do you remember that you were once one of us? Do you ever fear that you have wasted your lives? Do you know that we admire you? Do you know that we need you? O you who dwell above, do you know that we make you possible?

Other Failings

Descent is the most decisive way of failing to meet the challenge of the columns. More moderate ways include any attempt to make contact with other dwellers, any attempt to make contact with people below, and any breaking of silence through shouting, talking, or other distracting noises. Town regulations state that an infraction, once detected and verified, will result in immediate removal from the column top by trained guards. Records show that such incidents are extremely rare. Even rarer is a fall from the column, an event that has occurred only once in our history. In 1927 a young man of twenty-six plunged to his death, whether accidentally or deliberately has never been determined. The column, known as the Death Tower, remained empty for thirty years, before a young woman, unrelated to the dead man, ascended and remained for the rest of her life.

Town Regulations

From the very beginning our town has kept watch over its columns, but not until the 1950s was the decision made to formalize our oversight by recording all rules and regulations and depositing the record in the office of the First Selectman. The largest number of regulations are concerned with safety, of both the dwellers above and the citizens below. Inspections of all columns are conducted twice a year by teams of experts hired by the Commissioner of Public Safety. No column has ever been torn down, although the town is legally entitled to do so. Repairs deemed necessary to crumbling mortar, weathered stone, and cracked concrete must be attended to promptly. Townspeople and visitors are permitted to gather at the base of a column, where there are sometimes benches, and even to sit with their backs against the base, but they are forbidden to strike any hard object against the stone or concrete. This last rule came about when it was discovered that several teenagers were visiting the columns late at night with hammers and chisels in order to sell fragments as souvenirs to out-of-town customers. Other paragraphs of the town regulations define the behavior of citizens with respect to the dwellers above. No communication is permitted from below, including the flashing of mirrors, the display of signs with enormous letters, and the sending of written messages by means of balloons, kites, or birds. No toy drones are permitted in the vicinity of the columns. A small number of regulations govern what might be called decorum: no paint may be applied to the columns, no posters affixed, no objects of any kind attached in any manner. To a great extent, the regulations reflect the anxieties of those with a family member dwelling above. In practice, citizens of all ages respect the columns or ignore them altogether.

Waking

Day after day we wake from sleep. Suddenly the world streams in on us. We see! The forearm on the bedspread. The wood-shine at the top of the closet door. The streak of sunlight on the ceiling. Some say that our waking is no true waking but only another form of sleep. Is that what they are doing up there? Trying to wake from our waking?

Death

When a dweller dies, the town is responsible for returning the body to the world below. A problem that repeatedly arises is how to determine that the dweller has fully passed over into death.

The first sign that the end is near is the return of the food plat-form with all food untouched, but often a dweller ceases to eat for many days as life slowly departs. Current practice is to wait for a period of three days of untouched food before a doctor is lifted to the top. If the panel of the hut is closed, the doctor has permission to slide it open and examine the body inside. If, as is often the case, the dweller has not yet died, the doctor arranges the body comfortably and returns below. The visit is repeated once a day until death is complete. A frequent objection is that these visits, however well intended, destroy the privacy of the dweller, who has devoted a life to absolute solitude. Defenders of the visits argue that the body, though technically alive, is almost always unconscious. They point out that to delay the first visit for any length of time is to risk allowing the untended body to undergo visible stages of decomposition: bloating, green discol-oration, leakage of blood-filled foam from the nose and mouth. Supporters of the present system argue that physical decay is a matter of indifference to the dead body. We continue to debate the issue at town meetings. Once the body is removed, a worker cleans and sanitizes the upper surface, wipes down the inner and outer walls of the hut, and replaces the mat with a new one. The column is now ready to receive the next dweller.

Janet Powell

Even as a young child, Janet Powell loved everything about the columns. She would sit in her stroller, clutching a white bear, and raise her eyes higher and higher to the place where the column disappeared into the sky. Her mother and father, both grade-school teachers, answered her questions thoughtfully, with serious faces. By the time she entered fifth grade, Janet knew where she would spend her life, though she also knew that you weren't allowed to go up there until you were eighteen years old. During this phase she kept trying to catch sight of a dweller, sometimes staring up for hours at a time. Once she thought she saw a leg up there, extending from beneath a robe or gown, but a moment later there was nothing but sky. In high school she spent long afternoons visiting the columns, preparing for her new life. Toward the end of senior year her boyfriend broke up with her, complaining that she never paid any attention to him. She turned eighteen that summer, and on the morning of her birthday she vowed to begin life on top of a column on the day she completed college. After graduating from college she returned to our town, telling a friend that she had to settle a few things before leaving the lower world forever. For a while she lived with an older man, worked a number of odd jobs, joined a group that practiced tai chi, read books on the history of Buddhism. She decided to ascend at noon on the day before her thirtieth birthday. On that day she woke with a sore throat and a fever. Shortly before her thirty-fifth birthday, Janet Powell spent an entire afternoon and evening seated cross-legged at the base of a column, preparing herself for the long journey. Her parents, who saw her twice a week for dinner, no longer knew what to say to her. By the time she was forty, Janet Powell's dark hair was streaked with gray. One day she felt her first burst of anger at the columns, which were preventing her from leading any kind of life. That night she woke at three in the morning, dressed quickly, and hurried over to one of the columns, where she stood with her head bowed against the stone as she begged forgiveness. At fifty she was often seen in different parts of town, at stray hours of the day and night, standing by a column with her head bent back and her gray hair flowing over her shoulders. We wondered what drove her, we wondered what held her in place. Surely by now she must have known that she would never ascend. It was as if she lived in a middle world between two worlds, facing both ways. One morning at dawn a jogger found her lying unconscious at the foot of a column. She recovered, but now when we saw her around town she was bent over, feeling her way with a cane. Janet Powell died at the age of seventy-six, of pancreatic cancer, and was buried in the family plot. Those who wish for the destruction of the columns have turned her life into a cautionary tale, while others defend her as a tragic heroine. Already she is slipping into the past, as if she had lived two hundred years ago, though sometimes, walking along a sidewalk in the late afternoon and catching a glimpse of a distant column, we seem to hear a voice that whispers: "Do you dare?"

Heights

One decision a dweller must make concerns the height of the column, which in accordance with town regulations cannot exceed 140 feet. We nondwellers imagine ourselves choosing the tallest column, but in fact such a choice is uncommon. In the days of private payment, it was understandable that a family might wish to save money by paying for fewer stones, but even in the present era of public financing the columns rarely rise to the fullest permissible height. What might be the reason? One man, in an interview with our local paper, said that his sister had rejected the idea of maximum height, on the grounds that such a choice struck her as boastful and competitive, as if height were a contest you could win or lose. That desire, she said, was a sign that the climber had not yet broken free from the world below. It remains true that some dwellers do in fact choose the full 140 feet, perhaps in the hope of being more distant from possible distractions below. All these considerations remind us that we know nothing about our dwellers, who hover above us at every moment of the day and night.

Our Town Without Columns

It is possible that, at some time in the not-too-distant future, our columns will be taken down. Perhaps a fatal accident will prove decisive, or perhaps a new generation will turn against these all-too-visible structures that rise up like unpleasant reminders of a rejected past. When we try to imagine our town without columns, an anxiety comes over us. It isn't as if our town would then become like other towns. Rather, our town would cease to exist at all, as if life in our streets and shops and living rooms can take place only in the presence of our columns and their dwellers. And what if our town itself were to disappear, leaving only the columns? Wouldn't they gradually fade away? Don't they depend on the town being here, in order for them to be our elsewhere?

A Late-Summer Walk In The Park

A few days ago I took a walk along one of the wooded trails of the park by the river, stopping at the base of a column in a clearing not far from the shore. This spot is one of my favorite places in our town: the sounds of children, on the other side of the trees, playing in the water; the column of stone and mortar rising high above the treetops into the late-afternoon blue of the August sky; the familiar shape of each reddish-brown or speckled gray stone in the column's base. In the warm shade I sat down with my back against a broad oak, facing the column. At this angle I could not see all the way to the top, which was just as well, for I had no desire to catch a distant glimpse of the upper hut, or to think at all of the dweller living high above. Half asleep in the late-afternoon warmth, I imagined myself at the top of the column, sitting straight-backed with each foot resting on the opposite thigh as I stared out through the raised panel of my hut. It was an image I'd often had as a child, and it had begun to return recently. After all, I was fifty-nine years old, not far from retirement. I had had a good life, all things considered, but apart from my marriage I had pursued no passion to its conclusion. It was not too late. Even as I sat there dreaming my way to the top, where I would live far above the trees and the river and the rooftops of our town, I understood that I was not destined to be a dweller. But my understanding in no way interfered with the pleasure of the imagining. I would spend the rest of my life up there, opening myself wide to whatever might await me. At last I would discover what it was that some of us searched for, high over the town. I must have drifted off, for I was startled awake by the sound of voices. A young couple, holding hands, stood talking and laughing at the base of the column. I rose, wished them a good day, and left the clearing. As I continued through the park, I passed two other columns, but no need came over me to stop again. In my own way, I had just spent a lifetime at the top of a column. It was one of the things we liked to do, we people who lived below, we who loved the feel of the earth under our feet. In the warm air, heavy with the scent of pine needles, I could smell the river. I turned, saluted my distant column, and continued on my way.

A NOTE ABOUT THE AUTHOR

STEVEN MILLHAUSER is the author of numerous works of fiction, including *Martin Dressler*, which was awarded the Pulitzer Prize in 1997, and *We Others: New and Selected Stories*, winner of the Story Prize in 2011 and a finalist for the PEN/Faulkner Award. His work has been translated into eighteen languages, and his story "Eisenheim the Illusionist" was the basis of the 2006 film *The Illusionist*.

A NOTE ABOUT THE TYPE

This book was set in Adobe Garamond. Designed for the Adobe Corporation by Robert Slimbach, the fonts are based on types first cut by Claude Garamond (ca. 1480–1561).

Typeset by Scribe
Philadelphia, Pennsylvania

Printed and bound by Berryville Graphics
Berryville, Virginia

Designed by Michael Collica